Kissing Lessons

Kissing Lessons

STEFANIE LONDON

Entangled Publishing, LLC
10940 S Parker Rd
Suite 327
Parker, CO 80134
rights@entangledpublishing.com

Amara is an imprint of Entangled Publishing, LLC.

Edited by Lydia Sharp and Liz Pelletier
Cover design by Bree Archer
Cover photography by Asier Romero, popcorner, Staras, and blamb/
Getty Images

Manufactured in the United States of America

First Edition November 2020

To all the learners and collectors of weird and wonderful facts.

Chapter One

Fact: you are twice as likely to be killed by a vending machine than a shark.

"Who's missing a phone?" Audrey Miller held up an older-model iPhone with a cracked glitter case in one hand while she fished around in her handbag for her car keys. "And someone left the faucet dripping in the bathroom. Oliver, I think that was you."

The first day of school for her younger siblings was always chaos. There were costume changes to be assessed, bags to be packed, and nerves to be calmed in an extra level of insanity that Audrey was thankful only happened once a year. Out of the corner of her eye, she saw her youngest sister, Deanna, skid across the tiles in her socks, blond ponytail flying as she made a grab for her backpack. It had a hole in the bottom that Audrey had been meaning to sew up for weeks now.

Mental note: don't *give her anything valuable to carry until the backpack is patched.*

Not that there was much chance of that happening. Firstly,

Deanna was about as responsible as a Labrador puppy left alone with a tasty pair of stilettos. Secondly, the Miller family didn't own much of value.

"That's mine." Middle sister Georgie sailed past and grabbed her phone out of Audrey's hand. "Can I borrow your battery pack? I forgot to charge mine."

"I reminded you last night." Audrey looked up, her car keys still nowhere to be found. Georgie stood there, an expectant expression on her face. At seventeen, she was in a phase where she wanted to date and go to parties and generally act like an adult but without taking responsibility for any of it.

Audrey had never been given that option—not even when she was a teenager.

Rolling her eyes, she gestured for Georgie to go ahead and grab the battery pack from her bag. She had bigger concerns than her phone dying. Namely, if she couldn't locate her car keys, then her siblings would be late for school and Audrey would be late for work. And she might live among chaos at home, but nobody outside would *ever* see that. Being late was totally unacceptable.

"Oliver! I said turn that damn faucet off." She marched up the narrow hallway of their cramped house, knocking on her younger brother's door as she went past. She should never have gotten him those noise-cancelling headphones for his birthday. Not only had they maxed her credit card out, but now he was even more lost in his own world than before.

As Audrey reached the bedroom she shared with her sisters, she spotted her keys poking out from underneath a silk scarf on the middle of Georgie's bed—aka the bottom of the bunk she shared with Deanna. What on earth were they doing there?

"We leave in two minutes!" she called out as she headed back down the hallway. "No exceptions. If your ass isn't in that car before I start the engine, you'll be walking."

Oliver emerged from his bedroom, ducking to avoid knocking his head on the doorframe. He might be the exact age as his twin sister, Georgie, but that's where the similarities ended. Georgie was the shortest of all of them, and Oliver was six foot two and still growing like a weed.

"RIP my food budget," she muttered. The kid already ate like a horse, and it was only getting worse.

Snatching up her bag, she took a final glance around the room. The kitchen was a bit of a mess from the morning's cereal bowls, but otherwise it wasn't *too* much of a disaster zone. Well, so long as you ignored the overflowing recycling bin and the pile of laundry she'd dumped onto the couch while Deanna demanded she find her missing lucky socks.

"Miller family, roll out!" She held the door open as the kids trooped past her, the twins' heads bowed toward their cell phones as they tapped furiously with their thumbs. "Oliver, Georgie, Deanna... Where's Jane?"

Georgie snorted and lifted her head for the briefest second. "She left for college a year ago."

Oh yeah. Audrey shook her head as she locked the front door. She was so hardwired to count to four when checking on her siblings that she'd momentarily forgotten Jane had already flown out of the nest. Flown all the way to Duke, in fact, and was living her best life *far* away from Kissing Creek, a town with a stupid name and an even stupider reputation for celebrating all things romantic.

"All present and accounted for. Let's go." Audrey hoisted her bag up onto her shoulder and caught Oliver mock saluting her out of the corner of her eye.

She unlocked her car, affectionately known as Big Red. Not because at one time in the mid-nineties it had been a vibrant shade of vermilion, but because it had big red rust patches on both back panels. Sure, it wasn't pretty. But Big

Red was about the most reliable thing in Audrey's life, and she'd drive the damn thing until the wheels fell off.

"What's our fact for the day?" Deanna asked as she took her place in the front seat beside Audrey. That was always the rule: littlest kid gets the front seat on the first day of school.

"Oh no, I forgot to look up a fact." Audrey started the engine and eased the car away from the curb.

"No, you didn't." Deanna stuck a bony elbow into Audrey's side. "Tell us. We have to learn."

"Isn't that what you're supposed to do at school?" Audrey glanced at her little sister, trying to hide the smirk tugging at her lips. She was a miniature version of their mother—with her chipper personality and thirst for knowledge. Deanna even resembled her, with long blond hair and blue eyes so big she looked like a cartoon character.

Audrey had *also* inherited the long blond hair, but instead of blue eyes she'd gotten a rich olive-green from her dad. She'd also skipped out on her mother's naturally lean figure, too.

"It would be if the teachers actually knew anything," Georgie chimed in from the backseat with her signature teenage drawl. "I don't know where they find half of those idiots, I swear."

Audrey narrowed her eyes at the rearview mirror. She couldn't fully disagree, since there'd been a number of teachers with questionable education skills back when she was a kid, but she didn't want Georgie scaring Deanna off on her first day of high school.

"You're right, Dee. I *do* have a fact." Distraction—that was her go-to technique.

Deanna pumped her fist into the air. "My brain is ready."

Oliver chuckled from the backseat but didn't look up from his phone. Georgie listened on with interest, however. Despite her attachment to electronic devices and her generally sullen attitude, she was a sponge for information.

"You're twice as likely to be killed by a vending machine than a shark," Audrey said. She'd looked up that fact first thing that morning, when the house was still quiet and she'd had her coffee and breakfast in a rare moment of peace.

"No way." Deanna wrinkled her nose. "How does *anyone* get killed by a vending machine?"

"Darwinism?" Georgie joked.

"Actually, she's kind of right," Audrey replied. "There was one guy who shook a vending machine so hard it toppled over and crushed him to death."

After debating the silliest ways to die—top contenders included peeing on an electric fence, trying to hand-feed an alligator, and driving with your eyes closed—Audrey pulled Big Red up to the high school drop-off zone. Oliver and Georgie slid out of the back, eager to be away from the embarrassing car as fast as possible. Deanna stayed put for a moment, biting down on her lower lip as she watched the students streaming into the school.

"Don't be scared. You'll have a great time." Audrey kissed the top of her head. "Look, Celeste is here. Why don't you catch up to her so you can walk in together?"

Deanna's eyes lit up at the mention of her friend. "Good idea."

She slid out of the seat and hoisted her backpack onto one shoulder, slamming the door behind her. It was warm out already, the sun making her hair look like fibers of spun gold. At the last minute, she turned around and leaned in the open window of the passenger's side.

"I like your fact, by the way. Morbid, but interesting." She grinned before darting off into the crowd.

That was their routine. Every morning, Audrey would come armed with a fact, and Deanna would give her an assessment. Georgie and Oliver would both act like they didn't care about the ritual, but she knew they secretly enjoyed it. Even Jane, when she'd lived at home, had joined in.

Their life wasn't perfect by any means—they all missed their mother like hell, and they missed the man their father used to be. And they lived in the shitty part of town in a house made for a family half their size. But they were happy...and that was the thing that mattered most.

Switching her focus to the day ahead, Audrey followed the trail of cars exiting the drop-off zone and headed toward job number one: Kisspresso Café.

All people who lived in Kissing Creek would come to understand an important thing about their hometown. A place with the word "kissing" in its name can't *not* capitalize on romance. Because aside from sex, there's no greater marketing tool than love.

That's why almost three-quarters of the stores in town either had a romance-themed pun for a name or featured some kind of kiss mark and/or heart in their business logo. There was the fancy donut shop with the kiss-themed flavors: chocolate smooch, raspberry snog, and frenching vanilla. They'd even had a limited edition one called 'too much tongue toffee'. Then there was Italian restaurant *Mille Baci* (a thousand kisses) and the auto repair shop with the slogan: *kiss-proof your car!*

For someone who didn't believe in the whole happily-ever-after thing, it was a daily reminder of what Audrey saw as false advertising. But she'd never considered moving away. Kissing Creek was her home, and she had a duty to make sure each and every one of her siblings had the best possible trajectory in life. Which ultimately meant donning the cutesy pink polo shirt with the Kisspresso Café's logo, complete with embroidered red lip print, and tying a red waist apron over her jeans several days a week.

Truth was, she liked this job. Audrey had little time or budget for personal passions, but one she did indulge in was coffee, so her job as a barista ticked both the passion box and the money box. Plus, the Kisspresso Café was right at the edge of Harrison Beech College, which meant, for a few hours each day, Audrey could pretend she was a full-time college student without any worries in her life.

"One vanilla latte, one cappuccino, and two pink passion white chocolate mochas." Lana called the orders in her usual singsong voice from the front counter as she slid the empty takeout cups along the bench toward Audrey. "And a puppyccino for Ralf."

"Ralf is here?" Audrey peered around the pastel-pink espresso machine to look out the front window. Ralf was a Saint Bernard who loved the staff at the café. His owner, Andy, was a retired professor and a regular customer.

"Yep, and don't even think about running that drink out to him. It's my turn today." Lana folded her arms over her chest, and Audrey pouted. "I need to live vicariously, okay? The only pet I'm allowed in my dorm room is of the chia variety."

Audrey snorted as she picked up the single-shot portafilter and set it under the grinder with one hand while reaching for the milk jug with the other. "They still make those?"

"Sure. I have one shaped like Groot." She grinned.

Despite there being only five years' age difference between them, it felt more like a decade. Or two. At twenty-six, Audrey wasn't like most people her age—she worked two regular jobs, took odd jobs where she could, cared for her siblings, made sure the household bills got paid, *and* took night classes at the college to stop her mind from going to goop. Lana, on the other hand, worked a scant fifteen hours a week, often came into work hungover, and thought that trying to budget for a pair of Lululemon leggings was life's greatest challenge.

"Also, Jamie told me to mention that we have to crack down on people fraudulently using the college staff discount," Lana said. "If they look too young to be a professor, then we have to ask to see their faculty card." She hovered by the espresso machine, waiting for Audrey to finish making the puppyccino so she could take it outside. "Apparently we've been scammed on multiple occasions."

"Really?" Audrey wrinkled her nose.

She totally understood that many college students didn't have much spare cash. But if that was the case, why order coffee at Kisspresso? They could go to Dunkin' Donuts and get a coffee for two bucks instead. Or use the facilities in the student lounge. And Audrey might have been raised poor as dirt, but stealing was stealing…even if it was only a dime. Scamming a local business run by someone who gave plenty to the community was *not* cool.

"Yeah," Lana said, bobbing her head. "Jamie told us yesterday and asked us to fill in everyone who wasn't rostered."

"Duly noted."

Audrey waited for the espresso shot to finish and tapped the portafilter against the edge of the knock box, releasing the used grounds. Then she poured milk into the little silver jug and began to froth it, ignoring the thermometer attached to the side and instead gauging the temperature by how the jug felt against her palm. Audrey was an excellent barista, and she didn't mind saying that, because she had proof in the form of customers who wouldn't buy their coffee unless she was the one behind the machine.

Lana bounced on the balls of her feet, her gaze flicking to the front window, where Ralf was sitting in his usual spot with Andy. Rolling her eyes, Audrey fetched the whipped cream canister from the fridge and squirted some into their smallest paper cup.

"There. Now stop hanging around me like a bad smell." She shoved the cup toward Lana, who took off to go and see her favorite four-legged customer.

Audrey worked quickly, filling the drink orders and getting into the flow of her job. She'd read a book once that said job satisfaction came from believing that your role had a purpose. To Audrey, seeing her customers take that first sip, a smile on their lips—seeing them take a moment for themselves amidst their chaotic day—*that* made her feel like her job had a purpose. Sure, she wasn't curing cancer or putting criminals away or helping people make their lives better. But, in Audrey's opinion, the little moments mattered in life, too.

And that's what she did—she gave people little moments of joy.

"Vanilla latte," she called out as she poured the milk into one of Kisspresso's signature bright pink cups, moving her hand back and forth to create a perfect leaf on the latte's surface. "And a cappuccino."

As she was finishing up the pink passion white chocolate mochas—menu items that were better categorized as desserts than beverages, in her opinion—the café's door swung open. Only it wasn't Lana returning from her doggy visit. Oh no, this was a customer whom Audrey *definitely* hadn't seen before.

She knew that for a fact, because if the human form of every one of her sexy fantasies mashed into one perfect man had ever walked through the door before, she would have noticed.

He made his way to the front counter, raking a hand through his overlong hair as he surveyed the pastry cabinet.

Interest rippled through the café like an electrical current, with most female heads and a few male heads turning in his direction. The man ran a hand over his clean-shaven jaw, fingers long and slim like those of a piano player.

He wore a blazer with leather patches on the elbows, which should have seemed like he was trying too hard... but somehow it didn't. Dark denim jeans covered long legs, capped with a pair of Converse sneakers, and a fitted white T-shirt hinted at a lean yet muscular physique. Not bulky, like some of the gym bros Audrey saw at the smoothie place on Main Street. But more...economical. Sleek.

None of that compared to his eyes, however, which were a pierce-right-through-your-soul blue. They were eyes that promised to melt any form of logic or common sense a person might have until they were nothing but a mindless, willing vessel for pleasure...

"Like a sex robot?" She shook her head, then clamped a hand over her mouth when she realized she'd said it out loud.

The guy looked up, brow crinkled as he cocked his head to one side. His gaze caught hers immediately. Seconds ticked by as mortification trickled through Audrey's system, freezing her to the spot.

Relax, you weren't that loud.

"Excuse me," he said, blue eyes staring intently into hers in a way that halted her breath. "Did you call me a sex robot?"

Chapter Two

"I did *not* call you a sex robot." The woman behind the counter flushed almost the exact same color as the pink polo shirt displaying a cutesy lip-print logo.

She was gorgeous. Tumbling blond hair swept up into a bouncy ponytail, wide green eyes staring at him unflinchingly, and full lips all competed for his attention. There was something arresting about her, something strong and willful and so electric it grabbed Ronan Walsh by the balls. Add to all that a full figure with the kind of curves that could make a grown man weep, and he was momentarily robbed of his resolve to not even *think* about women for the next twelve months.

"She totally called him a sex robot." One of the younger women at a nearby table snickered and ducked her head behind a coffee cup big enough to caffeinate an entire college faculty. "How embarrassing."

"Can I help you with a drink?" the woman asked, trying to act like she wasn't ruffled. As she came closer, Ronan caught the name *Audrey* printed neatly on a white badge.

"Maybe a croissant or a bagel?"

"A coffee, black, in whatever is your biggest cup." He tore his eyes away from the barista to scan the bakery display. "And a blueberry muffin."

Audrey nodded and rang the items up on an iPad that served as the café's cash register. Kisspresso Café had been one on a list of recommended local businesses that his new boss had provided him when he'd checked into his visiting accommodation late yesterday. At first he'd almost walked straight past the place. Not because he'd missed it—a feat impossible to anyone who could see, thanks to a hot pink front door that looked like something out of a Wes Anderson movie. Rather, Ronan wasn't sure his long-haul-travel-weary eyes were ready for the visual assault.

But he'd quickly learned that pink and red were town colors and, therefore, were unavoidable. The college that he would call his workplace and home for the next twelve months had gone with the more universally appealing red for their school logo and for the uniform of their much-revered baseball team, the Flames.

"One coffee and a muffin," Audrey said. "To go?"

Ronan nodded. He could handle all the brightness for the five minutes it would take to get sustenance, but then he wanted to go back to his apartment and face-plant onto the couch.

Thank you, jet lag.

Audrey gave him the total, and Ronan pulled his wallet out of the back pocket of his jeans. "I've been told there's a discount for college staff?"

Audrey's eyebrow immediately arched. "Yes."

Hmm, was it a faux pas to ask? The information had been printed alongside the coffee recommendation in his welcome pack. "Great. I'm a professor there."

"I haven't seen you before," she said. "I'll need to see

your faculty card."

"Uhh…I'm new, so I don't get my faculty card until the office opens back up next week."

Audrey cocked her head. "You know, we've been warned about people like you."

"Sex robots?" The words leaped off his tongue before he could stop them. Someone behind him snorted, and Ronan cringed.

Great. His first day on campus, and someone was probably live-Tweeting this whole silly conversation.

"People posing as professors." She waggled her finger at him and made a teasing, tutting sound.

"Posing?" Ronan literally studied the very things which made people who they are—the very fiber of their motivations and morals. He would *never* scam someone. But this wasn't the first time someone had questioned him because he was younger than average. "I'm a professor at Harrison Beech College. I don't have my faculty card yet, that's all."

"You really thought you could get one past me by trying to look the part?" She shook her head. "The elbow patches were a good attempt, but don't you think they're a little cliché?"

Now she was insulting his fashion choices? He blinked. "What's wrong with elbow patches?"

"It's like you googled 'what do professors wear?' and then bought the first thing you saw." She bit down on her lip as if stifling a laugh.

Everyone was looking at him now, but luckily Ronan was impervious to embarrassment. Maybe it was years of growing up with his Irish grandmother, who was as blunt as a hammer.

Although he *had* googled that exact question before his first day as a professor in his late twenties. He'd been more insecure back then, feeling the age gap between him and his colleagues and his lack of life experience like a weight around his neck. These days, he'd learned to hold his own, academically and personally.

And he damn well liked his elbow patches.

"And besides," Audrey continued, gesturing to him. "You're so…"

He was certain he wasn't going to like this answer. "What?"

"Young."

He was thirty-four, to be exact. Clearly, he shouldn't have shaved his beard off before leaving the UK. The scruff had made him look older, more mature. But he'd wanted to make a good impression, and he could hardly turn up at his new job looking like he didn't know how to present himself. Still, maybe it was better to look older and a bit rough around the edges than to have a clean-shaven baby face.

He was going to toss his razor in the trash.

"Maybe I have a good skincare routine," he joked.

"Look," she said, holding up her hands. "I'm sure a man like you is used to getting what you want—"

"What's *that* supposed to mean?" He laughed at the absurdity of it. A man like *him*?

"Well…" Her eyes flicked over him, her cheeks growing even pinker. She liked what she saw; that much was obvious. "I mean, if you'd come in here claiming to be a model, now *that* I would have believed."

Ronan couldn't help but puff his chest out a little. First a sex robot, now a model. He'd never thought it was possible to be so flattered while someone was accusing you of theft, but here he was. "How am I supposed to prove to you that I'm a professor?"

This wasn't about the discount. Not at all—Ronan didn't need to save a dollar or two on his morning snack. His bank account was perfectly fine. But he was *far* too intrigued by this woman to walk away now.

"Ummm, what's something only a professor would know?" Audrey tapped a finger to her chin, and Ronan felt the curious stares of the entire café behind him. "What is pi to the first ten decimal places?"

"Three point one four one five…" Hmm, she had him there. "Well, I'm not a *math* professor."

Her green eyes searched his, mischievous and sparkling. "Okay. Which letter doesn't appear in any U.S. state name?"

That seemed almost too easy. But Ronan's mind whirred as he scrolled through state names, finding all the letters he thought of. He was stuck on blond hair and full, smirking lips, and his brain whirred like a tire bogged in mud.

"Are you trying to trick me, Audrey?" He leaned against the counter and folded his arms.

"I'm *not*," she said, planting a hand across her ample chest. She was having far too much fun with this.

"I don't trust you. It's a trick question."

"No, it's not," someone piped up from the back of the café. "There's no Q in any state name."

Crap. Ronan was officially rattled.

It was this woman—this gorgeous, quick-witted woman. Ronan's personal catnip was humor and a curvy figure, and Audrey had both dialed up to ten. He couldn't remember the last time a woman had gotten under his skin so damn quickly.

"I'll give you one more shot. Everyone deserves a third chance, right?" She planted her hands on the counter and leaned a little forward. "What is the official term for the hashtag or pound sign?"

Ronan shook his head. He should *know* this one, but she'd turned his brain into a pile of sludge.

"You'll have to forgive me," he said with a charming smile. "I've just flown in from Cambridge, and the jet lag is affecting the part of my brain responsible for storing trivia."

"Cambridge, huh? Fancy," she teased. "I'm going to put

that in the same category as the elbow patches. A good call, but a little cliché. You would have been better going with something less well-known."

As he opened his mouth to fire a comeback, the front door of the café opened and a young woman walked in, wearing an identical outfit of a pink polo shirt, blue jeans, and a red apron. Lana. She was the younger sister of one of his former colleagues when he was still working as a TA before he moved overseas. They'd asked him to keep an eye out for her on campus.

"Ronan, so nice to see you," Lana said with a big smile. "Sorry, it's Professor Walsh now, isn't it? I heard you were teaching here."

The café erupted in titters and whispers, and Audrey's face slowly drained of color until she no longer resembled the perky pink polo shirt that hugged her figure perfectly. And maybe it made Ronan a grade-A bastard, but damn if he didn't feel a little smug about the whole thing.

He greeted Lana and then turned back to Audrey. "That's right. I *do* go by Professor Walsh these days."

"The guest psychology professor," she said, scrubbing a hand over her face. "You're teaching the Wednesday night Brain-Changing Positivity class."

Ronan hadn't been sure the moment could have gotten any better, but he was more than pleased to be proven wrong. This was the gleaming, chocolate-dipped cherry on top of the sundae. "I take it that means I'll see you next Wednesday night."

She nodded, sucking on the inside of her cheek. Now her cheeks weren't simply pink—they were bordering on being as red as the lip prints he'd already spotted in the half the business logos around town. "Yes, that's right. I'll be there on Wednesday."

"See you then," he said as he handed a few bills over to

pay for his snack. "I'm *really* looking forward to it."

Later that night, Ronan forced himself to get off the couch. He'd napped for a few hours, his body completely confused about what time zone he was in, and he still wasn't sure whether the short sleep had made him feel better or worse. All he did know was that it felt like there was a small creature repeatedly slamming a pickax into the back of his eyeball.

Thank God he had a full week before classes started. He'd need it to shake the jet lag.

After downing a few painkillers with a glass of water, he showered and headed out into the balmy evening to meet his family for dinner. The walk to the restaurant took a good half an hour, but the air cleared his head, and by the time he made it to the bar and grill—which, thankfully, didn't have a stupid puntastic name—he was feeling more than ready for a family reunion.

When he arrived, he found his sister helping his grandmother out of her car. The visual struck him deep in the chest. Grandma Orna had always been a fearsome presence in his life—she was a gnarled root of a woman, hardened and impossible to bend. But with that stubbornness came a strength Ronan rarely found in others and a resilience that could only be admired. The last six years hadn't been kind. Her body stooped more than it did before, and her hand curled fiercely around the top of her cane. Her snow-white hair was still neatly coiffed, however, and she wore her signature slash of magenta lipstick.

"Don't stand there, Ronan," she barked in her Irish accent, which was still as thick as the day she'd stepped off the boat. "Come help your sister."

Keira looked up, her face blossoming into a huge smile.

She was still in her work outfit: a tailored navy pencil skirt, a white blouse, and heels that couldn't have been comfortable for the hour-long drive they'd made from Boston. She must have gone straight from the office to Gram's house.

"Here, let me get that." Ronan reached for the large tote bag dangling from Keira's arm and offered his free hand to his grandmother. "It's good to see you both."

He bent down to give the older woman a hug, and she felt smaller than ever. How had six years changed her so much? Would they have to start measuring her height in the doorway, like she used to do when they were kids, so he could tell if she was actually shrinking or if it was simply his worries dwarfing her?

"Would have been better if you hadn't gone to that miserable part of the world," she muttered, patting an arthritic hand on his back. "But I'm glad you're home."

Keira shot Ronan a look over their grandmother's shoulder and rolled her eyes. "I see we're going to continue with today's theme of deeply ingrained Catholic guilt."

Ronan snorted. "I expect no less."

Orna narrowed her eyes at him and stepped out of his embrace. "I'm glad you finally came to your senses."

It might sound harsh, but Orna had plenty of reason to detest the idea of her grandson going anywhere near Ireland. To her, it was a place full of betrayal and bad memories. She'd immigrated to the U.S. at nineteen, pregnant, claiming she was going to stay with relatives—although it was a lie—and she'd lived in a small, dirty house crammed with other young women who'd been cast aside for various indiscretions. And from nothing, she had forged a life.

"Where's Mom?" Ronan asked. "Is she heading over on her own?"

Keira's expression was all the answer he needed. "She's in the middle of a big project…"

Six years, he'd been away. Six fucking years without his mother returning his calls or texts for weeks at a time. Six years of her likely being happy that she didn't have to worry about him bugging her for some semblance of a relationship. He should have known she wouldn't show.

This is it. You're officially done.

"You don't need her," Orna replied in a clipped tone. "Come on. I'm hungry."

His grandmother would never coddle him—that wasn't in her character—but he knew that she didn't support the complete disinterest Merrin Walsh took in her children's lives. She hadn't even shown up at the hospital when Keira had given birth to her little boy, Lukas.

So why would she turn up for a dinner to welcome her son home?

"How're Lukas and Andy?" Ronan asked as they walked into the restaurant and got seated at a booth.

"Amazing." Keira smiled. "I can't believe my little man is two already."

"And *I* can't wait to meet him in person instead of only seeing him on a computer screen," he replied. "Looks like motherhood suits you."

"Thanks, Ro."

"Don't you mean motherhood suits Andy?" Orna said, picking up a menu and peering at it.

Keira's mouth tightened. Orna hadn't readily approved of her being back at work full-time while Andy stayed home with their son. It made financial sense, because Keira's career was incredibly lucrative. Both Ronan and Keira had been raised to be type A high achievers who were incapable of not working. Maybe there was something about trying to win the love of their absentee mother in there, or maybe that was just the researcher in him looking for meaning where there was none?

"I would say *parenthood* suits Andy," Keira replied in a frosty tone. Clearly the hour-long drive with their grandmother had worn her patience down.

Orna looked up and winked at Ronan from over the top of her menu, a wicked sparkle in her eyes shaving a decade off her age. Yeah, she was inappropriate and old-fashioned and stubborn as a bull. But Ronan's grandmother was one of the biggest influences in his life—hell, she was the reason he'd chosen to study resilience and mental fortitude for his master's thesis. Because for all her faults, she'd stormed through life's challenges like a Spartan warrior, and *that* was something to be admired.

"You shouldn't make jokes like that, Gram," he admonished.

"You two are no fun," she groused. The waiter interrupted their catch-up for a moment to take their orders and leave them with some fresh-baked bread and butter.

"I can't believe you're back," Keira said to Ronan as the waiter walked away.

"*I* can't believe you're living in a town called Kissing Creek." Orna made a face, her crow's-feet deepening with the disgusted expression. "When Keira told me, I thought she was pulling my leg. What a stupid name."

"Apparently they named the creek after a town in Bavaria called Kissing, where the founders were from. I read somewhere that one of the men wanted to name the town after his family name, but it was Leichenberg, which literally translates to *mountain of corpses*, and they thought it might bring bad luck."

Keira blinked. "That's dark."

Orna simply shrugged, as though naming a place Mountain of Corpses was completely fine by her. "So tell us, Ronan. Why'd you come back?"

"I told you when we Skyped," he said, meeting her hard

stare with a charming smile. "I got a job offer."

They both knew it was bullshit. The timing couldn't have been more obvious, because the offer had come in not a month after Orna had been rushed to the hospital with a stroke. And that had only been because Keira had found her and called 911. Orna had tried to call their mother repeatedly, and, as usual, Merrin hadn't picked up her phone. The news had rocked Ronan to his core—how could he be half a world away from the woman who'd raised him when she might not have too many years left?

Naturally, he'd found an opportunity to bring him back home. One that wasn't to the standard of his Harvard and Cambridge background, but it had been close to Orna and Keira and *that's* what mattered to him right now. The rest could be figured out later.

"I'm not sick," Orna said, ignoring his response. "I don't want you to throw your life away because I had a little visit to the hospital."

"It wasn't little," Keira mumbled under her breath, and she squeaked when the older woman jabbed a bony finger into her arm.

"I'm *fine*, okay? Fit as a fiddle, I'll have you know. And as I always say—"

"The older the fiddle, the sweeter the tune," Ronan and Keira recited in singsong unison. His grandmother was full of funny old sayings.

"That's right," Orna said with a nod. "Best you two remind yourselves of that; there's nothing wrong with growing old. Not everybody has that privilege."

Ronan leaned back in the booth and watched as Keira rested her head on top of her grandmother's, her brown hair—the same shade as Ronan's—mixed with Orna's snow-white perm. Despite their disagreements and how they often rubbed each other the wrong way, this was his family right here. His little sister, his grandmother. The three musketeers.

"Now," his grandmother said. "We need to talk about your marriage situation."

"Wasn't aware I had one of those," he replied breezily.

"You *don't*. That's the issue. I know I already have one great-grandbaby, but I'm not getting any younger."

"A minute ago, you were telling me you were fine. Fit as a fiddle, I believe you said." He winked at her, and Keira smothered a laugh behind a napkin. "And you don't look a day over sixty-five with those cheekbones."

Orna was eighty, but he knew she guarded that information like the key to a bank vault. "Flattery will get you nowhere, Ronan Walsh. And yes, I have some more time in me, God willing. But I don't have forever. Now, I know a young girl—"

"So do I." Ronan grinned. "Several, in fact."

Orna's end-of-her-tether huff made him swallow a chuckle. Truth was, Ronan didn't date much these days—he'd tried it once or twice, and it always ended up in tears. Never his. So he'd shifted his focus to his career, and his life had a lot less drama because of it. Now he was adding family back into the mix, and that would keep him plenty busy.

Romantic relationships weren't worth the hassle.

"Don't you want to be married, Ronan?" Orna asked, shaking her head.

"Not really," he replied honestly.

"But—"

"You never married, and neither did Mom and Dad," he pointed out with a shrug. "Anyway, Keira has the white-picket-fence thing totally covered. And honestly, I give her an A-plus at life. Gold stars all around."

His sister tossed him a look that said she would hate him forever if he dragged her into it. Oops. Too late now.

"That means something, coming from a professor,"

Ronan added with a mock serious face. "I couldn't possibly live up to the standard she's set."

"You fight dirty," Keira muttered.

"I only want you to have the good things in life that I never got myself," Orna said.

"I'm focused on my work, Gram." He reached across the table and clasped her hand. "And I love what I do. How many people can say they bounce out of bed in the morning because they love their job so much?"

"Life has to be more than work," Orna replied wisely. "Would it be so bad to settle down and make a family?"

Like the one he grew up in, where neither one of his parents ever seemed to love their children or each other? Like the family who kicked Orna out of her home for getting pregnant, or the rich man who paid her to move across the world like a fly to be shooed?

Uh, no thanks.

Keira's making it work.

An outlier. Every research study had those, and Ronan knew they weren't to be trusted. The *trend* was to be trusted. The bulk of information telling the same story, not the little red dot flying free in the white space.

And the trend told him that relationships equaled pain and suffering.

Chapter Three

Fact: an elephant's penis is so big it can rest on it like an additional leg.

Audrey rocked back and forth on her heels outside the classroom for her first lesson of the semester. Of *course* the subject she'd been most excited about was Brain-Changing Positivity with none other than Professor Walsh, former professor at Cambridge University in England and graduate of Harvard. First name, Ronan. Age, thirty-four. Height and weight...dreamy.

A crush on your professor? Really? Well, isn't that *more cliché than the elbow patches on his blazer.*

She bit the inside of her cheek. Luckily, her grades didn't matter. Unlike most of the students at Harrison Beech College, Audrey wasn't getting a degree. Hell, she wasn't even like the majority of mature age students in her night classes, who were doing it for career advancement.

She was learning for fun with no end goal in mind.

Most people would shake their heads at that, but

she'd always loved learning. Before her mother died, when Audrey's dreams were still intact, she used to fantasize about growing up and strolling through a leafy college campus, her arms filled with heavy books containing the secrets of the universe. These days, she satisfied that need with night classes on everything from depictions of women in film, to the politics of the British monarchy, to American postmodern literature, to philosophy and social media. Anything to keep her neurons firing.

Maybe taking classes for nothing beside the joy of learning *was* strange. But she was okay with that.

Which was all to say, her concerns about showing up tonight had nothing to do with grades and everything to do with total and utter personal embarrassment.

Sucking in a breath, she pushed down on the handle to the classroom. It was empty because she was a good ten minutes early. On purpose. At the front of the room, Professor Walsh was writing the class title and his name and email address on the whiteboard, arm stretched up in a way that put his lean, strong body on full display.

Ever since their encounter a week and a half ago, she'd been thinking about Professor Walsh. *Way* too much. Way too inappropriately. Way too…everything.

You're here to clear the air. Not ruminate on him being borderline offensively hot.

"Uh, hi," she said, hugging her bag to her body. Something about this man made her feel like she needed a physical barrier. He stirred things inside her that she'd promised herself wouldn't be stirred by anyone, ever.

"Audrey." He said her name before he turned around, as though he instinctively knew she was there, and for some reason that made her stomach do little somersaults. "You're a little early, but feel free to take a seat. I'm getting myself situated."

When he turned, she had to force herself not to gulp like some cheesy cartoon character with hearts for eyes. He looked...devilishly handsome. "You grew a beard."

He chuckled and ran a hand over his jaw. "Well, this is only the beginnings of one. I thought some facial hair might prevent any further confusion about which side of the desk I'm supposed to be sitting on."

"It looks good." The words popped out of her before she could stop them. Before she could even *contemplate* stopping them. She was prone to sharing facts, and it was totally and utterly a fact that the liberal sprinkling of bristles along Ronan Walsh's jaw was an unnecessary improvement to an already achingly handsome man.

"I was wondering if I might be able to take a moment of your time," she said quickly, hoping they could both gloss over her fawning. The air seemed charged somehow, like that feeling right before a storm swept through town.

"Sure. You might need to come a little closer, though," he replied in an amused tone. His accent was as intriguing as the rest of him—American, definitely, but there were some rounded vowels and a slight lilt that made her blood hum. Perhaps it was a souvenir from his time in the UK. "What can I do for you?"

"I wanted to clear the air about...what happened." Ugh, so freaking awkward.

How *did* one apologize for falsely accusing a person of attempted fraud?

"Because you called me a sex robot or because you told me I couldn't possibly be a professor?" A smile tugged at his lips, and it didn't seem unkind in any way.

"I did *not* call you a sex robot." Maybe Audrey should grab herself a shovel and start digging. If the earth wasn't going to heed her wish to open up and swallow her whole, then she might have to take matters into her own hands. "But yes, my assumption that you were not part of the college faculty was incorrect and unfair. Although, in my defense, the beard does make you look more…"

Attractive? Sexy? Like you've been plucked from my wildest dirty dreams?

"More…?" Ronan raised an eyebrow.

"Scholarly." Audrey nodded, trying to give herself a confidence boost. "I find beards to be quite academic."

Okay, now Ronan looked even more amused. Ugh, this was not going how she'd planned.

"I'm glad my facial hair gets your seal of approval," he said, his blue eyes flicking over her face. His curiosity was a magnetic pull. Nobody was ever curious about Audrey or her bland-as-oatmeal existence. Everyone in Kissing Creek knew her story—dead mom, deadbeat dad, future prospects that dwindled with each passing year. Girl from the wrong side of the tracks who wouldn't ever make anything of herself, because the longer you stayed in a situation like that, the higher the chance you'd be stuck there forever.

But *he* looked at her like she might be worthy of his interest—like she might have something worth saying.

"It's octothorpe, by the way," he said. "The official term for the hashtag."

Despite feeling an unwanted swirl of attraction rousing butterflies in her stomach, Audrey's chest got warm and fuzzy. "You looked it up."

He leaned back against his desk and smiled. And oh boy what a smile it was. "I couldn't have my professional capabilities questioned like that."

Audrey cringed. "I'm not usually so judgmental, Professor Walsh. I promise."

"It's fine. And no need to call me professor, okay? I don't need to be identified by the label," he said with a twinkle in his eye. "The elbow patches do that quite well enough."

Audrey laughed. "Stop. You're killing me."

"Okay, I cease fire." He held up his hands in good nature. "And Ronan is fine."

"It's a good name."

"Very scholarly to match my beard?" he teased.

"What happened to the cease-fire?" Audrey couldn't help but laugh. The man was charming, smooth. Yet kind. The kind of man she'd always been attracted to and yet would forever and always be out of her league.

Behind them, the noise of students trickling into the room reminded Audrey that they weren't alone. She instinctively took a step back, as though she'd been caught doing something wrong, even though there was nothing at all wrong with approaching her professor before class.

Don't you mean Ronan?

His name echoed in her head. What exactly about this man had turned her into a puddle? Maybe it was simply because he embodied the things she wished she had in her own life—success, education, an upward trajectory. Combine that with a delicious-looking package and of *course* she was attracted to him. It was biology.

An elephant's penis is so big it can rest on it like an additional leg.

Why exactly had she chosen *that* fact to share in the car ride to school this morning? Deanna had erupted in giggles, and there was a chorus of *eew*s from the backseat, but clearly Audrey had sex on the brain.

That's what happens when you go for three years without having a boyfriend. It's like sugar cravings—the more you ignore it, the worse it gets.

And she'd never been too good at ignoring cravings, sugar or otherwise.

"Anyway, thanks for your time," she said, awkwardly taking another step back, even though it felt like her whole body resisted it. "I'm really looking forward to this class."

Audrey didn't wait for Ronan to respond, but she felt his eyes boring into her back the entire way until she grabbed an empty seat. She'd chosen it carefully—not right at the front, because she didn't want to seem too eager, but not in the back, because she didn't want to get distracted by the slackers. She always picked an aisle seat if possible, since her hips required a little more room and she didn't want to get wedged in.

Plus, she needed to make a quick exit as soon as the class was done. Her father thought she was doing an extra shift at Kisspresso tonight, and they closed half an hour before the class ended, so she needed to hustle home in order to keep her cover from being blown.

One day you won't need to hide what you're doing.

That day would come the second Deanna graduated from high school and went off to college. Then *all* her siblings would be out in the world, and Audrey could finally live her own life. It would come soon…ish.

She leaned back in the chair and watched as Ronan introduced himself to the class, her stomach still twisting and turning as attraction wound through her system. Maybe it would be better if she concentrated on taking notes instead of looking at him. But for the next hour, she felt her eyes drawing upward at the sound of excitement and passion in his voice.

And whenever she *did* look up, she could swear he was looking directly at her.

Audrey pulled into the driveway of her house as quietly as she could, letting the tires roll slowly over the cracked concrete, headlights off and her radio silent. When she killed the engine, she sat for a minute in the darkness, quietly listening to an occasional passing car or dog barking. When nothing stirred in the house, she reached over to the passenger-side seat and grabbed her pink Kisspresso polo shirt.

She was now adept at the "quick change" in confined spaces and the pretzel-like contortions it sometimes required. Working quickly, she whipped off the cute white blouse she'd worn to class and swapped it for the uniform polo. Then she stuffed the blouse into her bag and put her apron on top to hide the evidence. Glancing at herself in the rearview mirror, she wiped her lipstick off with tissue and messed up her hair a little. She needed to look like a person who'd worked a fifteen-hour day and *not* like someone who'd thought way too much about whether they looked cute enough for class.

Audrey got out of her car and slung her bag over one shoulder. This was always the most difficult part of the day—coming home and having no idea what kind of wreckage she would find. It was the very reason she persisted with the cloak-and-dagger approach to her night classes. They kept her going, allowing her mind to keep full of good things instead of bad. And the Brain-Changing Positivity class had already given her *so much* to mull over. This week, they were supposed to take note of one thing that made them happy and one thing that made them sad every day, so they could analyze mood trends.

Her footsteps fell quietly as she approached the front door. Over the road, two people were screaming at each other, the sound floating through an open window. The dog three doors down continued to bark, its deep timbre a warning rumble through the night air. Weariness seeped into her bones as she shoved her key into the front door's lock—but she couldn't let any of them see it.

She was the pillar of this family—the rock—and she had to be strong.

Pushing the door open, she called out a hello. Deanna

was sprawled out on the floor, doing her homework, Oliver's noise-cancelling headphones perched on her head while the TV blared the baseball game, Red Sox versus Rangers. Boston was losing, which wouldn't end well for any of them. Her dad was leaning back in his chair, a beat-up recliner with holes in the upholstery and a permanent ass-shaped dent in the cushion. The kitchen was a mess of Chinese takeout boxes and dirty dishes.

Why was he spending money on takeout when she'd left a perfectly good casserole in the fridge? But asking that kind of question would only get her a lecture about how he was head of the family, even though he did absolutely nothing to take care of them.

"Hey!" Deanna pushed her headphones off her head and smiled as she got to her feet, scooping up her work and hugging it to her chest. The gesture made Audrey smile, because she looked like a Mini-Me version of her. "How was work?"

"Busy, little munchkin. I'm glad to be home." Audrey went to the cupboard that contained their washing machine and deftly tossed her apron in, which had her blouse bundled up inside it. "Did you have dinner?"

"Dad got us takeout," she said with a beaming smile.

"Did you eat any vegetables?"

"Rice."

Audrey narrowed her eyes. "You know that's a grain, not a vegetable, right?"

"If it grows from a plant, it's a vegetable, isn't it?"

"Marijuana is a plant," Oliver quipped as he walked past, grabbing a glass from the cupboard and filling it with water. "And that's not a vegetable."

Audrey shot her brother a warning look. "I appreciate the backup, but that's not an appropriate example."

"Hey, *you* were the one talking about elephant penises

this morning." He shuddered.

"Can you lot fucking shut up?" her dad bellowed from his chair. "Are ya blind or somethin'? The goddamn game is on."

"Come on." Audrey ushered her brother and sister toward the back of the house. Oliver immediately disappeared into his room with a scowl. Of all the kids, he was the most sensitive to his father's outbursts and had a tendency to crawl into his shell. That worried Audrey, but she didn't have enough fuel left in the tank to deal with it tonight.

"Can you help me with my homework?" Deanna asked.

"I sure can." She closed the door behind them, and Georgie acknowledged them with a slight raise of her head before rolling over on the bottom bunk to face the wall and continue her speed-of-light texting.

Audrey dropped down onto her bed, which faced the bunk that Georgie and Deanna shared. "Sit here with me. Let's figure this out."

"High school work is hard," Deanna grumbled as she flipped to the algebra section of her math textbook. "I'll never get this."

"Yes, you will." Audrey grabbed her little sister's face in both hands and forced her to make eye contact. "You will get this because you're smart and one day you're going to graduate and fly far away from here, okay?"

"But you're not going to fly away, are you?" Deanna asked, her blue eyes shimmering with worry. "You're not going to leave us?"

Audrey put a smile on her face that was so well-practiced, even *she* might fall for it in the mirror. "I'm not leaving. I promise."

It was a promise she'd made over and over, and it never failed to make her stomach sink a little every time.

Chapter Four

Ronan was officially lost. Well, not exactly lost in the traditional sense, since he knew he was on Main Street. But he was lost in the sense that he'd ended up here without meaning to. Was Kissing Creek nothing but a circular maze, forever pushing people back to the quaint little row of shops with their pink and red accents? How did all roads come back to this point?

It was like some unwelcome metaphor for the circular nature his life was taking, bringing him back to the US without him feeling like he'd made any progress at all.

Ronan shook off the ugly—and untrue—thought as he paused and looked for the nearest street sign. Perhaps he'd turned left when he should have turned right. For some reason, he'd decided to leave his phone back in his apartment in a personal mindfulness experiment. He did that a lot. Experimenting on himself, setting challenges to test his hypotheses about various things, was how he kept his mind in good shape.

Although admittedly, he'd conducted smarter tests than

wandering around an unfamiliar town without his phone.

Deciding to abandon his plans to find the secondhand bookstore that had initially set him out on this journey, Ronan walked along the strip and took note of the businesses lined up like colorful tin soldiers. The town had all the usual suspects—hairdressers and fruit shops and butchers and restaurants of different cuisines. There was an Irish pub and a pet supply store and a beauty salon and a gift store. He'd counted four bakeries so far, each with a different specialty and increasingly cutesy names.

His personal favorite was *All You Need is Loaf.*

But there was one store that stood out as being unlike the others. Whereas many shop fronts featured bright paint, artfully designed chalkboards, and welcoming slogans, Game of Stones had an imposing black door and a window shrouded with heavy purple velvet. It appeared to be a new age store with tarot cards and crystals. In other words, a store trading on bullshit, at best.

And fraud, at worst.

He'd conducted an experiment for one of his classes at Cambridge in which he'd asked students to read their horoscope before taking a decision-making test. They hadn't been real horoscopes, of course, and the variance in tone of these messages—ranging from positive to neutral to negative—had greatly impacted the students' test results. It frustrated him that smart people would allow themselves to be derailed by something that had absolutely no basis in fact or reality.

While he looked into the window display, eyes narrowed at the hunks of amethyst and the splay of ornate golden cards, he caught sight of something that made him pause. Or, rather, some*one.*

A woman disappeared from behind a counter, blond hair catching the light. Was that…?

Shaking his head, he wrapped his hand around the handle of the door and pushed it open. A chime sounded above his head, and an older woman looked up from behind the cash register. She had long silvery hair that hung in a heavy braid, and her shoulders were wrapped in a colorful shawl. Her fingers were cluttered with rings.

"Ah," she said as though she had an idea who Ronan was. He'd put money on this being her thing—tricking people into believing she had some psychic powers when it was nothing more than a keen sense of perception. "You're the new professor."

He tried to hide his surprise. Wait, was he wearing elbow patches again? Ronan resisted the urge to look down at his outfit. It would hardly be difficult for her to pick him out—Kissing Creek was a small town, and he was clearly too old to be a student. Especially now that his beard had filled in.

"I'm not looking for anyone to read my fortune," he quipped.

"No? What can I help you with, Professor Walsh?" Her green eyes danced over him.

She knew his name, too? Still, that could be easily explained, since there was an article about him in the local paper, which touched on the book he would be writing during his visiting position.

"If you tell me my birthday and my mother's name, *then* I'll be impressed." His gaze flicked over the glass cabinet containing all manner of witchy things—candles and pagan-inspired jewelry; books on herbalism, crystal healing, and birth chart interpretation.

"I'm not psychic," the woman said with a kind smile. "My niece said 'oh no, that's Professor Walsh' before she darted into the back office."

There was a sound of frustration from a small doorway behind the counter, and a moment later, Audrey appeared with a tight smile on her face. Her blond hair tumbled down around her shoulders.

"Thanks, Aunt Harriet," she said through gritted teeth. "Way to have a girl's back."

Niece? Interesting. Now that he looked closer, he could see the resemblance—wide eyes and ready, dimpled smiles. But Audrey's aunt had a slim frame and small shoulders swamped by the flowy fabric of her shawl and dress. It gave the appearance of the clothing wearing her rather than the other way around.

Whereas Audrey's curvy figure was the one in charge of her simple blue dress and cardigan, no doubt about it.

"Why don't you help the professor, dear?" the other woman said with a sly smile. "Show him those love intuition cards. Maybe he would like a sexual fortune reading?"

"Harriet," Audrey rasped under her breath, her cheeks turning a bright shade of pink. "Why don't you let him decide what he needs?"

"I'll be out back if you have any questions." Harriet stuck her hand out toward Ronan, and he took it, a stack of bracelets jangling on her arm as they shook. "Nice to meet you, Professor."

"It's Ronan," he said.

A second later, the woman was gone in a cloud of something densely perfumed. Patchouli. He recognized it from the one time he'd been allowed to set foot in his mother's art studio in the woods. Maybe that's why he hated all this hocus-pocus shit…it reminded him of his mother.

"I'm *so* sorry about that." Audrey shook her head. "She's…"

"Unique?"

"Uh yeah, that's one way of putting it." She laughed. "Another way would be that the woman doesn't have a filter and takes great pleasure in mercilessly embarrassing her family members."

There wasn't a hint of malice in Audrey's voice, only warmth and affection. "Are you two close?"

"Very. We don't always see eye to eye, but I know she has my back...unless there's an eligible man around, of course."

"How do you know I'm eligible?"

Audrey's gaze automatically flicked down to Ronan's hand, where, of course, he wore no ring. But she shook her head, pressing a hand to her cheek. "I didn't mean to say... that's not...I'm not assuming anything about you. It's your business, not mine."

"I *am* single." The words popped out before he could fully think through the ramifications.

What ramifications? It's not like you're hitting on her or asking her out on a date. There's no rule that says a professor can't confirm his relationship status.

And all of that was true. But Ronan knew he wouldn't be checking himself mentally unless there was some reason for the defense of his actions. Like, say that he found Audrey not only incredibly attractive but entirely intriguing.

He'd had a hell of a time getting through his class last Wednesday night. His eyes gravitated to her as if pulled by a magnetic force. He'd hunted out the details of her, like the way she scribbled notes with a furious curiosity that made him smile. He'd noticed the way she sucked on the inside of her cheek when he'd posed a thought-provoking question in class and how she'd twirled her hair, her gaze drifting toward something that nobody else could see. She got lost in learning. She was enamored by it.

And that only made her more attractive.

"Better keep that on the down low," Audrey said. "Unless you want women lining up around the block to see if they can snag Kissing Creek's newest bachelor."

"I'm not looking for anything but a chance to work."

"So no sexual fortune reading for you, then?" she teased.

He did *not* need those words coming out of her mouth—because the only sexual fortune he was interested in involved the woman standing right in front of him, and that was a very, *very* bad idea. Never mind the fact that he'd woken up with Audrey on his mind the last three nights since he saw her in class.

In fact, one particular dream had taken place at that very desk and rows of empty seats facing him while he took Audrey from—

Ronan coughed as if physically trying to dislodge the thought. "I like your earrings."

It seemed like the safest thing he could grasp in order to move the conversation on. Audrey's hand drifted up to her ear. The earrings were made of gold, with delicate wire wrapped around glossy black stones in a way that made them hang and catch the light. The effect was a striking contrast against her lighter hair.

"Thanks. They're obsidian."

"And what does obsidian do?" He raised an eyebrow.

"It's a protective stone that shields against negativity, but it's also a reminder that every person has lightness *and* darkness inside them."

"Do you believe in this stuff?"

She didn't strike him as the kind of person who put stock in woo-woo things like crystals and The Secret. Maybe she was only working here as a favor to her aunt.

"Do I believe that everyone has a light and dark side? Yeah. Do I think wearing pretty rocks is going to change my destiny? Not so much." She lifted one shoulder into a shrug. "But people find comfort and security in all kinds of things, so who am I to judge?"

"And where do you find comfort and security?" Ronan asked, leaning against the shop's glass counter.

She looked a little taken aback by his question. "In knowledge. Books. Actually, obsidian is quite interesting. They used it in Paleolithic times to make arrowheads and other tools, and it's formed when molten lava cools very quickly."

"I bet you'd be great at pub trivia," he said with a laugh. "I'd want you on my team."

"I've never done pub trivia before. Apparently, they have a great one in the next town over, but…I'm always working." She pressed her hands down on the countertop. "Anyway, I'm sure you didn't come in here to chat your Saturday afternoon away and hear my random thoughts on things."

Truthfully, he could quite happily listen to Audrey talk about anything all day long. She had the kind of voice that could lure a man out to sea if he didn't keep his wits about him.

Maybe this is your lack of social network talking.

All his friends were scattered across the world these days, following their research to far-flung places. His closest friend had a teaching post in Sydney, Australia, and the rest of the crew from his Harvard days were in various cities across the U.S., Canada, and Europe.

In Kissing Creek, he knew nobody.

"I could listen to you, actually," he said, and Audrey's shy smile lit a flame inside him.

"Is there something *specific* I can help you with?" she asked, her olive-green eyes looking straight at him. Up close, he could see her irises were speckled with a darker green and gold, and a heavy line of lashes framed the whole beautiful picture. "I'm not an expert in any of these things, but I might be able to point you in the right direction."

What about help starting over?

Starting over seemed to be his thing. He'd tried to reinvent himself in college, shaking off his unhappy home life and childhood. Then, when Harvard hadn't fulfilled him, he'd ventured to Cambridge and started building a life there, with even more space between him and the past. But while his work propelled him up in the ranks of his profession, his personal life was...sorely lacking.

And now he was here, in this little college town, with no specific future in sight.

"I'm lost," he said.

"Lost?" She cocked her head.

Ronan cleared his throat. He needed to get a goddamn grip on himself. He *wasn't* some bruised and damaged soul in need of a beautiful woman to fill the cracks in him. He *didn't* screw and drink his way through his problems, letting bad decisions override sensible thought. He was better than that. Better than the hedonistic parents who'd birthed him and didn't want the responsibility that came with it.

"Uh yeah, I came out without my phone, and I was looking for the Second Chance Bookstore, but every street in this town seems to lead back to Main Street." He raked a hand through his hair and let out a self-deprecating laugh. "It seems I'm perfectly capable of writing a complex thesis but not so great at navigating a few streets."

"Welcome to Kissing Creek," she said. "Where none of the streets make sense and everything has a pun for a name. I'm guessing you kept walking along Gertrude Street when you should have turned off at Rose. It's such a small little street that people often mistake it for a dead end, but it actually goes right through to the other side, and the bookstore is around the corner."

"Ah, that's exactly what happened."

"I could find my way there with my eyes closed. It's my favorite shop." She smoothed her hands down the front of her dress, which had a pretty gathered waist and buttons all the way up the front. There was a patch on one side where it looked as though a hole had been covered with some embroidery. "I can draw you a map if you'd like?"

"We're closing!" Harriet poked her head out of the back room. "You can walk him over."

Audrey's expression tightened, and then she swung her head back toward her aunt. "What are you talking about? It's only three-thirty and—"

"I'm not feeling well."

"But I can—"

"We're closing early. I'll count the cash." Harriet made a shooing motion that caused all the bracelets on her wrists to rattle. "Get out of here."

For a moment, Audrey didn't move, and Ronan got the impression there was some nonverbal communication passing back and forth between the two women. Eventually, it appeared Harriet won the silent battle, because Audrey sighed and turned to Ronan, a resigned expression on her face.

"How about I walk you over?" she said. "It looks like we're closing early after all."

Chapter Five

Tarot began as a card game and wasn't originally intended for fortune telling.

Audrey was going to plan a creative form of payback for her aunt over the next few hours. Not that she minded walking in the sunshine with Ronan at all—far, *far* from it. But that was exactly the point; her aunt was pushing her toward something she wanted but couldn't have. And while Audrey was intimately familiar with wanting things she couldn't have, flinging another unrequited desire onto the pile felt particularly cruel.

"So, you're a barista *and* a hawker of spiritual wares," Ronan said as they exited the shop. Audrey paused to flip the sign on the door, signaling that Game of Stones was now closed.

"Hawker of spiritual wares." She laughed. "I like that."

"What other hidden talents do you have up your sleeve?"

"I wouldn't say I have any talents," Audrey replied. They headed up Main Street, past her aunt's shop and the delicatessen and the craft store with a garland of rainbow pompoms in the window. "I mean, I make a good coffee, and I've been working hard on my latte art. But that's kind of it."

"What's your specialty?"

She tapped a finger to her cheek. "I can do a really cool bird with a feathery tail. Customers like that one. I do a lot of hearts, too."

"I'll have to come in again and get one of your specialties."

Audrey's stomach did a little somersault at the thought of Ronan coming to the Kisspresso Café specifically to see her.

Not to see you—to get one of your coffees. Just the same as all your other regulars.

Why did he have to be so obnoxiously handsome? It was really *very* inconvenient. Attending class each week would be a battle of wills to pay attention to what was coming out of his mouth and *not* how his arm muscles flexed as he scribbled on the whiteboard. Her mind didn't drift easily—Audrey was as focused as they came—but there was something about the deep timbre of his voice that lulled her into a dreamy pink haze.

Not to mention that the man had an ass like an actual peach.

Really? That's *what you're focusing on right now?*

Ugh. How shallow was she? It was particularly hypocritical, since she'd always felt it unfair that men wrote her off because she was carrying some extra weight. Or sometimes the opposite—that her weight was *why* they liked her, and it had nothing to do with what went on inside her head or her heart.

Yet now she was objectifying Ronan in that exact way.

Maybe it was simply a case of figuring out how to scratch her "itch." Sharing a room with her sisters did *not* lend itself to an active sex life—or any sex life at all. And these days, Audrey had too much on her plate to really put in the effort to find someone she had a connection with. Unfortunately, all that pent-up energy, coupled with the fact that Ronan was hot enough to fry a steak on, meant she couldn't seem to force her brain to think a single sensible thought around him.

"Come visit me anytime," she said, though her voice sounded a little higher-pitched than normal. Could she not act cool for once in her sorry life? "And what were you doing in my aunt's shop? You don't strike me as the type to be into all that."

He turned to her, his full lips quirking into a smile. "Funny. I thought the same about you."

"I'm there to help out. She's owned that shop since forever, but she's getting older. She needs to share the load."

That wasn't entirely true—more like her aunt was doing her a favor by giving her gainful employment and paying her more than she was worth so she could keep her siblings fed and clothed. Since Audrey refused to take money for nothing—aka charity, which felt utterly demeaning and rubbed against her sense of independence—they'd come to an arrangement where she worked at Game of Stones two days a week and helped out with the books.

But, for some reason, she didn't want Ronan to know all that. Because "all that" could lead to other things she didn't want to talk about.

"What's the weirdest thing someone has come in for?" There was a mischievous sparkle to his blue eyes, and her heart thumped insistently in her chest. The man could melt a grown woman with those eyes.

"Uh..." She forced her brain to shift gears. "We had this guy once who was in town for the weekend. He wanted a tarot reading done, but with his own cards, and they were kind of...graphic."

Ronan raised a brow.

She cringed at the memory. "Tarot has four suits, right.

Swords, wands, pentacles, and cups. These cards had...uh, phallic images for some of the suits. I'll leave it to you to guess what they used for *swords*."

Ronan laughed, and the sound was rough and raspy and delightfully at odds with his smooth voice. It sent a shiver down Audrey's spine. "What did you do?"

"I wasn't giving the reading, thankfully. We have a woman who comes in every weekend to take clients, so she ended up with him. He took the whole thing very seriously, and our poor tarot lady had to do the whole thing with a lot of very large, veiny penises staring up at her."

Ronan shook his head, still chuckling. "Veiny?"

"Uh, yeah." Audrey wrinkled her nose. "It was gross."

"I'll bet."

"It's funny. These days, we think of tarot as very hocus-pocus. But tarot originated as a card game back in the fifteenth century and wasn't widely used for divination until the late eighteenth century."

"I stand by my earlier assessment. If there's ever trivia in Kissing Creek, I want you on my team."

Her brain circled on "I want you" over and over, creating a sexy echo in her head. Yeah, right; a man like Ronan would never, ever want a woman like her. White trash, former trailer-park girl skirting the poverty line. A woman with nothing to offer. Did she seriously think a professor would be interested in a barista with a fountain of useless general knowledge?

"So, uh, the bookstore is down here." She pointed down Rose Street, which looked more like a glorified driveway than a road. "Take a left at the end."

He paused, eyes searching her face. The sun was high, and it was so warm Audrey felt like she was burning up under her cardigan. She only wore the damn thing to ward against the air-conditioning her aunt blasted to combat her hot flashes. But outside, under the intense contact of Ronan's delicious blue gaze, Audrey was seriously concerned that she might not-so-spontaneously combust.

"Would you like to accompany me?"

Damn. He spoke like a freaking Jane Austen hero, and that only served to ratchet her desire up a few more notches. The men she knew spoke in a series of grunts, and they most certainly didn't use words like "accompany."

"Sure." She was powerless to do anything but agree. "I love books."

You love books? Really? That's the best you could do?

Audrey had her nerd label all but stamped to her forehead. She devoured books like her life depended on it. Second Chance often had sales to clear out old stock where the books were a quarter each. She'd come home with a big stack every time, and there was something about the cracked spines and coffee stains and notes in the margin that she adored.

"I love books, too." Ronan grinned, and Audrey's heart thumped.

She would need to be on her best behavior today, because it was fine for Ronan to channel some Colin Firth–level sexiness, but she needed to keep her head on straight. Scratching an itch was fine, but *not* with her professor.

• • •

Ronan watched as Audrey slipped her cardigan off and slung it over one arm. The thin straps of her dress exposed rounded shoulders dusted with freckles and the sweet slope of her neck. He cleared his throat and forced his eyes ahead of him as they walked down the narrow street. It was almost an alley, with the backs of houses facing them rather than the front. One yard had a large lemon tree hanging slightly over the fence, bright yellow fruit dotting its full branches.

"What do you read?" he asked. Books seemed like a safe topic—something he could talk about for hours that would hopefully stop his mind from veering into any inappropriate thoughts about Audrey.

Your student, Audrey.

Yeah, he needed the reminder...which was highly unusual. In over a decade of some form of teaching, he'd never once felt tempted to cross the line. But there was something about Audrey that was like a hook in his brain, and he couldn't shake it free.

"Mostly nonfiction," she said. "But I'm open to any topic. True crime, history, travel memoirs, self-help, essay collections."

"It's admirable that you find time for recreational reading while you're studying. I know a lot of students find it difficult, given how much they have to read for class." It had certainly been that way for Ronan. He'd always been the kid with his nose in a book—something he'd been mocked for as a teenager. "Are you taking a full course load?"

"Umm..."

He allowed his gaze to slide back over to her in time to see her brows knitting above her nose.

"No, I'm not taking a full load," she replied. "I'm not actually working toward a degree."

That surprised Ronan. Sure, he'd noticed that she was older than the average student in his undergrad classes. He'd put her at mid-twenties, maybe a little older. There was a quiet maturity about her that set her apart.

"Oh? Is it workforce development, then?"

"For my jobs as a barista and hawker of spiritual wares? Uh, no." She laughed, but it sounded forced. "I don't really need too much development for those kinds of jobs."

She wasn't studying toward a degree or taking classes to enhance her employment opportunities. "Why *are* you taking my class?"

"For pleasure…of learning, I mean." She nodded as if reassuring herself. "I like to learn about different things. It's why I read and listen to podcasts and take night classes. Not all learning needs to be working toward something, right?"

They'd paused at the front of the bookstore, which looked like something he'd expect to find in the Shire. The low doorframe and tiny windows stacked with books had a distinct "hobbit hole" feel to them, and Ronan was sure he'd find some treasures inside.

"You're right," he said. "But it's not often I encounter a student in my classes purely for the love of learning. You're a rare breed."

She looked up at him like she wasn't quite sure what to make of his assessment—whether it was a compliment or not. "Rare. That's a new one."

They walked into the store, and it was as gloriously dusty and crammed as he'd hoped. Ronan had a thing for secondhand bookstores, probably because his grandmother was an avid reader and they'd spent many school vacations hunting out teetering piles of long-forgotten tomes and first editions of the Agatha Christie novels she loved so much.

Since he'd fled England with only a suitcase to his name, the bookshelf in his furnished campus accommodation was unacceptably bare. Besides, small towns might not be the most exciting places to live, but he'd come across some of his best finds in out-of-the-way places like Kissing Creek.

Audrey trailed her fingertip along a shelf of thick leather-bound vintage encyclopedias, her eyes flicking and assessing every volume she passed. The store was dim, since books filled every inch of the place, including being piled up high in front of the windows. There was a man near the door, sitting behind his desk with his head tipped forward, glasses perched precariously on the end of his nose.

Audrey held her finger up to her lips. "Mr. Hart likes to have a snooze in the middle of the day. He's almost ninety, but he refuses to let anyone take over the shop."

"Is this town straight out of a rom-com?" Ronan shook his head. "Don't tell me—somewhere there's a princess undercover as a regular girl."

"It certainly isn't me; I'll tell you that." Audrey snorted. "And are you intimately acquainted with rom-coms?"

"Not intimately, no. But I lived in a shared house with two other TAs at one point, and one of them watched those things on repeat. Christmas was unbearable."

"Oh, but they're so fun." Audrey clapped her hands together. "Secret babies and time-traveling royalty and small towns where everyone's always getting snowed in. And cute animals!"

"I don't think I'm the target audience, somehow." Ronan found himself moving farther into the store, the aisles narrowing so much that his shoulders bumped the shelves on both sides. He turned to his side to shuffle through a particularly small section. "This shop is a fire hazard."

"I know." Audrey sighed, a smile blossoming on her full lips. "Isn't it wonderful?"

"It really is."

They were standing closer than Ronan would have liked. Actually, that was a complete lie. They were standing close enough that Ronan liked it *very* much, because Audrey's hand brushed his as they reached for the same book. Her gaze shot up to meet him in a way that had his stomach knotting. Clearly, she'd felt that sharp electric spark, too.

"Sorry," she muttered, ducking her head. "You go ahead."

"No, you go." He gestured for her to slide the book out from between its shelf mates.

How was this whole scene so romantically charged? It was dark and cool and a little musty, but Ronan felt like he was in the basement of some castle, with a woman tempting as all sin tucked right beside him. The smell of her—like flowers and fresh air—mingled with the scent of old books and wood, and he had the very real vision of pushing her against the heaving shelves and kissing her senseless. Of pushing that pretty dress up her thighs and—

Hell fucking no. What's wrong with you?

Audrey was still looking at him, green eyes almost engulfed by black. Nostrils flaring a little. Her teeth dented her lower lip, and her breath skipped like a needle on a scratched-up record.

"So…you've lived here your whole life?" It was small-talk drivel, but that was better than having his mind run wild with fantasies.

"In the bookstore?" She smirked before turning to hook her finger into the spine of the book, sliding out to inspect the blurb on the back cover.

"You know what I mean."

"Yes, I'm a Kissing Creek resident from birth." There was a note of something dark in her reply, like she wasn't proud of admitting it. "Pink, white, and red runs in my blood. Why did *you* come here? I can't imagine Harrison Beech is high up on any professor's list of desirable colleges to teach at."

"Why do you say that?"

"We're close enough to Boston that most people move away, but not so close that we feel like we're part of the city," she said with a shrug. To some people, it might have sounded like a negative, but Audrey stated it as though it was simply fact. "And the average age might be mid-thirties, but don't be fooled. There are hardly any people here who *are* that age; it's simply an average of college students and retirees."

"What about you?"

She looked up, her eyes narrowed slightly. "Isn't it rude to ask a woman her age?"

"You brought up the topic," he replied.

"I'm twenty-six, and my birthday is at the end of the year."

He grinned. "Does that make you a Pisces?"

Audrey smirked. "Nice try, but Pisces is mid-February to March. Is that the only star sign you know?"

Busted. "Yeah. I was more curious to see if you knew about it, since you're such a collector of knowledge."

"I know about the star signs because we have books and astrological charts in the shop. For the record, I'm a Capricorn."

She replaced the book on the shelf and wandered ahead of him, her hips shifting as she maneuvered around a stack of leather-bound tomes that came up to her waist.

"What does that mean for the uninitiated?" he asked.

"I'm stubborn, persistent, practical, and a realist. Arguably the most boring of all the star signs, in my humble opinion. Well, all the earth signs get that unfair label, I guess." She glanced back over her shoulder. "That sounded like complete gibberish to you, didn't it?"

"Total gibberish." And *yet*, Ronan found himself once again impossibly fascinated. "What star sign would you rather be?"

"Leo maybe...but with less ego. Ooh, no, Scorpio. I want to be moody and mysterious and passionate." She grinned. "Highly unpractical and a little bit of a loose cannon."

"Ah, but you're much too sensible for that." Anybody could see it—Audrey was diligent and hardworking, and she took responsibility for her actions.

She might call it boring, but Ronan admired those traits. Who knew what his life might have been like if his parents had embodied a bit more responsibility?

Audrey laughed. "I'm afraid I am. Comes with the territory."

"And what territory is that?"

She blinked, the amusement in her expression evaporating and leaving behind something else. "Just my life."

"Being a barista and hawking spiritual wares?" He shouldn't prod; it was none of his business. But he wanted to know everything there was to know about Audrey, the mysterious girl with the beguiling smile.

"Putting food on the table for my siblings." Her gaze never left his, almost as if she wanted to gauge his reaction. Suddenly it all made sense—not studying toward anything because that was too much commitment, and the two jobs she seemed to enjoy but wasn't excited about. "Playing mom doesn't lend itself to being a passionate loose cannon."

Ronan's own mother would beg to differ, no doubt. "How many siblings?"

"Four, but one is off on her own adventures now. She's studying at Duke." Audrey's proud smile made Ronan like her even more. "The twins are seventeen and getting ready to start college applications. Deanna is fourteen. She started high school this year."

"I bet they look up to you," he said.

"They don't have much choice," she said with a rueful smile. "But I try to make sure they have everything they need. The wants are a little harder, but we make do. We're a good family."

We're a good family.

Her words had a hint of defensiveness to them, like she'd been told otherwise at some point and felt the need to stand in front of her family name with sword and shield.

He wondered what happened to her parents—were they sick, dead? Or just deadbeats, like his own? For a moment, Ronan felt a kindred connection with Audrey. Although he'd never had the responsibility of looking after Keira, as Grandma Orna had been there since they were born. And she'd been an entire family wrapped up in one person.

"And that's about as much talking about myself as I like to do, thank you very much," Audrey said, cutting into the questions forming a tornado in his head.

Ronan held up his hands. "Got it. No more personal questions."

They moved toward the back of the store, where yet more shelves sagged under the weight of a seemingly infinite number of pages and spines. He found the mystery section and scoured the Agatha Christie titles, looking for anything his grandmother might not own. She'd collected first editions of plenty of the later Christie novels from the sixties and seventies, but those from the thirties and forties were much harder to come by, often being snapped up by collectors and rare-book dealers to be sold for an exorbitant price.

"You're a mystery reader?" Audrey asked, peering around his arm.

"My grandmother is. She's got quite the collection, so I always keep a lookout for anything special when I find a new bookstore."

"You're looking for books for your grandmother's collection?" Audrey shook her head. "Could you be any more of a cinnamon roll?"

"A what?" He blinked.

"It's very sweet, that's all." She laughed.

"She was the one who taught me to read," he said. Orna had done it in her typical fashion, thrusting a book upon him when he hadn't been the least bit interested and forcing him to sit still until they'd made it all the way through.

Unlike a lot of grandmothers, she wasn't warm and fuzzy. She didn't fill her house with the scent of fresh-baked cookies, and she certainly didn't let her grandkids get away with whatever they wanted. But she'd prepared Ronan for the world—she'd loved him in the way she knew how, with her tough attitude and concrete work ethic and her survival mentality. She was the reason he got into Harvard when most were turned away. She was the reason he wouldn't stop until he'd achieved his lofty ambition for a tenured position at an Ivy League school and gotten his work into mainstream bookstores.

He owed her everything.

Just as Ronan was about to further question her on what exactly made him a "cinnamon roll," there was a commotion at the front of the store.

And the sound of something distinctly animal.

He swung his head toward Audrey, who'd frozen beside him. "What the hell was that?"

Chapter Six

Llamas don't bite, but they can spit up to fifteen feet.

"It's the llama," she whispered, her green eyes wide.

She said it with the same level of awestruck yet fear-filled reverence as if she'd announced that Satan himself had walked into the bookstore.

"A llama?" He raised a brow.

"*The* llama." She sucked in a breath. "We only have one — our college baseball team's mascot. She's mean."

"Aren't llamas supposed to be all fuzzy and cute?"

Audrey made a scoffing noise. "No. You're thinking about alpacas, which are sweet-natured little bundles of fleece and eyelashes. They wouldn't hurt a fly. I *love* alpacas. But llamas… They'll cut you."

For some reason, he had this vision of a llama wielding a butcher's knife, *Psycho* style. "I'm sure you're exaggerating."

He walked past the rows of books. There was a startled yelp from the front of the store and something that sounded like a stack of books being knocked over.

"Stay back, Lily!" Mr. Hart yelled.

Ronan glanced back over his shoulder at Audrey, who shrugged as if to say: it's your funeral. He'd seen llamas before...well, not in person. Only in memes that his colleagues liked to send around occasionally. Then there was his friend who'd gone to South America and posted a bunch of pictures with him and the furry creatures to Facebook. They didn't look *that* scary.

"Lily...don't you dare!"

Ronan exited the aisle in time to see Lily, whom he could only assume was the shaggy beast taking up most of the space in the front of the bookstore—thus blocking the exit—nudge a pile of books, sending them toppling over.

"You confounding animal!" Mr. Hart was shakily getting to his feet. He was protected by a large, heavy banker's desk, complete with hunter green leather insert and matching lamp. "Go on, shoo! Get out of here."

But Lily merely looked at him with the disdain of someone who knew they were in the position of power. She stretched up to her full height, and Ronan gulped. Okay, so maybe she *did* look a little mean. And damn if she didn't weigh over three hundred pounds. At her full height, he'd guess her to be a hair under six feet tall, meaning she could look him right in the eyes.

Her coat was mainly white, with patches of a warm brown on her face, neck, and hindquarters. For a second, he swore her eyes flashed at him.

"Do they normally get that big, or is she special?" Ronan turned around to look at Audrey, only to find her hiding behind a smaller bookshelf, the top of her blond head poking over the top. "Coward."

"Coward?" she gasped. "You can *see* that thing, right? She's a monster."

"Audrey, dear. Is that you?" Mr. Hart peered into the

bookstore, trying to locate the source of the feminine voice. "Can you call the farm? She's making a mess of everything again."

Lily snorted, as though insulted that her "decorating skills" weren't being admired. As if in retaliation, she lifted her hind hoof and kicked at another stack of books, sending them flying.

"Dammit!" Mr. Hart slapped his hand down on the desk. "Why do you hate me, llama?"

"I'll see if I can get her to back up and go through the door." Ronan took a step forward, hands outstretched, and the llama immediately swung her head toward him. "Whoa girl, easy."

Behind him, Audrey could be heard talking to someone on the phone. But Lily didn't seem content to wait for her owner to come collect her. Oh no—she seemed determined to destroy everything in her path.

"Stop!" Ronan clapped his hands and immediately regretted it. Lily looked at him, her head slightly lowered, as if she were about to charge him. "It's okay, girl. We just want you to leave the books alone."

He used his best teacher voice—the one he'd leaned on many times when a student was crying in his office about how they were going to fail...usually because they'd left things to the last minute, he might add. It was equal parts soothing and steady, designed not to raise blood pressure.

But clearly Lily did *not* want to be calmed.

Instead, she made the most bloodcurdling sound that Ronan had ever heard. "Uh oh."

"You made her angry," Audrey said from behind the bookcase. "It's not good when she gets angry."

"Is that what they're supposed to sound like?" Ronan blinked.

The llama let out the same bleating, hollering sound,

which could only be described as Chewbacca on helium crossed with angry cat gurgling. In other words, a sound that would haunt him for the rest of his life.

Lily took a step toward him, her big body squeezing between the bookshelves and Mr. Hart's desk. The space was cramped, even for humans. But for the llama, if she went too much farther in, she'd risk getting stuck.

That wouldn't be good for anyone.

Maybe she was scared. Animals were wired to defend themselves, right? If he didn't treat her like a monster, then perhaps she wouldn't act like one.

"There's a good llama." Ronan took a step toward Lily, and she tossed her head, glaring at him. Could llamas glare? It certainly felt like it. "Let's go outside. It's sunny outside; you'll like it better out there."

"Don't get too close," Audrey advised from behind her barricade. "She—"

Audrey's advice was cut short by the llama drawing her head back and spitting right in Ronan's face. The moisture hit the side of his cheek, as instinct had made him turn his head, and now it was sliding down to his jaw in a slow, soggy trail.

"She spat in his face!" Mr. Hart shoved his glasses back up his nose and made a sound that could only be classified as chortling. Unabashedly gleeful chortling.

Ronan dragged his hand across his left cheek, unsure whether that made it better or worse, because now his arm was sticky, too. "Score one, llama."

Lily looked smug as hell, her deep black eyes fringed by white eyelashes trained steadily on him. Her ears stuck straight up, flicking like she was keeping close tabs on everything around her. Her bottom teeth stuck out a little and might fool one into thinking she was cute, if a little derpy.

But Lily was not *cute*.

"That wasn't very nice, but I get it. You're feeling

threatened."

Lily brayed as if to say: *no, I'm* not*!* But llamas weren't inherently aggressive...were they? Ronan held his hand out, allowing her to sniff him. That's what he'd always done with dogs, and it seemed to work. And really, besides the occasional interaction with a friendly canine on the street, his experience with animals was zip.

"We can be friends," he said to the llama. She sniffed the back of his hand and tossed her head again. "Please don't spit on me."

Thankfully, she didn't. This time she nudged his hand with her nose and stomped her feet. What the hell was that supposed to mean? He took another step forward, and the llama shifted, her rear knocking into a bookcase so that it rattled precariously.

"I think she's stuck." Ronan skirted into the aisle closest to the llama and tried to see if he could move some of the shelving.

The entire bookstore was made up of single, mismatched bookshelves that looked as though they'd been rescued from charity shops and estate sales and front lawns. That meant none of it was bolted together. Talk about a safety hazard. Between all the paper in this store, the loose shelving, and the dust...this place was a 911 call waiting to happen.

You can worry about getting crushed to death after *you've avoided being spit on...again.*

Bracing his shoulder against one of the shelves, Ronan tried to nudge it forward. The damn thing didn't budge. Clearly he needed to get back in the gym. Sucking in a breath, he tried again, and this time the unit moved a few inches.

Lily stomped her feet.

"Don't get mad. I'm trying to help you." He heaved again and budged the shelf a few more inches.

It was enough that Lily could turn, whereas before she'd

only been able to move forward. Or potentially backward... could llamas walk backward? Add that to the list of things he didn't know. Thankfully, the animal took the opportunity to swing herself around, knocking more books over in the process and heading back the way she'd came. On her way out, she tossed her head and kicked back at the doorframe in some kind of parting shot.

• • •

Audrey was about to call out for Ronan to keep watch on Lily, because she'd been known to zigzag across the road, putting herself and others at risk. But as Ronan disappeared, following the llama out the bookshop's only entry and exit, she heard the sound of Lily's owner out front.

Breathing a sigh of relief, Audrey crept out from behind her protective wall of books. Mr. Hart was standing behind his desk, a frown on his wrinkled old face. "I hope you and your boyfriend are going to clean up this mess, missy."

"He's not my..." She sighed and shook her head. "Of course, Mr. Hart."

There was no point trying to correct the man—most days he didn't remember anyone's name, let alone who'd been in and out of his store. Hell, he might not remember Lily being in here, and then he'd wonder if a tornado had blown through. It was sad, really. She remembered the excitable, bespectacled man who somehow knew every single book in this place and the exact person who should read it.

Kneeling down in front of the desk, she started collecting the books and putting them back into piles, having no idea if there was any rhyme or reason to the order. A second later, Ronan walked back through the door. He had a wad of tissues in his hand and was cleaning up his face.

"I met Lily's owner," he said with a slight frown.

Audrey stifled a smile and kept about her work. "First impressions?"

"They're perfectly suited."

She snorted. "Truer words have never been spoken. Devon Huxley is, uh...efficient in his personal dealings."

"Meaning he likes dealing with people to be over as quickly as possible?" He shoved the tissues into his back pocket. "Yeah, I got that impression."

"You were very brave...with Lily."

"Brave or stupid, it's a fine line."

"I'd say stupid," chimed in Mr. Hart as he settled back into his chair. Audrey and Ronan exchanged amused glances a second later as the sound of snoring filled the bookstore once again.

Ronan shook his head, chuckling to himself, and set about sliding the bookshelf back into place from the opposite side. From her position crouched on the floor, Audrey watched, her hands fluttering uselessly over the books as her heart thumped in her chest. Ronan's body was...magnificent.

His arms bulged, the muscles flexing and working, as he pushed into the bookcase. The way he was angled, leaning in with his shoulder and bracing his legs, made his ass look like *David*-esque perfection. Audrey groped for another book to add to her stack, her fingers brushing nothing but air.

"Might be easier if you were looking at what you're doing." Ronan's voice jolted her back into the present, and she snatched her hand to her chest as though she'd touched something hot.

"I *am* looking," she grumbled defensively, scooting along on her knees to the next upended stack of books.

Yeah, you were looking all right.

"I know you can't keep your eyes off me, what with all the llama spit glistening on my face."

Audrey grinned. "How could you possibly know that was

my personal catnip?"

"I could tell that about you from the moment you accused me of being a scam artist. I thought to myself, she's a llama-spit woman through and through."

A deep, genuine laugh shot out of Audrey—so loud, in fact, that there was a startled snort from behind the desk and a brief pause before the quiet snoring started up again. "The professor has a sense of humor, I see."

"It came free with my elbow patches."

Okay, so he was hot, strong, sweetly looked for books for his grandma, *and* had an epic sense of self-deprecating humor? *That* was an unprecedented combination. So unprecedented, in fact, that it had only previously existed in Audrey's head, filed in a box marked "perfect men who don't exist."

Ronan nudged the bookshelf again, sliding it mostly back into place. How the hell he could move the damn thing when it was packed with books was beyond her.

Well, it wasn't *quite* beyond her imagination. Something told Audrey she'd have to make an effort *not* to imagine it when they were back in class next Wednesday.

"So tell me," he said, bending down to collect a few books that had toppled off shelves in the move. "What do you know about llamas?"

"Are you going to quiz my knowledge on everything now?" She looked up at him, ready to meet the challenge.

"I'm curious how long it will take before I find a topic you don't know anything about."

"Llamas have a gestation period of three-hundred and fifty days. They don't bite, but they can spit up to fifteen feet." She shuddered. "Actually, spitting at humans is rarer than people think, and it's often a sign that the llamas were over-socialized during rearing. Typically, llamas spit at each other, but if they've been overhandled as crias—which is what you call baby llamas—then they tend to treat humans as they would other llamas. Hence the...glistening."

Ronan bobbed his head. "Well, that shut me up, then, didn't it?"

"The spitting or my facts?" She got to her feet and dusted her hands down the front of her dress.

He served up the most delicious lopsided smile that crinkled the corners of his blue eyes and made him look even sexier than he already did. "Both."

Why did he have to be her professor? Even if it was only a visiting, temporary thing. Why couldn't he be some hunky tourist in town for a month...or four? Why couldn't he be the new owner of a bakery or restaurant or the hardware store?

Why did the universe see fit to constantly tempt her with things she couldn't have?

Happiness is wanting what you get.

Her mother had told her that once when Audrey was young and crying over the fact that she had old sneakers instead of the cool new ones the other girls wore to school. Her mother was one of those serene people who could always find the silver lining in things. Since she was young, Audrey had tried to emulate her.

It's better that he's off-limits, because you know *you don't want anything serious. What would you do, anyway? Invite him back to your house?*

The very thought of it sent a shiver down her spine. No way would she *ever* bring a man home—not with her father causing the house to reek of beer and cigarettes. Especially not with the fact that privacy was a premium she couldn't afford. Not to mention the fact that she didn't want him to know she lived in the bad part of town...for some reason, that made her pride cringe.

Therefore, it was easier *not* to go there. That was why Ronan was her professor, so she would know that getting close was not only ill-advised but pointless.

"Do you want to grab a coffee?" Ronan asked as they finished up with the bookstore. He was looking delightfully rugged now, with hair mussed and shirt slightly askew. The bookstore was silent except for the quiet snore of Mr. Hart up front.

Audrey could all but hear the pounding of her heart and the fact that she very much *did* want to have a coffee with Ronan droning like a chant in her bloodstream. She couldn't remember the last time she'd been so attracted to a man. He was smart, gorgeous, and hard-bodied. Funny.

Happiness is wanting what you get.

"I have to get home," Audrey said with a perfectly practiced smile. "Maybe next time."

But it was a lie. For the sake of her heart, there would never be a next time.

Chapter Seven

The most innings ever played in a Major League Baseball game was in 1920 when Boston played 26 innings against Brooklyn.

Audrey leaned back against the side of Big Red, breathing in the cool, early-morning air. There were only a few cars scattered throughout the parking lot for the Chinnery State Park, signaling she was one of a handful of early birds ready to seek out nature while the rest of the town slept the wee hours of Sunday morning away. Come rain, hail, snow, or shine, she met her best friend, Nicole, every Sunday morning in this very spot.

A familiar car turned into the parking lot, and Nicole pulled up beside her. A second later, she got out of her car, dark hair tied into a messy topknot and a silver thermos glued to her left hand.

"Good morning, sunshine," Audrey said in an artificially perky voice, because she knew Nicole would hate it. "You're looking bright as a spring sunrise."

"We both know *that's* not true." Nicole narrowed her hooded eyes and groped around for the sunglasses perched on her head. She wore a pair of leggings with a baggy sweatshirt that said *fries before guys*. "And don't tease the zombie. It's cruel that you make me get up this early."

"Come on, time's a-wastin', girl. Let's hit the trail." Audrey marched toward the entry to the reserve, ready for her weekly dose of soul refreshment.

A green sign listed the several trails that cut winding paths of varying difficulty through the dense, quiet forest. They usually took the long, easy trail that allowed plenty of time for their boots to crunch over the packed earth, snapping twigs and disturbing leaves, working up an appetite for the breakfast at Nicole's place that always followed. The whole time, they talked, sharing triumphs and worries and excitements, cheering each other on with the kind of sisterhood that Audrey found necessary for survival.

The forest was peaceful. *This* was why they sacrificed sleep on a weekend morning—for the shift of light as the sun came up, dusky tones filtering through the tall oaks and pines, lighting the path ahead of them. It was for the scent of the leaves and cool earth, for the sound of heartbeats and breaths and birds tittering. She sucked in deep lungfuls of the clear air until her head was free of cobwebs and doubts.

"You're always here first," Nicole said, sipping her coffee. "I'll need to start staying up the night before to beat you."

Audrey laughed. "Maybe I'm more eager to get out of my house than you are."

"Can't say I blame you. The thought of sharing a bedroom with two teenagers gives me the heebie-jeebies."

"The girls aren't that bad."

"It's common knowledge—all humans under the age of eighteen are to be avoided." Nicole was an only child who'd grown up without much family to speak of and had zero desire to start one of her own. "Although I'm sure you disagree with that, Miss Mother Hen."

Audrey rolled her eyes. "I'm a nice person, so sue me."

"Too nice." Nicole shot her a look. "You put up with *way* too much shit, my friend. Speaking of which, how is your dad? Is he trying to be less of an asshole these days?"

She focused on putting one foot in front of the other. "He's fine."

Audrey didn't have the mental fortitude to make excuses for him today. He'd been in a mood last night, yelling at Deanna for "making too much noise" while she listened to music in her bedroom…like any other teenage girl would do on a Saturday night. But there was some prideful part of Audrey that made her feel like she *still* had to defend him. If for no other reason than she remembered the man he used to be.

"Every day is different, but he's working on things at his own pace."

Nicole looked at her with brow furrowed, most likely because she smelled Audrey's reply for what it was—bullshit. "Those are a whole lotta words that don't say a damn thing."

"Grief doesn't go away overnight."

"Your mom has been dead for fourteen years, Audrey. I'm not saying he should get over it, but acting like a wounded bull and lashing out at his own family is not okay." Despite Nicole's bluntness, she was a softie at heart. And as fiercely protective of Audrey as she had been since they became friends in the fourth grade when someone was bullying Audrey for her weight. "When is *your* turn to grieve?"

"I'm fine." Audrey put on her most indulgent smile, like her friend was talking nonsense.

"Have you been to visit her grave yet?"

Audrey bit the inside of her cheek. This was well-worn territory between the two of them. She could tell Nicole to mind her own business, but Audrey knew it wouldn't stop her friend asking the tough questions.

And Audrey would be lying if she didn't admit there was a part of her that felt deeply guilty that she'd never visited her mom's grave. Not since the day they buried her. But there was also a part that caused Audrey to freeze up every time she even thought about setting foot in the cemetery. It was almost like she was worried that something might happen—like a floodgate might open or something might break inside her. The only way she was able to power on taking care of her siblings and putting up with her father was if she stayed positive.

And visiting her mom's grave would *not* be positive.

"She wouldn't want me crying over things," Audrey said. "She's gone. Looking at a plaque won't magically change that."

"People don't visit cemeteries hoping to resurrect the dead," Nicole deadpanned. "But it's...healing."

"Not for me." Healing for Audrey was *doing*, not wallowing. Not thinking or remembering or indulging in melancholy. And it most certainly wasn't crying, which was what would happen. "You know I like to keep busy."

"It helps you avoid things you don't want to deal with," Nicole grumbled.

"Can we *please* talk about something else?"

Her friend looked like she was going to argue, but instead she slung an arm around Audrey's shoulders and squeezed. "Sorry, Audrey. I didn't mean to give you a hard time, I just worry about you."

"I know." Audrey brushed aside the thoughts about her parents and forced herself to turn to the positive. "Let's talk about you. Any wins this week?"

"You mean other than not killing my boss or any of his army of sycophants?" she quipped, taking a long drink from her thermos.

"I'd say zero murders makes it a good week." Audrey grinned. "Gotta celebrate all the wins, even the little ones."

"Amen to that." Nicole shook her head. Her sigh echoed through the forest, drowned out only by the soft, even thump of their footsteps. There was something magical about this place—something special in the intimacy of being surrounded by thick trunks and dense greenery, the cozy blanket of scents like earth and pine and crisp air, and the quiet stillness.

"I had dreams once, you know." Nicole's voice didn't waver. "I had dreams of being a Hallmark cliché—I was going to start my own business and buy a big house and marry a guy who wanted to fuck me every night."

"Pretty sure there's no fucking in Hallmark," Audrey said with a snort.

"Don't you ever feel…" She stomped her foot, trying to loosen some of the moist earth that had gathered there. "Like time is slipping away from you? Like those dreams might up and leave if you don't do something about it?"

The question struck Audrey hard in the chest. It was like being run through with something cold and impenetrable. Realization. That's what the feeling was—the realization that her dreams *were* getting away from her. That by the time her siblings were all safely out in the world, there might be nothing left in Audrey's future except serving coffee and selling crystals.

What matters is making sure Deanna, Oliver, Georgie, and Jane all make something of themselves and that you do your mom proud.

"Aren't dreams a bit…" Audrey lifted one shoulder into a shrug. "Self-indulgent? That sounds harsh, and I don't mean to be. Maybe I mean more that dreams are for people who've got survival sorted out."

And she hadn't yet. Not quite.

Nicole looked at her curiously. "You don't think you've got survival sorted out?"

"It's a work in progress."

"You can still dream even if you don't have the basics locked down." Nicole shook her head. "Hell, dreams are what make survival worth it. It's the light at the end of the tunnel."

"It doesn't feel like a light to me." Sometimes, dreams were more like a noose. "All I'm saying is that I'm grateful for what I have. I could have less, so I don't want to waste time thinking about what I'm missing out on. It's not productive."

Namely, she didn't want to spend any more time mooning over Professor Ronan Walsh. Since their trip to the bookstore yesterday, he'd been on her mind. Constantly. In fact, she'd burned the family's dinner last night because she couldn't stop thinking about him.

That's why dreams were dangerous. You could spend a whole life chasing something that wasn't meant to be, only to end up missing out on the joy of what was right in front of you.

She forged on ahead, leaning into the slight incline of the earth. Audrey enjoyed the brisk walks and getting her heart rate up, even if nothing ever seemed to budge her weight.

That was one of those things—she *could* be unhappy that her genes meant even smelling a cheeseburger caused the pounds to stick to her hips and waste time wishing for slimmer thighs and a smaller waist. Or she could, as she chose to, be grateful for the fact that her body was strong and allowed her to work, to get out and enjoy nature and to fill out the chest area of all her tops very nicely.

It was all about perspective.

"That's very practical," Nicole said, catching up to her easily.

"Exactly."

"But don't you want *more* than practical?"

Yes.

"No." Audrey shook her head resolutely. "Practical is important. Being happy is important. And I can't be happy if

I keep wanting what I can't have."

"I think it's sad that you believe you can't have dreams." Nicole's dark eyes narrowed with worry. "You deserve dreams."

"I'd rather have reality."

She loved her friend dearly, but they were very different people. Nicole was driven by her restless dissatisfaction and a hunger for more. Audrey was driven by responsibility and duty. Therefore, sacrifices had to be made. And she was more than happy to let go of lofty ideals in the pursuit of something tangible.

Her one little concession would be a dirty dream or two about Professor Ronan Walsh, because Audrey *was* human, after all.

• • •

The following Thursday, Ronan found himself wandering the Harrison Beech college campus after his work had gotten the better of him. It felt so small compared to Cambridge and Harvard, and so…new. Unlike the centuries-old universities of his previous experience, Harrison Beech had opened its doors in 1958. Some of the newer buildings weren't erected until the nineties, and one particular upgrade had been completed a scant five years ago, with modern architecture and lots of glass.

It was a nice college. Not prestigious, but the staff seemed passionate, and he'd met plenty of students who were eager to learn. There were definitely worse places he could have ended up.

He made a start toward the sports stadium, which housed the baseball diamond. There was an exhibition match on tonight, and he got the sense it was a big deal and that it might be good form for him to show up. Besides, he'd spent the last few hours sitting in his office and staring blankly at the pile of research in front of him, trying to figure out how to make it tell a cohesive story. He needed a break.

Kissing Creek felt like a detour on his life map—almost as if he'd taken a wrong turn but was enjoying the scenery enough to take the long way around to his next milestone. Of course, being close to his grandmother was essential. In fact, he was heading to Boston this weekend to see her and finally meet his nephew in person.

There was something hanging over his head, though—a worry about being back home. About seeing his little sister in her new role as mother and wife. How would that make him feel? He'd always felt a bond with Keira, like they were kindred spirits weathering the same life storms and protecting each other.

How many times had he held her while she cried after their mother left yet again? After she missed another birthday or Christmas?

Yet Keira had gone on to do the complete opposite of what Ronan expected: she'd built a family. She'd trusted herself enough not to turn out like either of their parents. She'd risked giving her partner the power to hurt her. To leave her. All because she loved him. It was encouraging, to see how she'd grown and changed as a woman. Yet Ronan was floating through his personal life, using his work as a distraction while calling it a dream.

The stadium had people of all ages streaming inside. Most people wore red. He spotted T-shirts with the local team's logo on front—a llama head with a flame surrounding it.

Lily.

At one point, he would have said a llama was a stupid choice for a team's namesake—weren't all teams supposed to be named after fierce things, like bears and cougars and other things that would frighten Dorothy the second she stepped off the yellow brick road? Only now, Ronan knew better.

He'd back Lily in a fight against most things.

Ronan followed the crowd into the stadium. Food vendors were lined up in a neat row, ready to feed the hungry masses. He spotted hot dogs, pizza, and even a cute little pink pop-up stall that appeared to be selling donuts.

He was headed toward the bleachers in front of left field when he caught sight of a familiar blond head.

Really—it's Audrey's head *that you noticed first?*

Ronan shut his snarky inner voice down. Okay, so maybe he'd noticed Audrey's body being spectacularly hugged by a denim dress. The fabric was soft and well-worn, and it fluttered around her legs as she walked. A red ribbon decorated her ponytail, and she wore a red belt at her waist.

"Audrey!" He called her name without thinking, and much like anything to do with her, it was based on instinct rather than rational thought. It was almost as if there was something inside him that was magnetically drawn to her—like he couldn't *not* call out if he saw her. "Hi."

She whirled around and blinked. "Ronan, hi."

God, she was so pretty. Like *really* pretty. A sheer red gloss made her lips shine, and she had a pair of chunky black sunglasses perched on her head.

"You look great." *Not appropriate, professor.* "I mean, I like the way you've incorporated the team colors into your outfit."

She looked genuinely pleased at the compliment. "Thanks. Someone stole my Flames T-shirt, so I had to get creative."

Her eyes darted over to a teenage girl who was heading toward them, a spitting image of her. "This is my little sister, Deanna."

"Nice to meet you, Deanna." He stuck his hand out. "I'm Ronan."

"*Professor* Ronan," Audrey added.

"Hi." Deanna smiled up at him. She was all arms and legs and big, inquisitive eyes. But there was no denying the resemblance in the small, freckled nose, heart-shaped face, and ready smile that matched Audrey's. Deanna peered at him curiously. "Do you know a lot of things, then? I bet you have to be smart to be a professor."

"Your sister certainly seems to think so," he said, shooting Audrey a knowing smile. She laughed and made a mock awkward expression. "She likes to quiz me about things professors should know."

"Oh yeah?" Deanna looked at her sister with interest. "Do it now."

"We shouldn't." Audrey shook her head.

"Go on," he said with a smile. "Ask me something."

"What's the most innings ever played in a game of baseball, and when did that game take place?" Audrey asked. "Bonus points if you guess which two teams were playing."

Shit. Of *course* it would be a baseball-themed question. Ronan didn't follow baseball too closely—which, coming from Boston, was basically a criminal offense. "This is a terrible time to admit that I have never sat through a full game of baseball."

Both of the women looked at him like he'd sprouted a second head. "Not once?"

"Not once."

"That's almost…blasphemous." Audrey blinked.

"Go on and guess anyway," Deanna said, grinning like an evil little sprite. Looks like she shared a spark and spirit with her big sister as well as all that blond hair.

"Based on my limited knowledge…" And even calling it limited was generous. "I feel like a record number of innings would probably have been set a long time ago. Maybe pre–World War II."

Ronan caught a flash of surprise across Audrey's face, a subtle quirk of her eyebrows that told him he was on the right path. He might know jack shit about baseball, but reading people was definitely one of his skills.

"I'm going to guess 1920s," he said. It was a total stab in the dark, but Audrey's expression was carefully arranged not to give a thing away...which in itself was giving something away. The lack of smugness told him he might be right. "Number of innings..."

Hmm. Baseball had nine innings, right? Or was it eight? *You'll never be allowed to enter Boston ever again.*

"Let's say thirty innings, and the game was Boston versus..." Crap, what was one of older teams again? "New York."

"Well, well, well." Audrey bobbed her head. "Not bad for a fake professor."

Ronan laughed. "That's not nice."

"Can I tell him?" Deanna asked, looking up at her sister, who nodded. "The most innings ever played in a Major League baseball game was in 1920 when Boston played twenty-six innings against Brooklyn. Although, that was the Boston Braves, not the Red Sox. *And* back then, Brooklyn were the Dodgers, until the team moved to L.A."

"Wow, that's impressive." He blinked. "Do you like baseball?"

"Sure." Deanna shrugged in that noncommittal way that only a teenager could. "I like hot dogs more."

Audrey laughed. "Subtle. Okay, let's get you some food, and then we can take our seats."

Deanna skipped ahead and grabbed a place in the line at the hot dog stand.

"Now I have two of you quizzing me," he said with a shake of his head as they walked slowly toward the food stands.

"You can quiz me back," Audrey replied with a sweet

smile. "Since you think I'm a trivia genius and all."

"Challenge accepted. Figure out something that Audrey doesn't know…" He tapped a finger to his chin, and she laughed. "How many parts of the human body are unable to heal themselves?"

She looked at him almost like she was insulted. "Depends on how you want to count them, but if we do it as a collective, then it's one. Human teeth are the only part of the body that doesn't repair itself."

Damn. "Okay, don't get too cocky. That was a warm-up question."

Audrey's eyes sparkled. "You're going to have to try harder than that."

"How many extra bones does a baby have than an adult?" he asked.

"Ooh, that's a good one." She sucked on her lower lip as she thought, eyes narrowed in concentration. "I feel like I read an article about this a while back. It was a lot. I know their skulls are not fully formed so there's flexibility for the birthing process."

"Final answer?"

"Hmmm. I feel like it's high double-digits, in the nineties maybe."

"It's ninety-four. Babies have three hundred bones and adults have two-hundred and six."

Audrey snapped her fingers in victory. "Another win for the trivia genius."

"I was unprepared. Next time I see you, I'll have some harder questions up my sleeve."

"Deal." She smiled at him in a way that made him feel warm inside. They had this connection between them—a glimmering little thread based on attraction and a mutual love of learning and knowledge. "Bring your A game next time."

They joined Deanna, who was already ordering her hot dog—extra cheese, onions, and every sauce. She took the liberty of ordering one for her sister, too. Plus two large Cokes. He caught Audrey frowning a little out of the corner of his eye as she pulled her wallet from her bag and looked inside.

There was definitely something going on with Audrey. The comment she'd made last weekend about "playing mom" and having lots of responsibility, putting food on the table for her siblings, not working toward anything with her education…

"Deanna," Audrey said softly, as though she didn't want him to hear. "We shouldn't…"

"I've got it." Ronan pulled his wallet out of his back pocket and smiled at the cashier. "Could you add another dog to that order?"

"Sure." The cashier gave him the updated amount.

"I can't let you pay." Audrey placed a hand on his arm, and her green eyes met his. The touch—so innocent and so human—shot sparks through him in a way that was totally out of alignment with the action. It was like his body had its awareness dialed up to a hundred, and even the smallest contact felt like fireworks. "That's not right."

"It's nothing."

But clearly it was to her. To her family. He almost wanted to slap himself for the careless comment. Twenty bucks to him was inconsequential. Sure, as a professor at a smaller college he wasn't earning a fortune, but he came from means. His artist mother might not have bothered to spend time with him at any point in his life, but she'd left him and Keira very comfortable financially.

That was a comfort Audrey clearly didn't have.

"I mean…" He scrambled for the right thing to say. "I owe you for the other day."

She raised an eyebrow skeptically. "Oh yeah?"

"For showing me to the bookstore and..." He was clutching at straws now. "Helping me clean up after the Lily incident. A few hot dogs is the least I can do."

He handed a few bills to the cashier and passed the bulging hot dogs to Audrey and Deanna. The younger woman's eyes widened, and she sank her teeth straight into her meal.

"Oh my God," she said with her mouth full. "It's wicked good."

Audrey laughed and ducked her eyes. "Thank you, Ronan. You didn't have to do that."

"Sure, I did." They grabbed their Cokes and made their way to the bleachers. "I could have walked right into Lily's trap without your sage advice."

"The advice I dispensed from behind the cover of a bookshelf?" Audrey laughed.

"You were the smart one in that situation. *And* you called Lily's owner." He took a long sip from his drink. "I'd say you deserve more than stadium food for that."

She looked at him, her olive-green eyes flicking over his face as if she was trying to figure something out. As if she was waiting for a hidden motive to reveal itself. There was something so guarded about Audrey. A veneer, impenetrable and sunny, hiding the real her underneath.

He chose not to take it personally. As someone who generally kept people at arm's length, he understood that driving and deep-seated need for self-preservation. Instead, he bit down into his hot dog. "It *is* good."

"See?" Deanna shot him a knowing look. She had a dot of yellow mustard on the corner of her lip. "Told you."

The bleachers were already starting to get full, and they found a spot with enough room for the three of them to squeeze in. As he sat, he was acutely aware of Audrey's thigh pressing against his. With her hands occupied by food and drink, her skirt rose up her legs as she sat, and although she tried to subtly pull the hem down, she didn't have any luck.

"So, how do you two know each other?" Deanna asked as they settled in. "I can tell you're not from around here."

"How's that?" Ronan looked down at himself. He didn't look *that* different from the average person in Kissing Creek, especially since he wasn't wearing his elbow patches today.

"You're…" She wrinkled her nose, and it struck him as so like Audrey. "Fancy."

He laughed. "Fancy?"

"I think she means clean-cut," Audrey supplied. "Well, aside from the beard."

"You don't like the beard?"

"Oh no, I do." Pink colored her cheeks, and Ronan decided then that he wanted to see her blush more often. There was something so honest about it, a reaction that even she, with her careful veneer, couldn't hide. "It suits you."

"Thanks." He was aware that Deanna was watching the two of them very closely, her brow crinkled as though she might be drawing her own conclusions. Better to correct that. "Actually, I'm Audrey's—"

"Customer." She cut him off and shot him a pleading look out of Deanna's line of vision. "Ronan gets his coffee at Kisspresso."

Okay, *that* was a little weird. Sure, she wasn't lying, since he had gotten his coffee at Kisspresso most mornings and Audrey had served him whenever she was in. But the more obvious answer—which he'd been about to give—was that he was her professor. Yet, for some reason, she didn't want her sister to know that.

It seemed the more time he spent with Audrey, the more questions he accumulated. And that was only going to make it more difficult to keep his distance.

Chapter Eight

Mistakes had been made.

Mistake number one was stopping to chat to Ronan when he called her name. Not because she didn't want to talk to him—she definitely did—but because having Deanna beside her added a whole new level of risk.

Mistake number two was wearing a dress she knew was a little on the short side when she sat down. But laundry day had come and gone three days ago, and Audrey hadn't found a spare moment to do it. In fact, she'd contemplated canceling on the exhibition match tonight so she could catch up with housework—since the place was starting to look like a dump site—but Deanna had been so excited she hadn't found it in herself to say no.

Hence, her clueless little sister had tried to bleed her dry at the hot dog stand, which made Ronan step up to pay and left Audrey feeling embarrassed and…grateful. She didn't like feeling grateful, because that felt a whole lot like she owed someone something, and Audrey didn't like being in anyone's debt.

"I like the pink passion mochas at Kisspresso," Deanna said, her face brightening. "But Audrey says I can't have them too often."

"Too much sugar. This"—Audrey gestured to the Coke that looked almost as big as Deanna's head—"is a special treat."

Rolling her eyes, her sister took a long slurp from her drink, as if trying to prove a point. Audrey let it slide. She had bigger things to worry about—namely the fact that Ronan was probably wondering why in the hell she'd prevented him from telling Deanna that he was her professor.

Hers.

The word circled in her head like a vulture.

But her thoughts were cut off by the raucous cheer from the hometown fans. The Flames mascot, a guy dressed in an unfortunate skintight red suit with a wig made to look like flames, was leading Lily around the field to signal that the game would be underway soon.

"That's a brave man right there," Ronan said with a shudder. "You could not pay me enough."

"Because of the suit or the llama?" Audrey bit into her hot dog and chewed, happy for the distraction from more dangerous topics of conversation.

"Both. One, there's no way I'm getting near that creature again unless absolutely necessary. Two, it would take a lot of money for me to put my junk on display." He cleared his throat. "Not that I'm ashamed of what God gave me."

Oh *lord.* Audrey did not need to be thinking about anything that God gave Ronan Walsh below the belt. Trying to combat the sudden rise in her body temperature, she pressed the Coke cup to her cheek.

Ice cubes, work your magic. Now, please.

But Ronan was clearly determined to backtrack, his cheeks suddenly as red as hers.

"I mean, any man would feel uncomfortable having it all hang out in front of an audience, regardless of size." He cleared his throat. "I'm going to stop now."

"Please," Audrey said, half mortified and half trying not to choke on the laugh she was holding back.

"I usually have better social skills than this," he muttered. "I swear there's something about you that turns me into a babbling fool."

Her heart skipped a beat. *She* made *him* turn into a babbling fool? Surely it was the other way around. There was no way Ronan could be attracted to her the way she was attracted to him. And it wasn't because Audrey didn't think she was attractive. She had confident days and those where she avoided the mirror, like any other woman.

But this didn't have anything to do with looks. It was everything else. Why would a professor with his pedigree be interested in a worker bee with no future?

"So, what's the story with the Flames?"

Thank God, a change of topic. "They're good. They made it to the College World Series a couple years ago, and they're hoping to have a shot at it again this season. Last season, they had a few unfortunate injuries that let them down. But they've got an amazing pitcher they think could make the majors and a promising first baseman from a prospect camp a few years ago. We've been waiting for him to start."

"Oh, that Jackson guy?" Deanna let out a big sigh. "All the girls at school totally stan him."

Ronan's brow wrinkled, and he leaned closer to Audrey. "Stan?"

She laughed. "It means he has lots of fans."

"Apparently his Instagram is almost at ten thousand." Deanna munched on her hot dog. "That's a lot."

There was more action on the field as the players started filing out, an announcer calling names from both teams and inviting the crowd to cheer. The stands were getting fuller, and someone squished themselves down next to Ronan with a friendly "'scuse me," forcing him to move closer to Audrey.

"Your sister makes me feel old," Ronan joked. "And apparently I'm supposed to be a millennial."

"How old are you?"

"Thirty-four."

"That's young for a professor, especially one who taught at Cambridge." Like she needed to be any *more* impressed by Ronan.

"So young I occasionally get mistaken for a student." He winked. "Yeah, it's young. Sometimes that works against me."

"People don't respect your opinion?"

"Being an outstanding professor requires life experience as well as a good academic record," he said in a mock-stuffy voice before shaking his head. "I've got what it takes, without a doubt. That's why writing my book and furthering my research for the next year will be really important. It's a pivotal moment in my career that could mean the difference between getting a tenured position at an Ivy League school and being stuck..."

He trailed and shifted in his seat. The message was clear enough. "Being stuck here?" she said.

"That's not what I meant."

"Yeah, it is." Audrey swirled her Coke around in the plastic cup, half-melted ice cubes swishing on foamy brown waves. "Kissing Creek doesn't provide the kind of life some people aspire to. It's a slower pace, here. Everybody knows your business."

"No joke. My first meeting with the senior faculty members proved they'd searched every inch of my history, right down to my favorite beer."

"I believe it. And besides, you've seen what the world

has to offer. You've been overseas and experienced exciting things. Why would you want to stay here after all that?" She said it as though reminding herself.

People with prospects who came into this town didn't often stay. Sometimes they'd collect a spouse on the way out, whisking some lucky person off to greener pastures. Heck, Audrey had even had such an offer herself. A hunky Canadian named James had chatted her up at work, and they'd gone on a few dates, shared a few nights together, and then he'd packed his bags. He'd asked her to go to Vancouver with him, said he thought they might have a future.

She'd been younger then—twenty-two—and the possibility of exploring a new country and making her own life had tasted like candy on the tip of her tongue. But when she'd explained to him that she couldn't leave her siblings, that maybe he could stay here with her for now—long enough for her to get her siblings out—he'd laughed and said he couldn't afford to "waste" the best years of his life in Kissing Creek.

For a town that loved all things romance, it was a great irony.

"Do you like living here?" he asked.

"My family is here, and I love my family, so...yeah, I like living here." She nodded. "The people here are kind for the most part, and I have steady work."

"Ah, that's right. Cappuccinos and crystals." When he smiled, it went all the way to his eyes, setting off a flutter in Audrey's tummy. "You're a very interesting woman."

"Because of the cappuccinos and crystals?"

"Because of all of it—the random facts, the mystery... everything."

Around them, the crowd got to their feet as the home team trotted out to their positions on the field. But Audrey and Ronan were stuck, asses glued to the bleachers as they looked at each other. Nobody had *ever* called Audrey

interesting before. Nobody had ever looked at her like that—
with intensity. With curiosity. In a way that told her she
mattered.

Her head blocked out all the noise around her, and her
gaze dropped to Ronan's mouth. It was perfect—full lips
made for kissing and straight white teeth that needed a *ping*
sound effect when he smiled. Sandy-brown hair covered his
jaw, though it was neatly trimmed, in keeping with the rest
of him. Would it feel good scratching against her skin if they
kissed? Would he taste sweet like Coke and earthy like man?
Would his hands fist in her hair and—

"Did you see him? Did you see him?" Deanna grabbed
her arm, ripping Audrey from the intimate moment. Her
little sister shook her drink so violently the lid popped off
and some of the sticky liquid sloshed over the edge. "Oh my
God, there he is!"

"You're literally a bag of hormones," Audrey grumbled
as she stood. She could still feel the heat of Ronan's gaze on
her as he got to his feet beside her.

"Go Flames!" Deanna bounced up and down on the spot.

"I should never have given you so much sugar."

The crowd settled, and out of the corner of her eye,
Audrey noticed a man with salt and pepper hair approaching
them.

"Ronan! I didn't know you were coming to the game."
The man grinned. "We've got a spot for staff on the other
side. You should come sit with us; I'll introduce you around."

Ronan looked at Audrey, but she shooed him, letting him
know he should go and network.

"I'll see you around," he said to Audrey, getting to his
feet.

"Thanks for…" She trailed off as the words stuck in her
throat. Thanks for what? Paying for the drinks and dogs? For
keeping her company? For looking at her in a way that stirred

up things she wanted to ignore? "Just thanks."

"You're welcome." He smiled his crooked smile and then left her sitting there, her body grieving the warmth of his thigh pressed against hers.

After the game was over—where Audrey and Deanna almost lost their voices screaming as the score remained neck and neck until the bottom of the ninth—they followed the crowd away from the diamond and toward the parking lot.

"You like that guy," Deanna said, a delighted smile on her lips.

"The first baseman? Yeah, I thought he played a good game. He's got good reach, considering he's not as tall as Thomas from last year."

"No, silly." Deanna giggled. "The professor."

"Ronan?" She tried not to react. Her little sister was like a sponge for information, and she picked up on subtle emotions and feelings that most adults totally missed. "Sure. He's nice."

"You *like* like him."

Audrey rolled her eyes. "That's a lot of likes for one sentence."

"But you do, don't you? I can't blame you. He's cute."

"He's *twenty* years older than you."

Deanna shrugged. "Sure, I mean, he's old. But that doesn't mean he's not cute."

Audrey couldn't deal with this right now. "Well, it doesn't matter, anyway. We have rules against dating…customers."

"Why?"

"It would be inappropriate."

"Why?"

Lord give her strength right now. "That's the rules, okay?

It's not allowed. I don't like it, either."

The words tumbled out of her so fast and so strong it almost stopped her in her tracks. Of course, she wasn't talking about the rules of dating a customer. It was *his* job that was the concern. Which seemed stupid to her—sure, she was his student. But she wasn't studying for a degree or even career development, which meant him giving her better grades—or penalizing her if things went south—didn't mean a damn thing. The grades were inconsequential.

Hell, she didn't even have a high school diploma. It wasn't like taking one night class a semester meant anything more than something she needed to stay sane. She learned for her own personal enjoyment, and that was it. Him being her professor meant nothing in the grand scheme of things.

Rules are rules.

Deanna looked up at her, brow wrinkled and her blue eyes narrowed in sisterly worry. "Maybe your boss would give you one of those…inceptions?"

"Exceptions?" Audrey laughed and shook her head. "No, baby, I don't think that can happen."

It flitted across her mind for a brief moment that maybe she could switch classes—then it wouldn't be as much of an issue, right? But she was 100 percent getting ahead of herself now, because all Ronan had done was show some polite interest in her.

And look at you with those incredible blue eyes like you're the only woman in the world.

Wish fulfillment and maybe a hint of desperation; it wasn't anything more than that.

The parking lot was, to put it not so delicately, a shit show. It would take them forever to get onto the road. Thankfully, there was no need to rush tonight, since her dad knew exactly where they were. Baseball was an acceptable reason to be out of the house, and with Deanna in tow, Audrey wasn't likely to be "whoring around," as he'd insultingly put it.

"I think I can see Big Red." Deanna squinted and pointed ahead of them. "Next to that green truck."

"Good eye." They made their way over but didn't bother to get in the car. Audrey was happy to avoid going home for as long as possible. Plus, she feared her beloved vehicle was one love tap away from falling apart at the seams. She'd rather give it ten or fifteen before attempting to navigate the traffic.

She listened to Deanna talk happily without taking a breath until the parking lot was finally clear. Seriously, the girl could keep up a steady stream of words. Audrey would put money on her being able to pass that SEAL test where they have to sit on the bottom of the pool and hold their breath for an eternity, since it was clear that Deanna's lung capacity was better than most.

"All right, munchkin. Time to scoot." She unlocked the front door and dropped into the driver's seat, reaching over to yank up the lock on the passenger side. "I need to get you home before you turn into a gourd."

This little game had started when Audrey had used the accurate quote and Deanna had demanded to know why it was always a pumpkin and not other types of fruits and vegetables. So now, every time she used the phrase, a new word was exchanged at the end.

"Oh, *gourd*. That might be my new favorite." Deanna slid into her seat.

"Even better than durian?"

"Possibly, but durian is definitely up there. And rambutan, too."

Chuckling, Audrey stuck her keys into the ignition and turned. Big Red made a weak-sounding sputtering noise and failed to turn over. Ugh. The old gal was struggling these days, and she'd made the kids late to school once this week already. Audrey *really* needed to get the car fixed, but her schedule had been fuller than normal, with extra shifts at Kisspresso to cover a coworker's vacation. She'd literally hopped from one commitment to the next, with this baseball game being the only thing she'd done this week that wasn't eating, sleeping, or working.

Even studying hadn't factored in. She was behind in her reading for Ronan's class already.

"Come on," she muttered as she tried again. Yet Big Red whined and whined and failed to start.

Deanna bit down on her lip. "It's not working?"

"It'll be fine. She's just...old and tired." Audrey tried again. The car sounded like it had contracted a chest cold and wheezed its way through another attempt. But nothing. "Shit."

She slumped back in her seat, shutting her eyes for a moment to think of a solution. When she opened her eyes, a figure was striding toward them.

Ronan.

Hastily, before she could embarrass herself any further in front of him, she tried the car again. Nada. Biting back a curse, she balled her fists. Being without a car *wasn't* an option. The area of town they lived in meant the kids couldn't walk to school—it would take an hour and a half. At least. And even though the twins were old enough to drive, they couldn't afford another car, so it was Big Red or bust.

Kissing Creek had a few taxis and even a couple of Uber drivers, but on game nights they were always snapped up quick. They had exactly three mechanics, though only two did regular cars. The other mechanic specialized in motorcycles, since there were plenty of those around here.

"Come on, you big hunk of rust." Audrey tried again, groaning when the car failed her once more.

"Maybe you flooded the engine?" Deanna supplied less than helpfully.

"Do you even know what that means?" Audrey asked, trying to keep her tone in check. It wasn't Deanna's fault, and the teenager shook her head. "Then zip it."

Ronan had made it to her window now, and when he knocked, Audrey let out a sigh. She couldn't ignore him, no matter how mortifying it was.

She rolled down the window and pasted on a cheery smile. "Hey."

"Car trouble?"

"At what point does it become trouble?" she quipped. "We're having a slow start is all."

Ronan raised a brow. "By the sound of that engine, I don't think you're going anywhere tonight."

"Are you a mechanic as well as a professor?" She didn't mean to sound snippy. "Sorry, this car has been giving me trouble all week. I'm a bit frustrated."

"Can I give you a ride home?"

"No!"

The word shot out of her before she even had time to think. And it didn't have anything to do with being close to Ronan again or getting in a car with him. But him giving her a ride home would mean seeing where she lived, and *that* was a treat she reserved for absolutely nobody. It was one thing to be a little swoony and pink-cheeked in front of an attractive man. It was quite another to show him you lived in a dump.

Her heart could not handle that level of shame. Not with this man.

"I would hate to put you out," she clarified, her heart thumping for all the wrong reasons. "Do you even have a car here?"

"I've got one on loan from a family member. It's parked in the staff lot on campus, so I can easily get it. It's no trouble."

Outside, the sky was dark, with stars already beginning to twinkle. Deanna would be a mess tomorrow for school if

Audrey didn't get her home soon, because on days when she started at eight she had to drop the kids off by seven thirty, which meant leaving the house just after seven. Not an ideal situation for teenagers who liked to sleep as long as possible.

"A jump start should get us going. I can call…" Dammit. She was so rattled she'd forgotten the guy's name, despite the fact that he'd been fixing Big Red since all the way back when she was a kid and the car was driven by her parents. "The mechanic."

"It's almost ten o'clock."

Audrey bit down on her lip. It *would* be rude to call a family home and drag someone out of bed when she had a perfectly good option in front of her.

"But I need my car first thing tomorrow. I've got work early and school drop-off."

"We could borrow Mrs. March's car?" Deanna suggested. "It sits there in her driveway all day long, and she's always offering to drive us to school."

The older woman who lived next door didn't have much, but her heart was made of solid gold. And she *did* always offer to drive the Miller family around, probably because she didn't have any family of her own and they always took her Christmas cookies and stopped in to check on her.

"Let me help," Ronan said. There was that crinkled, lopsided, *gorgeous* smile again. "I promise it's no trouble."

"You got a cape tucked into the back of your sweater or something?" she asked softly.

Ronan chuckled. "Nah, it's totally self-serving. I was taking a shortcut back to campus and saw you guys waiting here, so I wanted to say thanks for keeping me company earlier. It's not easy moving to a small town and being the new guy. So will you let me help you?"

Audrey's eyes flicked to Deanna, who made a show of yawning so obviously that her ploy to get her big sister and

Ronan in the same car was entirely transparent. "Sure. That would be great. Thank you."

"Give me five minutes, and I'll bring the car around. It's getting cool out, and there's no need for you to walk in the cold."

Audrey watched Ronan walk away, feeling giddy and sick all at once. When was her body going to get the memo that *nothing* would ever happen between them? That a man like him was nothing more than a fantasy to stop her lady parts from shriveling up and dying?

That, like every other man who'd walked into her life, he would discard her at some point—whether it was the hunky Canadian who'd left her behind or the man who called himself her father and acted like anything but—and Ronan was no different. He'd made it clear that Kissing Creek was a stepping-stone on his way to the top.

And Audrey wasn't foolish enough to let herself be a figure in anyone's rearview mirror.

Chapter Nine

One man became a millionaire by selling fake dog testicles made out of silicone.

Ronan pulled his car into the parking lot shared by the baseball, swimming, and gym facilities, half expecting Audrey not to be there. But her beat-up red car sat there, the lone occupant of the otherwise mostly empty space, with two figures inside. He wasn't sure why it had taken so much convincing for her to accept his lift, although he guessed that even in small towns women were reluctant to get into cars with men they didn't know.

But he and Audrey weren't strangers.

Maybe it's because you can't stop looking at her and she thinks you're a creepy old man.

Okay, firstly, eight years' age difference didn't exactly make him an old man compared to her. And secondly, he'd heard the intake of breath when he'd slid closer to her on the bleachers. He'd felt the shift in her energy, the way she looked at him when she thought no one was watching. He knew how to read people. And while Ronan might not be the best person *in* a relationship, he was aware enough to know when someone was attracted to him.

Why are you doing this to yourself? You know it can't go anywhere.

Maybe that's why she appealed to him. There was a strange and intriguing dichotomy with Audrey, in that she was both dangerous and safe. Dangerous, because being with her would at best tarnish his image and at worst ruin his career. But that was exactly what made her safe—the risk was too great, so he was forced to keep his distance.

He pulled up beside Audrey's car, and the two women joined him, Audrey sliding into the front seat and Deanna in the back. Deanna was tapping away at a phone, which he recognized as Audrey's because it had a distinctive crack in the right corner of the screen. She wore a pair of white earbuds, the cord dangling over the front of her Flames T-shirt.

"Thanks for rescuing us," Audrey said.

"No problem at all."

He pulled onto the street, and Audrey gave him the basic directions. The sky was pitch-black now, and the streetlights rolled past with measured frequency, lighting up the gold lengths of her hair for a moment before dropping them back into darkness again. His headlights swept across the quiet street. There was a lone person riding a bicycle, and most of the houses had glowing windows, but it was so still. So peaceful.

"And uh…thanks for not blowing my cover before." Audrey kept her voice low, though with the sound of whatever was blaring from Deanna's headphones, she wouldn't have heard a damn thing anyway. Ronan fought the urge to tell her to turn it down or else she might damage her hearing.

Maybe you are an old man after all.

"Your sister doesn't know you're taking my course?"

"My whole family doesn't, actually." She glanced out the window—or maybe she was looking at the reflection shimmering in the glass. "We, uh...don't have much money."

Ronan bobbed his head, unsure whether he should confirm that he'd picked up on that already. "Right."

"I work two jobs, plus picking up whatever extra bits and pieces I can, and everything goes to the family...except I put aside enough to take a single class every semester." She glanced at him. "I know that probably seems incredibly selfish."

"That you save a little money to educate yourself? No, I don't think that's selfish at all."

She pointed ahead to the next street he needed to take. "As it is, my aunt pays half. She's the only one who knows about it, and she's always tried to encourage me to keep studying."

"Your aunt who owns the crystal shop?" For some reason, that surprised him, but he guessed that was his personal bias showing. She reminded him of his artist mother, who thought all schools were societal indoctrination camps.

"Just because she believes in astrology and crystals doesn't mean she undervalues education," Audrey said. "It's possible for belief and knowledge to exist side by side."

"Have you tried getting some official support for your studies?" he asked. "Many colleges have scholarships and other types of student-assistance programs. I'm not sure about Harrison Beech, but—"

"I'm not eligible."

He steered onto another street as Audrey directed him. "Why? I'm sure if you can prove that you're in a low-income house—"

"I'm *not* eligible." This time her words had a little more bite, and Ronan blinked. When he didn't ask anything further, she sighed. "Sorry, I didn't... I know I'm not eligible, okay? It's not an option for me. Not at this college, anyway."

And if she was supporting the family, then Harrison Beech probably *was* her only option. Even though he didn't know Audrey that well, he couldn't imagine she would leave her siblings to go and study in some other town. Her loyalty and care glowed like the brightest star, and it was easily one of the most beautiful things about her.

"They don't have scholarships?" Ronan shook his head. "That's ridiculous. Education should be available to everyone."

"They *have* scholarships. But I didn't finish high school, so therefore I'm not eligible, because that's one of the criteria." Her gaze was glued to the passenger-side window now, like she couldn't stand to look at him. "It's fine. I made the right decision for my family, and I wouldn't go back and change it, even if I had the chance."

Ronan didn't consider himself an overly emotional person, but listening to the resolve and marble-like commitment in Audrey's voice was like scraping a knife over his heart. This woman, who clearly loved knowledge and learning more than anything, hadn't been able to finish high school.

Of course he realized that she said she *didn't* finish high school, like it was her choice. But Ronan could put the pieces of the puzzle together—dead mother, four younger siblings, no mention of a father figure...her choice wasn't exactly a choice.

"I love my family," she added fiercely. "I would do anything for them."

"That comes across very clearly. They're lucky to have you."

He turned down another street, and suddenly it felt like Kissing Creek was a world away. Instead of the rows of neat redbrick homes with gambrel rooves and tidy lawns, the houses here were smaller and simpler. Some were in a state of disrepair, with broken mailboxes and peeling paint. Others were tidy but plain. One house had a group of men standing out front, smoking and drinking with music blaring.

"It's a bit farther up," Audrey said. She was smiling too much now—like it might distract Ronan from what he was seeing.

"I'm not judging you, Audrey," he said.

"I have no idea what you're talking about."

She'd shared a little of herself tonight, but each piece was like extracting a tooth. She was so eager to take information in, but she guarded information about her own life like a dragon protecting its gold. No doubt people in the past *had* judged her. He was well aware how money changed people—his mother had been a broke artist in the beginning, and she'd been softer, then. But the more money she made, the more fame she accrued in the art world, the more selfish and self-invested she became, always wanting more, more, more.

"It's there, next to the house with the yellow car."

Ronan pulled up on the side of the road and killed the engine. He wanted to say so much—to reassure Audrey that he didn't think less of her because she hadn't finished high school and because she didn't live in the nice part of town. Frankly, her tenacity and resilience were better qualities than anything money could buy.

But he got the feeling that trying to reassure her would only make her more uncomfortable, so he kept his mouth shut.

"Thanks again for the ride," she said, her hand drifting to his arm for the briefest touch. Yet as innocent and simple as it was, the gesture electrified him. It burned him from the inside out. Her olive-green eyes looked almost golden under the streetlights, and her features were sharpened by shadows. "You've got a kind heart, Ronan Walsh."

Unwilling to say anything that might ruin the moment, he simply nodded and watched as Audrey turned around to her sister, who'd fallen asleep in the backseat, phone dangling precariously from one hand. Deanna woke with a groggy shake of her head, and they bid him goodbye.

He stayed in his car for a moment to make sure they got inside safely, drumming his fingers on the steering wheel and cycling the night's events through his head.

Dangerous or safe or both? Whatever Audrey was, she'd officially burrowed under his skin.

. . .

Audrey's Fridays always felt like three days rolled into one. She started work at eight, opening Kisspresso and making sure the townsfolk were well caffeinated, and finished shift number one around three p.m. Then it was onto shift number two at Game of Stones to manage the store from three thirty until the store closed at eight. By the time she fixed up the register, balanced the books, and dusted, it would be after eight thirty. Staring down the barrel of such a long day was exhausting, even when she was only three hours in.

"One extra-shot latte and two caramel iced coffees coming up," Audrey said.

She swiped her hands down the front of her apron, wincing at the mark on her wrist. A soft bruise was blossoming under her skin, and she tugged down the sleeves on the white long-sleeved T-shirt she'd worn under her uniform polo shirt despite it being hot enough to walk around without any sleeves at all.

She lost herself in the meditative process of making the orders, hands drifting from portafilter to milk jug to ice scoop. Last night had been a strange, mixed bag of things. Having time alone with Ronan—well, if you didn't count Deanna passed out in the backseat—had made her feel almost like a normal twenty-something woman on a night out.

It had been so long since she'd gone on a date, she'd almost forgotten how delightful that fluttery feeling was.

Except it wasn't a date.

And the fluttery feeling had been lost the second she'd set foot in her house. Audrey shook the negative thoughts off, stopping herself before she got dragged down. There was no time for bad feelings today; she had customers to serve and two shifts to get through.

"One large Americano, no room," said the young woman behind the cash register as she scribbled on the takeout cup and slid it along the bench to Audrey. "Two cappuccinos, one with an extra shot."

Audrey's head snapped up at the familiar order. She'd been so in the zone, she hadn't even noticed Nicole walk into the café. "Hey girl."

"Hey yourself." Nicole waved as she handed her company credit card over to the cashier. Today she had on a fitted black pencil skirt and a silky blouse in rich red. It was a far cry from her weekend attire of leggings, hoodies, and messy buns. "I was hoping you'd be in. The boss prefers it when you're behind the coffee machine."

Nicole walked over and propped herself on one of the stools that hugged the far side of Kisspresso's main counter so they could chat while Audrey worked.

"You almost missed me. I was finishing up these orders before my morning break," Audrey said.

"Good, you can walk me back to the office." Nicole grinned. "How was the game last night? So bummed I had to miss it."

"The new first baseman is great." She hit the portafilter against the knock box and dislodged the used puck of coffee grounds. "Deanna was *very* excited to see him in the flesh."

Nicole snorted. "Lovelorn already, and she's only fourteen."

"Tell me about it. She's ninety-nine percent hormones right now." Audrey put up the orders and called them out. "How's work going?"

"I've thought about murder approximately five times this morning." She cocked her head. "Which is down from my lifetime average, so I guess that's good."

"You've got to get out of there. The place is going to crush you." Audrey paused to look her friend in the eye so Nicole knew she meant business.

"And what am I going to do, huh? Get a retail job and earn half of what I'm earning now, and probably *still* end up being miserable." Nicole smoothed a hand over her dark hair, which she'd pulled back into a simple twist. It showed off the tiny gold hoops in her ears. "At least now I can afford my own place, which halves my murderous thoughts every day because I don't have to live with my mother."

"What about your dreams?"

Nicole shot her a look. "The ones you said were pointless?"

"I didn't say they were pointless." Audrey placed the Americano and two cappuccinos into a little reusable holder that Nicole always brought with her. "Come on. Let's walk."

Audrey undid her apron and called out to her colleague that she was going on her break. After hanging her apron up and grabbing her phone, she followed Nicole outside. Kisspresso was just off Main Street, along the road that housed the college's main entrance. It was leafy and pretty, and today the warm air ruffled the branches of the trees overhead.

"I remember what you called them," Nicole said. She carried the tray in one hand, and her shiny nude pumps clicked against the pavement. "Self-indulgent. I'd argue that's worse than pointless."

"Only because women are trained to think their purpose in life is to serve others," Audrey said, knowing full well that she upheld that stereotype. "But I was more talking about the rest of it. The Hallmark stuff. Husband, the house, white picket fence."

"So it's fine to dream about a career change but not a family?" Nicole raised a brow. "Although I understand why you think that way."

"I guess I've seen the dark side of families more than most. The bits they cut out of those movies. My family life would be film on the cutting-room floor." She shrugged. "And I'm okay with that—not everybody gets to have the happily ever after. But…"

"Wanting is dangerous."

"Yeah. I find it easier to do what's necessary, and that way I have a purpose, which makes me happy. I'm not chasing some grand thing that may or may not be real. Instead, I'm chasing something that's actually possible. Something tangible."

They walked down Main Street toward Nicole's office building. There were fewer trees here, and the sun beat down relentlessly, bouncing off the shiny shop-front windows and making Audrey squint. Sweat beaded along her hairline, and she swiped at it with the back of her hand.

"Why on *earth* are you wearing a long-sleeve top under your uniform?" Nicole asked as they walked. "It's hot as dog balls out here."

Audrey faked a laugh. "And how do you know dog balls are hot, huh? Got some weird fetish I don't know about?"

"Ew." Nicole screwed up her nose. "Don't even joke about that."

"You were the one who started talking about animal genitalia. Actually, did you know there's a guy who became a millionaire by selling fake dog testicles made out of silicone?"

"I'm sorry I said anything." Nicole rolled her eyes. She looked like she was about to say goodbye, since they were now paused in front of her workplace, but at the last minute, her eyes narrowed. "You only do that when you're hiding something."

Audrey stiffened. "What? I share facts all the time."

"Not facts about balls, though."

"Ah, you'd prefer something more to the point, so to speak. I have a fact about elephant penises—"

"What's going on?" she demanded.

"Nothing."

"Pull your sleeves up."

Audrey's stomach sank, but she wasn't going to get into this now. Better to go on the defensive. "You're being ridiculous, and I am *not* a child. I have to get back to work—"

"Did he hit you?"

The question socked Audrey right in the chest. She knew what people thought of her father—that he was a drunk. That he was violent. That he hit his kids. Only part of that was true. Yes, her Dad had been in a lot of bar fights, and he was rough. And yeah, he drank too much. But he didn't hit his children.

"No," she said through gritted teeth.

Nicole bit down on her lip, her eyes shimmering with worry. "Please talk to me, Audrey. We've always promised we wouldn't do secrets. Especially not when one of us was hurting."

"I'm not hurting." The words came automatically. Because people who let themselves hurt sometimes couldn't get back up again, and Audrey *always* got back up after life dealt her a blow. "I'm fine."

"What happened?"

An open question, dammit. Nicole was right—they *had*

made a promise. A pact, in fact. They'd linked pinkie fingers and sworn they would protect each other. Them against the world.

"Big Red broke down after the game last night," Audrey said with a sigh. "I ended up getting a lift home from my professor."

Nicole raised an eyebrow but didn't interrupt.

"He's young enough that he doesn't look like a professor, and Dad saw him out the window and thought I'd been on a date and that I'd used Deanna as cover."

"What's wrong with you being on a date, exactly?"

"I had stuff to do around the house, or I could have taken an extra shift instead." She knew it didn't sound reasonable. "My priority is to take care of my family, not go on dates."

"Your words or his?" Nicole's jaw ticked.

"Don't." She shook her head.

"So why the long sleeves?"

"I tried to walk away from him while he was still talking." *Yelling.* "I shouldn't have done that."

"So what? He grabbed you?" Now her nostrils were flaring. That was *not* a good sign.

"I shouldn't have walked away. It was disrespectful." The line of red around her wrist wasn't so bad. It would fade in a few days. "He doesn't hit us."

"I don't know why you keep defending him, Audrey. I really don't." Nicole swallowed, and her eyes looked glossy, like she was holding back tears. "If you keep moving the line of what you'll put up with, he'll keep pushing until you're accepting things you should *not* accept. I worry you're already there."

"I don't expect anyone to understand."

They didn't remember her father like she did. They didn't remember the man who slow danced with her mother in the kitchen of their trailer when it was just the three of them, before the other kids were born. They didn't remember the man who turned up with flowers and a roguish smile, who left love notes taped to the refrigerator. They didn't remember the man who cried when his last daughter was born, when he lost his wife.

Those broken howls would haunt Audrey forever.

That man still existed. He *had* to.

"I'm fine," she said, placing a reassuring hand on Nicole's arm. "It was a one-off incident, and I provoked him. I know he's not perfect, but he doesn't get physical with us."

Usually.

She could tell her friend wasn't appeased, but Audrey really did have to get back to work.

"You know you can *always* come and stay with me. You and the kids." Nicole's dark eyes bore into her. "All of you."

"In your one-bedroom apartment?" Audrey shook her head. "And where are we going to sleep, huh?"

"I'll have every one of you in my bed, and I'll sleep on the floor if that's what it takes to keep you safe."

"Do you trust me?" Audrey asked. After a moment, Nicole nodded. "Then I'm telling you I'm fine. Everything will be okay; it was just a bad night. Now, I *really* have to get back."

"Call me tonight."

"I promise."

Audrey headed back in the direction of Kisspresso Café, all her "normal girl" feelings well and truly dead. Knowing she'd have class with Ronan again next Wednesday was keeping her going, however.

Around him, she *could* be normal, if only for a moment.

Chapter Ten

By the time Wednesday rolled around, Ronan had found himself fully entrenched in life in Kissing Creek. He'd been here a little over two weeks and already had a "usual" at the Kisspresso Café: an extra-large Americano, no milk, and a berry muffin. Raspberry, blueberry, blackberry—it didn't matter. He liked that hit of fruity sweet with a strong-enough-to-punch-you-in-the-face coffee. He'd also returned to the secondhand bookstore to scour for Agatha Christie novels without a demonic llama hovering over him. Mr. Hart was a kind old gentleman and had promised to bring in a copy of *The Clocks* from his personal collection.

To his surprise, Kissing Creek felt like home. Or at least, as he kept telling himself, home until he decided what to do next. Part of him still felt as though he should be chasing the prestigious Ivy League tenured professor dream, but there was a smaller part of him that wondered what it might be like to stay in a small town like this.

The highlight of his week, of course, was his Wednesday night Brain-Changing Positivity class.

"One of the things I want you to take notice of this week in your journaling is the impact of positive and negative messages on your mood. Now, you might not think you're so exposed to these messages, but digital-marketing experts estimate that the average American is exposed to between four and ten thousand messages a day." Ronan swept his gaze across the room, heart full at the sight of so few empty seats. "If you're an avid social-media user, then you're likely at the higher end of that. Add in the conversations we have with friends and family, memes, TV shows, movies, video games, we're exposed to—and absorb—so many more messages than we realize."

Ronan let his eyes linger on Audrey for a moment, the top of her blond head forward as she scribbled in her notebook. Unlike a lot of the other students, who took notes on laptops and tablets, she was old-school. She used one of those four-color pens to neatly map out her notes in a simple spiral-bound notebook. There was something charming about it. And about the way the tip of her tongue edged out of her mouth as she wrote.

"I want you to keep your journals with you all week, and every time you notice a message that impacts your mood, make a note of it. Also make note of whether you're seeing more positive or negative messages. As you all know, our brains are finely tuned relevancy engines, and we automatically filter out much of what we see. Some of us might be more wired to expect—and therefore notice—the negative. Next week, we'll be talking about how you can actively change the way you see the world. On that note, I'll leave you to your evenings. Don't forget there's a short personal essay due next week, and my office hours are available in your student portal if you need to come and speak with me. Thank you, everyone."

The sound of bags rustling and laughter and chatter filled the room as the students started packing up to head home.

Ronan sat on the edge of his desk, waiting for everyone to file out. Naturally, as they had the past two weeks, his eyes drifted to Audrey. He could always spot her in the crowd, no matter how full the classroom was. Today she wore her hair in a long braid, and it hung over one shoulder. She had on a simple white T-shirt, a pink cardigan, sneakers, and a pair of jeans with a rip at one thigh. That little flash of skin, framed by frayed denim, had taunted him all class.

As if she'd detected his attention, her gaze suddenly rose and met his, cutting all the way through the movement of people eager to get home. Ronan swallowed. He'd been thinking about her since the baseball game last Thursday night, about how vulnerable she'd been and yet how tough. He'd thought about her simple home and how her shame was palpable, even though she had *nothing* to be ashamed of.

Over the weekend, he'd looked into the scholarships. Sure enough, without a completed high school diploma, there was no way she could apply for any at Harrison Beech College. He'd contemplated seeing if there was anyone he could talk to. Maybe they might make an exception for her. Audrey's thirst for knowledge was a professor's dream. And she deserved to study if that's what she wanted to do.

It's none of your business.

Audrey took her time packing up her things, lingering while the rest of the students filed out. Soon she was the last one remaining, and she slid her bag up on one shoulder.

"Have you got a question about the assignment?" Ronan asked, pushing off the desk and walking toward the neat rows of chairs.

"No." She shook her head. "Although I'm a little worried that I might not have much to journal as far as the messages go. I don't use social media, and I spend my whole day working. I can't remember the last time I watched TV."

"I think you'll be surprised what you see, once you start

paying attention," he said. "Even if you're getting messages from café customers instead of Facebook ads. Besides, I imagine your aunt's store is *full* of messages."

"That's a good point." She nodded. "I didn't want you to think I wasn't trying."

"I doubt anyone could ever accuse you of that," he said. "Your investment in your own learning is admirable."

She toyed with the strap on her bag. "I'm enjoying this class. It's giving me a lot to think about."

"If you're interested, there's an event going on later this week that's kind of a 'meeting of the minds' between professors and students. The new Dean has asked all the attending faculty to bring a student guest so they can mingle and share their thoughts on the university and curriculum and things like that."

"And you want me to be your guest?" She sounded shocked.

"I do."

He hadn't planned on asking Audrey, actually. Not because he didn't want to spend time with her—far from it. But he'd been worried about the optics of a young male professor bringing a female student along, especially if it was clear to anyone they had chemistry. But maybe if more of the faculty got to know Audrey, they might consider giving her flexible options for further study. It could help her situation and, in his mind, that made it worth the risk.

"I would love to, but I'm working at my aunt's shop on Friday." Her face fell.

"No chance she'd give you the afternoon off?"

"I could ask," she said with a nod. "Or maybe I could finish early? I'll ask her."

"I'll leave it up to you, but the offer is there."

"Thank you." She looked at him for a moment longer, and Ronan had the sensation that he was standing at the edge of a cliff.

That's how she made him feel—wild, free, dangerous. He could almost feel the wind in his hair.

Audrey curled her hands over the back of the chair in front of her, as if steadying herself. Or maybe it was as a barrier. They both knew it was wrong to be dancing around each other like this. But they kept drifting together, like magnetically attracted beings unable to resist the pull between them. Did she keep thinking about him the way he thought about her?

Audrey's lips parted. He wasn't close enough to touch her—there were two rows of chairs between them. And every part of him ached with the distance. His body shouted at him to get closer, to touch. To kiss her. How easy it would be to close the door to the classroom and flick off the lights so they could pretend nobody was here. He could reach for her in the dark, sliding his hands over her delectable curves and—

The door opened with a bang, and one of the cleaning staff walked in, a pair of earbuds in her ears and her head bobbing to the beat. She looked startled when she noticed there were still people in the room. "Sorry," she said, plucking one of the buds from an ear. "I thought you were all done."

"That's okay," Ronan replied. "We're finishing up."

Audrey let out a long, slow breath and then punctuated the sound with one of her dazzling smiles. "Thank you for the offer, professor. I'll let you know if I can make it."

Professor. Not Ronan.

That was a line in the sand if he ever saw it.

"Thank you, Audrey." He turned and headed back to the desk. By the time he'd scooped up his phone and stuffed his laptop into his leather satchel, she was gone.

Just as Ronan was walking outside, his phone started buzzing, and Keira's picture—one of her holding her chubby-cheeked son—flashed up on the screen. He frowned and swiped his thumb across the screen. It wasn't like his sister to call late.

"Hey, what's up?"

"Ro." His sister's voice was tight, tearful. "I'm sorry to call late. I hope you're not still in class."

"What happened? Tell me."

"It's Gram. She had a fall." Keira sucked in a shaky breath. "A neighbor found her and called an ambulance."

Ronan's heart lurched. "Is she okay?"

"She broke her arm and hit her head. I...I don't know much more than that. I'm on my way to the hospital now."

"Text me the address. I'll be there in an hour."

Ronan hung up the call and sprinted across campus, panic flooding his system. But freaking out wouldn't help now. All he could do was be grateful that he'd taken the position at Harrison Beech and that he wasn't sitting in another country, half a world away, feeling guilty as well as useless.

God, he'd forgotten how bad the traffic was in Boston, even when it was past ten p.m. That's what happened when there was a Red Sox game on at Fenway Park—the city turned to sludge.

Ronan jogged from the hospital parking lot into the stark gray-and-white building, the sterile snap of antiseptic hitting his nostrils the second the glass doors slid open with a soft *whoosh*. A polite nurse directed him to the room where his grandmother was being kept. He spied her from the door, looking small and frail among the starched white bedsheets and pillows. She had her eyes closed, her thin lips open slightly. Even from here he could see the bruise blossoming on her forehead and one more under her eye.

Keira wasn't in the room. She must have gone to grab

a cup of coffee or have a restroom break. Ronan moved forward quietly, hands shoved into his pockets.

"Don't be hovering at the door like a meek child," Orna said, cracking one eye open. "If you've come to visit, then you need to come into the room."

Ronan bit back a smile. If Orna was bossing people around, then she couldn't be feeling *too* bad. The day his grandmother was quiet and passive, *that's* when he'd be worried.

"Looks like you took a punch." He walked over to the bed and sat where she patted the top of the sheets with her good hand. "You getting into bar fights again, old lady?"

She laughed, and the sound was dry and croaky, so Ronan reached for a jug of water that was sitting on a moveable table and poured her a glass. She accepted it eagerly.

"Maybe that's what I should tell people," she said. "I was defending my honor."

"Or maybe you're actually Batman. I'd believe it."

She narrowed her cloudy gray eyes. "You shouldn't believe in fairy tales, Ronan. That way lies the devil."

"Now I *know* you're feeling okay, if you're spouting that superstitious crap." He rubbed a hand up and down her good arm. The other, which was wrapped in some lightweight kind of cast, was tucked against her body. "And Batman isn't a fairy tale."

"But he turns into a bat, no? Isn't that a fairy tale?"

"He doesn't actually..." Ronan shook his head. This was what his grandmother did whenever she didn't want to talk about something—she diverted his attention. "Where's Keira?"

Orna wrinkled her nose. "Gone to get me a decent cup of coffee. Not this dishwater shit they serve here."

"Okay. So, what happened? You fell?"

"No, I was dancing with a leprechaun, and he turned me

too fast." She rolled her eyes. "Yes, I fell."

Ronan shot her a look. "Tell me what happened."

"Why? So you can make the decision that I'm too old to live in my own home?" She glared at him.

"That's not what I'm trying to do." He raked a hand through his hair. He loved his grandmother to bits—alongside Keira, she was the most important person in his life. But her stubborn Irish blood made her tough as nails and twice as sharp. "I promise."

"I was making tea and carrying it out to the sofa. I caught my foot on the cat and fell."

"You tripped over the cat?" It sounded like something out of a bad slapstick comedy.

"Don't you dare laugh at me, Ronan Walsh. I'm still strong enough to clip your ear." She looked down at her cast. "I bet this makes a good weapon, too."

He'd known ever since he was a kid that Orna's bark was *far* worse than her bite, and her threats of "clipped ears" never amounted to anything more than a good telling off. Most of the time, he'd deserved it.

"Dare I ask how the cat fared in all of this?"

"She's a tough old nut." Orna smiled. "That's why we work so well together. Mrs. Boyle from next door is going to look after her until I get home."

Thank God. The last thing that Ronan needed right now was for some grumpy old cat to be foisted on him.

"I'm glad you're okay," he said seriously. "You gave me a heart attack."

"Your sister gave you a heart attack. I told her not to call you."

"Why?"

"Because…" It was a rare moment when he saw how vulnerable his grandmother was under her tough, life-worn exterior. None of them were too good with showing their emotions—all too proud and too self-protecting. But he could see it now: the fear. The concern. The dread. "You've got bigger things to worry about than me."

"Gram." He squeezed her hand. "I love my job...but it's just a job."

"No, it's not just a job. You said so yourself when we had dinner. Your work is who you are, because what else do you have?"

The comment struck him in his chest, like an arrow flying out of nowhere and piercing his skin. She was right. Work was the entirety of his life. Beyond it, he had no real relationships outside his family, no close connections, no hobbies. Any spare moment he had when he wasn't teaching or working on his research was spent reading, which was really more work disguised as relaxation.

The only time he'd done something different was when he was with Audrey. He felt like a different person with her— someone who had a fuller, more well-rounded life.

"I have my family." He flattened his lips. "That means whenever you need me, I'm here."

Ronan felt another presence in the room, like they were being watched. If it was Keira, she would have rushed in, and if it was a nurse, then they wouldn't be waiting for a tender moment to be over, no matter how rare. A prickling sensation crawled down Ronan's spine. Awareness, tension. He felt his muscles bunch, and then a familiar scent hit him— sandalwood and patchouli. It twisted in his gut. He didn't even need to turn around to know who was standing there.

"Mom." He uttered the word almost as if it was a curse.

If Merrin Walsh heard him, she didn't respond. Ronan looked up, and, no matter how much he prepared himself to face her, seeing her was no less uncomfortable than being grabbed by the throat. She hadn't changed much—a few more gray hairs, giving her mousy brown halo of frizz a distinct silvery sheen. But her blue-gray eyes—*his* eyes—were unchanged. She still wore the same shapeless artist smock in rumpled linen over flowing pants. She still wore necklaces layered around her neck and a single chunky resin bangle on one arm. She still had that aloof, gauzy air about her, like an impenetrable bubble of her own making, keeping the world out and her dreams in.

And she still smelled the same.

"Orna." Merrin had always called her mother by her first name, as though wanting to distance herself from the label she did everything in her power *not* to embody. "Are you okay?"

Ronan got up from the bed and took a step back, jamming his hands into his pockets. He watched the awkward interaction between his mother and grandmother—a stilted peck on the cheek, neither sure where to put their hands.

His mother glanced furtively over to him. "Hi, Ro."

Ronan's nostrils flared, and he gave a curt nod but found there was a boulder sitting on his chest that prevented him from speaking. So, it took multiple hospital visits to get his mother to show up. Good to know.

Merrin toyed with a long, silver feather dangling from a chain around her neck. "I'm sorry I didn't get here sooner. The traffic from Gloucester was..."

Ronan walked out of the hospital room to give his mother and grandmother a moment alone. More importantly, *he* needed a moment alone. He hadn't prepared himself for a reunion tonight, and there was so much—and yet so little—he wanted to say. Sighing, he sagged back against the hospital wall and spotted Keira returning with a cup of coffee in each hand, the colorful plastic lids a stark contrast to the relentless white of the hallway.

"You called her?" he said as Keira came up to him, handing over one of the cups. She'd clearly gotten one for him and one for Orna and nothing for herself, because that was how his sister operated.

"Mom?" Keira's blue eyes met his, unwavering. Ready to be challenged. "Yeah, I called her."

"Why?"

"Because she's family and she deserves to know."

Ronan sipped the drink, but it tasted like sawdust. "Is a DNA link all that's required to be considered part of this family?"

"Ro." Keira frowned. "Come on."

"No, I'm serious. Could I walk away now and not bother to put any time in with you or Lukas or Gram or anyone, but you'd still keep me up to date even though I'd done *nothing* to earn it?"

Maybe it was the worry festering in his brain about his grandmother getting old. But his resentment was hot and angry, and it was so close to the surface he was sure that if he turned his wrist over he would see it bubbling in his veins.

"Can we not do this now?" Keira asked, her brows knitted together. "I was scared, okay? Mrs. Boyle called me, and then I called the hospital, and they said they couldn't give me a status, and...I had to leave Lukas with a friend because Andy was finally having a night out with the guys and I didn't want to take that from him."

Keira had to juggle so many things, and she'd always been the meat in the sandwich, as Orna used to say. Stuck between her strong-willed grandmother, flighty mother, and angry brother. Ronan had mellowed over the years, losing his fiery teenage streak...for the most part. But now he felt like he had all those years ago—frustrated and hurt that his mother felt like she could flit in and out of their lives as it suited her.

"I'm not angry at you, Keke." He used her childhood nickname so she would know they were okay. There could never be bad blood between them. "I...I don't know why she thinks she can pick and choose when to be involved."

He glanced back into the room to see Merrin and Orna talking quietly. Merrin was sitting on the bed, but they weren't touching.

"She's making more of an effort these days," Keira said.

"How?"

"She's called a few times and wanted me to put Lukas on the phone. She sent a card for his birthday, though the date wasn't quite right." Keira bit down on her lip and cradled Orna's coffee between her hands. "She even mentioned coming to Boston for a weekend soon so she could see him."

That hurt. His texts and calls had gone unanswered since before he left for England, but Merrin was suddenly making an effort with Keira because she'd had a child? Ronan didn't resent anything Lukas had. Far from it. That little boy was going to have more love than either he or Keira had ever had, and Ronan would be sure to contribute to it every chance he got.

"I'm glad she's making an effort for Lukas's sake."

Keira nodded. "Don't worry. I'm not fooled into thinking she would have done it if there wasn't a grandchild in the equation. But I want him to have the chance to get to know her."

"You're not worried that she'll come into his life and then leave?"

"I expect she will." She sighed. "But what other choice do I have? Should I let perfect be the enemy of good?"

"I'm not sure she's reached 'good' yet. She's barely scraping into the adequate category." Ronan took a long draw of his coffee, willing the caffeine to work its magic on his weary brain. "If that."

"Will you never forgive her?"

Ronan wasn't sure he wanted to answer that question, because his gut told him a resounding no. Forgiveness wasn't something he gave out easily, but mainly that was because he never put himself in a position to be hurt in the first place—hence his work-driven, singular-focused life. He'd learned his lesson hard and fast: relationships lead to pain.

People were selfish creatures because survival necessitated it.

Do you think Audrey is selfish, with all she's sacrificed for her family?

An anomaly. Something that couldn't be trusted, even if Audrey tempted him with her ray-of-light personality. But he wouldn't be fooled—not into trusting Merrin's return, nor into thinking that his stance on relationships might change. Ever.

Chapter Eleven

Zombie spiders exist.

On Friday, Audrey wrapped up her shift at Game of Stones a few hours early and walked along campus. She'd worn her favorite jeans today—the ones that she'd had to patch multiple times but that made the most of her ample booty, and a pretty blouse in sage green that made her eyes pop.

Was it a perfect day? Or did it only seem that way because the luxury of an afternoon doing something fun for herself was so out of the ordinary?

The weather was postcard-ready, with blue skies and bright sunshine amplifying how green and lush the Harrison Beech campus was. She passed a group of students lounging on the grass under a huge elm tree. They were studying and talking, scrolling on their phones and laughing. They were so…carefree.

At their age, Audrey had already been working two jobs and struggling to deal with her younger siblings, who needed a hell of a lot more care back then. Deanna had been at the start of tweendom. And Jane had been venturing down a worrying path of smoking and skipping class. She'd managed to keep them all in line. To make sure they knew they were loved and that life had more to offer them than a carbon copy of their father's spiraling despair.

Shaking off the troubling memories, Audrey jogged up the steps of the science building and pushed the door open. From memory, the faculty offices were the first hallway on the right. As she rounded the corner, she caught sight of Ronan.

He was wearing the blazer with the elbow patches, and his hair was long around his ears. His beard looked a bit heavier than usual, not as clean-cut as she'd seen him before. Audrey gulped. For some reason, that extra roughness—the hint of imperfection—made him seem so much more touchable. Desirable.

He was so...unabashedly masculine. *Devastatingly* attractive. And yet she knew inside he was a kind soul and had a good heart. In her mind, that was an irresistible combination. A *rare* combination.

"Audrey." His face lit up into a friendly smile as she approached, and his reaction set off butterflies in her stomach. "I'm so glad you could make it."

"Me, too." Audrey nodded, trying to stifle the giddy grin that wanted to burst forth.

It's one thing to pretend to be a normal twenty-something woman for an afternoon. It's quite another to revert to being a giddy teenager.

"We're over in the humanities building for this event." He gestured for them to head back the way Audrey had come.

Outside, it felt amazing to be in the sunshine, a handsome man by her side. She noticed the curious glances aimed in Ronan's direction as they walked. That seemed to happen a lot. Audrey had caught several students mooning over him during the Brain-Changing Positivity class and felt a little prickle of possessiveness burrow under her skin.

Which seemed stupid now—she was here at his invitation.

"I thought of another trivia question for you," he said, their footsteps falling in time.

Audrey grinned. "You're determined to trip me up, aren't you?"

"You questioned my honor. It's only fair." His smile was warm and sexy, and for a second Audrey feared she might melt like ice cream on hot pavement.

"Hit me."

"What animal has cube-shaped poop?"

Audrey burst out laughing. "Seriously? *That's* your question."

"Ah, it's all about strategy." Ronan held a finger in the air. "I had to find something that was general trivia so I wasn't cheating by asking something too esoteric. However, I figured a classy woman like yourself might not be intimately familiar with the shape of animal excretions."

"That's very tricksy." Audrey bit down on her lip.

"Tricksy like I've got one over you?" His eyes glittered mischievously, looking even bluer in the warm afternoon sunshine.

"Nope." She couldn't help the big, smug smile from spreading across her face. "Cube-shaped poop comes from the wombat."

"Dammit!" He slapped a hand down on his leg.

"You forget—I have four younger siblings, and I know exactly what facts will entertain them. Although I appreciate you calling me classy," she added. "Even if you're wrong about that, too."

"You're classy. I see how much effort you put into dressing nice and presenting yourself well."

He noticed that? Audrey's heart made a weird little thump in her chest. Of course she believed in presenting herself well—it was a defense strategy as much as a personal standard—but she had to admit that she'd made even more effort than usual since starting Ronan's class.

"We're in here," he said, breaking into her thoughts. They walked up to another of Harrison Beech's older buildings, and he held the door for her like a total and utter gentleman.

"So, what's the whole point of this meet-and-greet thing?" Audrey asked.

"I understand that the college feels the relationship between faculty and student body could be improved." Ronan raked a hand through his brown hair, but it flopped stubbornly back into place, and Audrey swallowed a comment about how her current student-teacher relationship was more than fine. "So, they're doing a series of events where professors bring students they feel can provide useful insight into improving the 'student experience' and help shape some kind of program that's being put together."

"Why on earth did you bring me, then?" she asked. "I take a single night course each semester. For fun, I might add. I definitely *don't* represent the average student."

"All students deserve to have a voice," Ronan replied. "Why should it matter that you're not full-time? Your experience is valid, and you have as much right to be here as anyone else."

That warmed Audrey's heart. It was tiring to constantly feel like an anomaly. Like an asterisk. Like the odd one out.

"But don't you think they care more about the students who bring a lot of money into the college?" she asked.

"They might, but I don't." Ronan flashed his faculty ID to the woman manning the desk outside the room where the meet and greet was being held. He bent forward to sign his name on a form, and Audrey tried really, *really* hard not to stare at how good his butt looked in a pair of blue Levi's.

Tried...and failed.

Clearing her throat and wrenching her eyes away from Ronan, she peered into the room. She'd never been in this building before. It looked like a club room of some kind, with wood paneling on the walls, deep green sofas dotted around the room, and a wall of bookshelves at one end. It had an old-world-society feel to it, and it seemed out of character for the rest of the university.

Ronan lead her into the room and handed her a "hello, my name is" sticker with her name written on it.

"Professor Walsh!" An older man with dark hair approached with his hand outstretched. "Welcome. And which wonderful student did you bring with you today?"

"Audrey, this is Professor Matsuda. He teaches Japanese language and history. Professor, meet Audrey Miller. She takes my Brain-Changing Positivity class."

"Nice to meet you." Audrey extended her hand, and Professor Matsuda clasped it in a firm grip.

"Tell me, what have you learned about the brain?" he asked. "If I was a student myself, I would definitely be taking this class."

"I've learned a lot about the tangible impacts of positive messaging on productivity and concentration," Audrey replied. "And how we can actually teach our brain to filter information for the positive rather than the negative."

"Fascinating!" Professor Matsuda nodded. He was a well-dressed man, with neat slacks and loafers, and he smiled readily.

Audrey released a breath. She hadn't even realized that the tension in her body had been rising to the point that she was holding it—but if she allowed herself to think honestly for a moment, she *was* a little intimidated being here. Despite Ronan's words about her having the same right as everyone else.

She knew she wasn't much value to the college. But Ronan

made it feel like she belonged—like she had something worth saying.

Professor Matsuda's eye caught on something behind Audrey. "Ah, Kate. Excellent, you're here."

Audrey turned and caught sight of a woman in a simple navy shirtdress and wedges with straps that wrapped ballerina-style around her ankles. She had dark hair and darker eyes and looked so effortlessly glamorous that Audrey suddenly felt like a cave troll having a bad hair day.

"Professors." Kate shook their hands in turn. "So nice to see you both."

"Audrey, meet Dr. Kate Kissinger. She completed her PhD last year, and now she's working with Dr. Kirmayer," Ronan said. "Audrey is taking my Brain-Changing Positivity class."

"Ah, you're an undergrad." Kate stuck her hand out with a friendly smile. "I'm glad we have a mix of students here today. Sometimes they only open these opportunities up to the post-grads, so I'm very glad we're moving past that."

Audrey could tell the other woman had meant it as a compliment, but instead the words were like termites attacking her confidence. Gnawing away at the rose-colored lenses she'd been looking through a moment ago.

Was it poor form not to correct Kate's assumption?

Oh no, I'm not even an undergrad. I can barely afford one class a semester as it is, and I don't have my high school diploma.

She couldn't force herself to say it out loud. Guilty as she felt lying by omission, the mortification of admitting the truth would be worse. So much worse.

"You finished your PhD last year? That's impressive," Audrey said. "How does it feel to be done?"

"You know, I actually felt a little bereft at first." Kate shot her a knowing look, and for a moment Audrey let herself pretend that she belonged. That she was one of those people who could share in-jokes about school and know what it was like to be working toward a monumental personal goal. "Study has been my whole world since I was a little girl. All I ever wanted was to get to the next level, and I actually fell into a bit of a slump after it was done."

"That's very common," Ronan chimed in. "Post-PhD blues are a real thing."

"Absolutely." Professor Matsuda nodded empathically.

"But then I had the opportunity to come back to Harrison Beech and help out with Dr. Kirmayer's research, which honestly was a complete lifeline."

"How does it feel to be called doctor now?" Ronan asked.

"Exciting, but also…I'm still me. Just with a few extra letters to my name." Kate looked at Ronan in a way that made Audrey's gut clench. It was so full of admiration and respect.

"Kissinger from Kissing Creek," Audrey said, the words tumbling out of her mouth in an attempt to divert her brain. "That's…well, I bet that stands out."

Kate looked at her a little strangely. "I'm not from Kissing Creek, actually."

Audrey knew that, of course, because Kissing Creek wasn't immune to the foils of small-town living—namely that everyone knew everyone else's business. As a college town, half the residents were transient because of their attachment to Harrison Beech. The other half were lifers who would, more often than not, be there from birth until death.

That meant a lifer would always know if another person was like them. Or, in this case, not.

"Tell us about the experiment you were running in the science building the other day," Kate said. "I saw you setting up."

"I was testing the impact of positive messaging on resilience." Ronan's eyes lit up the way they always did when he talked about his work. "The students were coming in for 'speed trials' of a lateral-thinking activity. We put a call out for students who enjoy puzzles and problem-solving to come along and test their skills."

"So, they believed it was a lateral-thinking puzzle, but what was it actually?" Audrey asked.

"Well, before the test commenced, we exposed them to a kind of message. The control group received purely informative material about the puzzle, thus a neutral message. Group A received a negative message, and Group B received a positive message. Then we timed them completing the puzzle."

Audrey frowned. "But what if one group is naturally better at solving problems than the other, regardless of messages?"

Ronan smiled and placed a hand on Audrey's shoulder. "The puzzle is broken, so they *couldn't* solve it. We were testing how long they attempted the activity before giving up."

"Oh." Audrey frowned. "Isn't that a little...mean?"

Kate laughed. "That's research."

"Of course we have them all booked to attend a 'results session' on Monday, where I'll explain what the exercise was about and debrief them. Don't worry," he said with a kind smile. "We're not here to damage anyone's self-confidence."

"Good." Audrey nodded. "They might not be mice in a lab, but we should still treat them properly."

Kate looked at Audrey with a curious expression but then turned to Ronan. "How did you come up with the messaging?"

"Positive messaging was easy. YouTube videos of kittens did the trick. But the negative was harder," he said. "In the end, I went with a news story about a family whose house had been destroyed in a tornado. But we're running another session on Monday, before the first group comes in to be debriefed, and I think we can do better. Maybe I should have asked my resident trivia expert."

Ronan looked at Audrey with a cheeky smile that went all the way up to his heavy-lashed eyes.

"Audrey knows everything about everything," he explained, and Audrey wished for a moment that she had something to hide behind. She *hated* being in the spotlight.

But Professor Matsuda looked on with interest. "Really, a trivia expert!"

"Not really," Audrey said, shaking her head. "I'm—"

"Help a professor out," Ronan teased. "I need something more effective than a tornado story."

He wanted her input. Her brain scrambled. Negative messaging? She was the *last* person he should ask about that, because she did everything in her power to keep that stuff as far away from her as possible. She stayed off Twitter, didn't read the comments on any article. Hell, it wasn't like she had time for that stuff much, anyway.

"What about zombie spiders?" she blurted out.

The other three people looked at her for a moment, none of them saying a thing. God, she really was a weirdo. It was all the time she spent looking up silly facts to share with her siblings. Some days, it was the only thing she had time to read.

"There's a type of wasp in Costa Rica that attacks spiders and paralyzes them. Then it lays eggs inside the spider, and two weeks later, the spider wakes up, and larvae have taken over its brain. They force the spider to create a strange web so they can burst out and use the web to create their own special nest."

Kate blinked. "That's…horrific."

"I love it!" Professor Matsuda clapped his hands together. "I have to tell Dr. Altman about this immediately."

Professor Matsuda turned and disappeared into the

crowd. Kate followed after saying a polite goodbye, leaving Ronan and Audrey alone for a second.

"Zombie spiders, huh?" Ronan nodded.

"So it's kind of like...well, fascinating. There's a documentary on YouTube." Audrey interlaced her fingers. "Sorry, it was all I could come up with on the spot."

"Only you would know that." He chuckled. "Come on. We probably should meet some more people and talk about your college experience."

"You mean you don't want to keep talking about zombie spiders?" Audrey laughed.

"I'm worried if I do, I might not ever sleep again."

Two hours later, Audrey had done her best to dodge specific questions about her educational status while giving her honest feedback and trying to be as helpful as possible. Not an easy juggling act.

But this latest professor was...a challenge.

"Audrey Miller, hmm." He tapped his finger against his chin. "Why does that name seem familiar?"

"Well, I believe it's the seventh most common surname in America," Audrey said with a tense laugh. "And my first name isn't exactly unusual, either."

"What's your father's name?" The professor rubbed a hand along his jaw, fingers catching on the liberal dusting of salt-and-pepper bristles.

"Patrick. Again, pretty common."

She wasn't sure if the professor *did* know her family or not. He wasn't a long-time Kissing Creek resident, but he had been here for at least the last five or six years. So it was possible he'd encountered Patrick Miller. Maybe at a bar.

But she sincerely hoped not.

"I'm sure it will come to me," he said, waving his hand. "And tell me again, what are you studying?"

"I take Professor Walsh's Brain-Changing Positivity class." That was her line; she would usually then follow up with something fun she'd learned and steer the conversation away from herself and toward Ronan's research. But this time, she was beaten to the punch.

"Yes, but what field of study are you in?"

"Oh, I take a bit of this and a bit of that. Honestly, I'm still trying to figure out what I want to do." Audrey felt her face grow hot. What was she even doing here?

She could pretend this was her life all she wanted—but the reality was that Audrey didn't belong here. *That* much was evident. Everyone else was all too proud to spit out their majors and their career plans and life goals like they were fairies shaking glitter dust around.

The professor narrowed his eyes. He seemed to be catching on to the fact that she was dodging the question. Out of the corner of her eye, Audrey caught Ronan watching them. He was chatting with a PhD student, but she could feel his gaze flicking over to her every few seconds, like he was keeping a lookout for her.

Audrey swallowed.

For a moment, resentment welled deep in her stomach, thick and hot, like sticky, black tar. If only her siblings didn't depend on her so much. If only her father could pull himself together and actually be the parent they all needed him to be. If only her mother hadn't died giving birth. If only her father hadn't pushed for one more baby, then maybe none of this would ever have happened.

She immediately regretted the thought—because Deanna was precious to her. She loved her sister with all her heart, and she would do *anything* to protect her. Everything to protect her. Even give up her future. Even swallow her sadness down so many times that she worried one day she might stop feeling anything at all.

"It's important to figure that out," the professor said. "I know many students are tempted to take this subject and then that subject. But your degree should be crafted in a way that you graduate with well-rounded knowledge in your chosen field."

"Yes, I completely agree."

At that moment, Ronan walked over, his blue eyes searching Audrey's face as though he'd sensed the tension. He nodded at his colleague.

"And which bachelor's degree are you working toward, Audrey?" the professor asked.

"Uhh…" Oh God, she really didn't want to lie. "Well…"

"I'm so sorry to interrupt your conversation," Ronan said smoothly, "but I have Audrey's cell phone in my office, and I need to get it to her before I head out tonight."

"Oh." Audrey blinked, startled that he'd come to her aid.

"You left it in class on Wednesday." His voice was a little stiff, as though he hated lying as much as she did. But it was out there now, and she wasn't going to call him out in front of another faculty member.

"Uh yes, thank you." She nodded and turned to head out of the room as quickly as her feet would carry her.

For someone who thought her opinion mattered and her experience was valid, Ronan certainly had jumped in to stop her from admitting that she wasn't working toward a degree.

Maybe he sensed how uneasy you were.

Or maybe he knew where the conversation would go— much the same as it had done when he'd driven her home after the baseball game. Why would anyone who'd dedicated their life to academia accept that she wasn't doing everything in her power to further herself? It must baffle them. Perhaps he was simply saving her from feeling obligated to explain herself.

Whatever the reason, Audrey would make it a point not to get stuck in a room full of professors ever again.

. . .

Ronan followed Audrey outside, and he had to quicken his pace to catch her. "Audrey, wait. Sorry, I…"

What are you going to say now, huh?

Why had he opened his big mouth? He'd seen the inquisitive look in Professor Martell's eyes and the panic flaring in Audrey's, and he'd butted in. Overstepped. He lied to a colleague for no good reason. Dammit. There had been some protective impulse that had burst to life inside him, and his brain didn't have a fighting chance.

Audrey paused and turned. Her olive-green eyes narrowed at him, as though suspicious. Ronan already felt like a complete tool. Why did he keep *doing* this to himself? He should forget about Audrey and her delectable curves and her sweet smile and curious mind and the goodness that poured out of her like molten sunshine.

He should forget about all of it.

Only…he couldn't.

"I appreciate you giving up your afternoon," he said. The sun was getting lower on the horizon, and Ronan's stomach grumbled. He'd skipped lunch to deal with a student who was freaking out about a grade, and now he was paying for it. "And the start of your evening."

His stomach rumbled again, this time even more aggressively than the last. The sound made Audrey laugh.

"Maybe next time there's an event like this, we should bring snacks," she said.

We.

Ronan nodded. "I have to admit, I wasn't expecting it to

go on quite so long. They're a chatty bunch."

"I think it's good they want to hear from students. I had an...interesting time," she said. "But it would definitely have been better with snacks."

"Would you like to come with me? Uh...for food, I mean."

Can't you leave it alone?

"I thought you had somewhere to be." Her eyes were luminous, and her lips were softly parted, plush and full. "After we get my phone, that is."

For someone who was supposed to be so adept at reading people and situations, he sure was acting like an idiot today.

"Truth be told, I..." Shit. "I don't have anywhere to be."

"Must be hard being the new guy in town." There was something strange about Audrey's tone—but he couldn't quite put his finger on what it was.

For all Ronan's research and experience, he was still better with data about people than people themselves. Not that he didn't have social skills—he did. But there was something about the nuance of personal relationships that eluded him. He could *read* people, but putting those readings into action...

Well, that didn't always pan out.

Remote, his ex had called him. A workaholic and an enigma. It had hurt, because they were all things he associated with his mother.

"I'm not good with networking," he admitted. "I'm more a working-quietly-in-a-dusty-library kind of guy."

A genuine smile drifted across her lips. "That sounds wonderful."

"So...food? Do you want some?"

Audrey sucked on the inside of her cheek as if weighing up the pros and cons. Maybe she had to get back to her siblings and ensure they were fed. Or maybe she was going to visit her aunt. Maybe she wasn't interested in—

"I'd love to," she said with a nod. "But I have one tiny, little request."

"Name it."

"Let's get out of Kissing Creek."

Chapter Twelve

Flamingos turn pink from eating shrimp.

Audrey felt all the tension leave her body the second Kissing Creek was in the rearview window. She couldn't even remember the last time she'd seen the *thank you for visiting Kissing Creek* sign, which meant she hadn't made it to the edge of town in months.

Or was it years?

Despite the awkward moment at the end of the meet and greet, Audrey found herself biting back a giddy grin as she sat in the passenger seat of Ronan's car. The roads were quiet, and they zipped along the highway toward a town that was perched along the coast, closer to the New Hampshire border. Forever Falls was the only other town in Massachusetts that came close to rivaling Kissing Creek for silliest town name... and that was saying a lot, since their great state was home to such gems as a town called Sandwich.

But while Kissing Creek leaned into gimmicks to differentiate their town, Forever Falls didn't need anything like that. Audrey had been there several times as a kid, and it was one of the most beautiful places she'd ever seen. They had a boardwalk along the beach strung with fairy lights and dotted with ice-cream stands. The quaint old buildings had a storybook look about them, and there was all the natural wonder you could cram into a single town. It wasn't surprising that tourists flocked to the small town every summer, swelling their population for three months of the year.

"Apparently the pub in this place is really good," Ronan said as they navigated the roads. The sun was fat and low on the horizon, bathing everything in red and gold. "I've been itching for a good pub meal since I got back."

"Not the same as England, is it?"

"Unfortunately, no. I mean, don't get me wrong, there are some things that we do *way* better here, but nobody does pub food like the British. I'm pretty sure I existed solely on fish and chips and Guinness the entire time I lived there."

Audrey glanced at Ronan's cut physique and rolled her eyes. "Only a man could do something like that and not put on a pound. All I have to do is look at a pint of beer and I feel my pants getting tight."

"I do have a fast metabolism," Ronan admitted. "I hated it when I was a kid."

"Really?" It felt like a real treat having Ronan all to herself, and getting to learn about him—even mundane things like his metabolism—felt special. The warmth of joy wound slowly through her system, loosening her. Uncoiling her.

"Oh yeah, I was that skinny kid who was all elbows and knees until I hit my teenage years. Even then, it took a while to get going. I was never really into sports much." He turned to her and shot her a grin. It was hard to imagine Ronan as anything but the roguishly handsome man with the panty-searing grin he was now.

"Me neither." Audrey wrinkled her nose. "I can't even tell you how many times I faked being sick to get out of swimming. I was pretty sure the teachers thought I was a hypochondriac."

"You didn't like swimming?"

"I didn't like being in a bathing suit in front of my peers." Back then, Audrey *had* been self-conscious of her body, even if she wasn't as curvy as she was now. "I was the only thirteen-year-old wearing a D-cup bra with booty before booty was cool."

Maybe don't talk about your tits and ass, weirdo.

"I guess all teenagers are self-conscious," she barreled on, heat filling her cheeks. "Kids can be cruel."

"Were you teased?" He frowned so seriously and yet so comically that Audrey had to laugh.

"Uh, yeah. I've always been on the, uh…chubby side." Audrey had probably left chubby behind twenty pounds ago, but these days she was comfortable with her body. "Took me a long time to accept myself for how I was. I used to wear really baggy clothes to try and hide myself, and I would never let anyone take my picture."

Ronan's eyes were trained on the road as they approached the welcome sign for Forever Falls, but she could see the concern in his eyes.

"Raising my little sisters is actually what made me learn to love myself," she said. "Especially Deanna. She would hang on to every word I said and observe every little thing I did, and one day I realized that if I kept hating my body, then there was a good chance I'd teach her to do the same. I wanted to be better for them, so I decided to change how I viewed myself. It wasn't instant, by any means, but I worked really hard at it."

"I imagine you work hard at absolutely everything," Ronan said softly.

"I try."

They followed the signs directing them to the Forever Falls main strip. Although not as busy as during peak season, the main strip was still bustling. People walked hand in hand, some eating ice cream from cones or cups. The patios of several restaurants were full, lit with glowing lanterns and twinkling fairy lights, and neat rows of cars lined the curb.

They continued past it all, with Audrey glued to the window like she was a child seeing another country for the first time. Was it a little pathetic? Definitely. But who knew how long it would be before she had a night out again?

A thought flickered in the back of her mind, a worry whispering that her dad would be pissed. But he was out tonight. It was his monthly poker game with his friends, and he never came home before one or two in the morning, often drunk. Always smelling of cigars. All she had to do was return before midnight; then she'd have a buffer to get into bed, and he'd be none the wiser. The kids were elated to have the house to themselves.

It was almost like fate had engineered what Audrey needed most—a night without responsibility, without duty. A night when she needed no more reason to do something than simply that she wanted to do it.

"Looks like you can park around the back," Audrey said as they approached the town's popular Falls Inn & Pub. The building was old, rumored haunted, and perched on a slight hill so that it overlooked the boardwalk and beach.

Ronan followed Audrey's advice and pulled into a small driveway that cut between the pub and the building next door, leading out to a small parking lot at the back. They grabbed one of the only available spots and made their way inside.

That's when Audrey spotted a chalkboard propped up against the wall near where staff waited to greet them. In pretty chalk lettering, the night's events were spelled out:

Pub Trivia—test your general knowledge skills and win big!

"Bar or bistro?" asked an older woman with curly hair and big earrings.

Audrey's eyes lingered on the chalkboard, and Ronan placed a hand at the small of her back. "Where's the trivia being held?" he asked.

"At the end of the bar. It's almost full, but I'm sure we can squeeze you in." She smiled and plucked two menus from a holder. "Follow me."

Audrey beamed as she followed the woman into the crowded bar area. It was full of people young and old, families and couples and groups of friends. There were casual tables dotted around the room and people seated at a long, curved bar that ran the length of the room. At the other end, the space opened up somewhat, and Audrey could already hear the trivia host getting the night started.

"You got here just in time," the woman said, setting the menus down at a small table jammed into a corner. There wasn't even space for them to sit across from each other, so Audrey had to wedge herself into the side of the table, and her knees brushed Ronan's as they sat.

"Latecomers!" The trivia host waved to them from the front of the room. He was a young hipster guy with circular glasses and a thick ginger beard. "Welcome, folks. My trusty assistant will get you some pens and paper to write your answers down. Make sure you put your names at the top."

"Oh my gosh." Audrey clapped her hands together. "This is going to be *so* fun."

"Damn straight, and you're my cash cow, okay?" Ronan nudged her with his elbow. "I expect that big brain of yours to help us take home the grand prize."

"You don't even know what the grand prize is," she said.

"Don't care; I just like to win."

"Oh, you're one of *those* guys," she teased. "Win at

any cost, huh? Who would have thought you were hiding a ruthless personality under those elbow patches."

"You have *no* idea." He leaned forward, and Audrey caught a whiff of his cologne. It was crisp and manly, like wood and lemons and a hint of something musky. "You don't make it to Harvard without having a ruthless streak."

Hmm, maybe Audrey needed a little more ruthlessness in her life. It wasn't a quality she'd ever considered to be a positive trait, but right now—staring into Ronan's clear blue eyes, the heat of his body drawing her closer, their limbs brushing—she thought it might be the most perfect trait ever. Ronan went after what he wanted. He *got* what he wanted.

She wanted that for herself. "I like to win, too."

"Good," he said as the trivia assistant came past the table and set down some printed-out sheets with spaces for each answer and a few pens. "We've totally got this."

"All right, everyone, are we ready?" The trivia host paused to let the crowd cheer for a minute.

He was quite the showman, and it was clear the trivia was a staple for the pub. There seemed to be lots of people who knew one another, some good-natured smack talk flowing between tables. Most of the groups appeared to be in their twenties through forties, clusters of beers and other drinks clogging the tables. One woman bounced a little girl of about five on her lap, and she high-fived a man sitting on the other side of the table.

Is this what Friday nights looked like for people? Friendship, fun, frivolity. For a moment, her chest ached. It wasn't often she got to see exactly what she'd sacrificed staring her right in the face.

"Okay," the host said, snapping Audrey out of her reverie. "Question number one...flamingos are born with gray feathers. So what do they consume that turns them pink?"

"Oh, I know this one." Audrey reached for the piece of

paper and grabbed one of the pens. Ronan leaned forward to see what she was writing, his arm pressing against hers in a way that made it hard to breathe. "Flamingos eat mainly shrimp, larvae, and a type of algae that are full of carotenoids that turn into pink and orange molecules in the digestive tract. They literally turn into the color of what they eat."

Ronan shook his head, laughing. "I *knew* you'd kick ass at this."

Feeling a little high on the power of being her own woman for an evening, she shot Ronan a saucy look. "I'm sure I'll perform better if I have a beer in my hand."

"Whatever the lady wants." He signaled for a waitress to come over and quickly ordered them some drinks while the other tables were arguing over the answer to question one.

It was amazing what being outside Kissing Creek did for Audrey's confidence. She found herself sitting up straighter, leaning in closer to Ronan without worrying that she shouldn't be doing it. She felt like she could tease and flirt and be a young woman in her prime. Tonight, the world was her oyster, and she intended to grab the opportunity with both hands.

Consequences were a problem for tomorrow.

• • •

Audrey was magnificent. Hell, she knew everything about everything. Sabermetrics, Welsh folklore, rock and roll history, anatomy, pop culture. Everything.

"You have rendered me utterly useless," he said, leaning back as they paused before the final round of questions. "I think I've answered two whole questions, and I'm pretty sure you let me have one of those."

A flirty smile flitted across her lips. "I might have."

"I am *going* to find a question that stumps you," he said.

"Eventually."

"I won't hold my breath," she teased back.

"Why do I feel like I need to beat my chest or hoist a table above my head to make up for it?" He frowned and picked up his beer. "I don't often feel like I need to prove myself."

"I have that effect on you?" She blinked. "That's ridiculous."

"Why?"

"Because I'm…" Something dark flickered across her face, or maybe it was a trick of the light. "*You're* the one with the Harvard education and the list of accolades a mile long."

"Education doesn't make someone smart, you know. It's simply a way to guide that intelligence toward something purposeful. But not having an education can't take intellect away from you. Plenty of influential people in history never finished school."

Fresh drinks arrived at the table, and Audrey sipped her beer before setting it down on the table and looking into the clear amber depths. "Then why did you interrupt me today, when that professor was asking me about which degree I was taking?"

"I…" Why *did* he do that? It was none of his business. "You looked uncomfortable."

"I was, but I can take care of myself."

"I have no doubt." He nodded. "It was…instinct, I guess. I didn't want you to feel bad. But that wasn't my place. I'm sorry."

She smiled at him, but this time there was something utterly, heartbreakingly vulnerable about it. Audrey had a lot of smiles, he'd come to realize. Some were real and some were armor and some were a diversion. It was like her parents had taught her that there was only one acceptable facial expression. Not that he could judge her—Ronan wasn't exactly forthcoming with his emotions, either.

Except tonight. Tonight, he felt like he could say anything.

"Why are you looking at me like that?" he asked.

"You have this incredible, perfect life, and, honestly, I'm a little jealous. I can't imagine what it would be like to see the world and study things that interest me and have people want to listen to what I have to say." She swirled her beer, watching the liquid shift and the foam cling stubbornly to the inside of the glass.

"My life is *not* perfect—trust me." Ronan took a swig of his own beer. "I had a...messed-up childhood."

Audrey leaned forward. "Really?"

People were still coming and going from the bar and restroom while the trivia host walked between the tables, chatting with people. He could give Audrey the short version; they had a few minutes.

"My mother is a very creative person. She's done everything from painting to poetry to live performance art. She's very...internal. Living in her own world, I guess you could say." He sucked in a breath. "When I was eleven, she bought a cabin about an hour or so outside Boston and decided that she needed to go into a 'lockdown' to complete her latest project. But she seemed to forget that an eleven-year-old and a four-year-old can't look after themselves."

He remembered that feeling of hopelessness, when his mother still wasn't home. Keira had been hungry and crying, the fridge bare because Merrin regularly forgot to shop for groceries. She'd often order pizza and leave it on the table for the kids while she worked—never eating with them. He'd found a dusty can of baked beans in the cupboard and heated it up in the microwave for Keira—but there was no bread to go with it. She'd slept in his bed that night, her little shoulders heaving with sobs as she repeatedly asked where their mother was.

"Two days later, when we'd both missed school, the

principal called our grandmother, and she came right over. I remember her and my mom having a huge fight when my mom came back. They were screaming at each other."

"So your mother…left you there?" Audrey pressed a hand to her chest. "That's awful."

"She claims that she told our father—who was even more useless than she was—that he was supposed to come get us. But he claimed they never talked about it." Ronan sighed. "And really, he was never part of our lives. He never lived with us, and I could easily count on one hand how many times I saw him in a year with several fingers to spare."

"What happened after that? Did your grandmother move in?"

Ronan shook his head. "Not right away, no. She and my mom didn't get along too well—they had very different ideas about how things should be done. My Gram is kind of intense. She's very opinionated and strong, which I love her for, but she can rub people the wrong way. So we stayed in the house with our mother disappearing more and more, until one day she told us she was moving to the cabin full-time."

Audrey's eyes widened. "Were you supposed to go with her?"

The laugh that came out of Ronan's mouth was the most bitter, sharp-edged sound he'd ever heard. For a moment, he wondered if it was wise to share something so deeply personal with another person. He'd never told anyone about this—not even his ex. Partly, it was because the past was the past. Rehashing it wouldn't change anything.

But more than that…he felt a little ashamed. Ashamed that his mother hadn't loved him enough to stick around, and ashamed that he'd been so hurt by her actions. As a child, he'd been…what had his dad called him one time? Soft. It had lit a fire in Ronan's belly, made him want to be the best at everything he did. He might not be the most physical person, and he didn't have a tough-guy bone in his body. But he would be the smartest. He would be the most successful, and he would do it without help from either of his parents.

"Uh, no. My sister and I were an 'impediment' to her creative process, as she liked to tell us on a regular basis."

"My God." Audrey shook her head.

"She told us that we could stay in the house—since she was very good at her job, it had been paid off, and she would send us money to cover the bills."

"How old were you?"

"Fifteen. I couldn't even drive yet." He shook his head. "But I was afraid to tell my grandmother, because it felt like admitting that I couldn't take care of my sister and myself. We lasted three months before she found out and moved in."

"Oh, Ronan. I'm so sorry."

He lifted one shoulder into a shrug, suddenly feeling very exposed. "It made me who I am today."

"For what it's worth, I think you turned out pretty damn impressive." Audrey's eyes lowered, and she cradled her beer, a hint of pink spreading across her cheeks. She opened her mouth to say something else, but she was cut off by the squeal of the microphone as the trivia host stood up at the front of the room.

"Sorry, folks. Hope that woke up those who were napping in the back," he joked. "Put your thinking caps back on for the last round of the Falls Inn and Pub trivia. We've got a couple of smarty-pants sitting in the corner who are beating all my regulars by a country mile."

The host pointed toward Ronan and Audrey, who laughed and raised their beers in good-natured competition. Audrey's eyes darted over to him, an expression of unadulterated joy and pride on her face.

Ronan decided that *this* was Audrey at her most beautiful—when she was brimming with confidence and full of the knowledge that she was holding her own.

"Question number thirty, what does HTTP stand for?"

Ronan didn't even bother to reach for a pen; he simply sat back and watched Audrey work, eyes glittering as she nailed question after question after question. By the end, their score sheet was neatly filled in, and they sat around waiting for the scores to be tallied up.

"Folks," the trivia host said from the front of the room. "I think we have a Falls Inn and Pub trivia record. With an unprecedented score of forty out of forty questions correct, we have newcomers Audrey and Ronan!"

Audrey's eyes lit up. "Oh my gosh, every single one? I wasn't totally confident about the jellyfish question. It was a guess, really, but—"

Ronan leaned in and whispered into her ear. "I think we have to go up to the front. You can gloat when we get outside."

"I'm not gloating...okay, maybe a little."

"Come on, let's claim your prize." He stood and held a hand out to Audrey, trying to resist the urge to haul her into his arms. She looked radiant. Sparkling. Like the world was at her feet.

Something stirred inside him. It was wanting, but not the kind of wanting he'd experienced in the past. Usually, wanting was about the physical. Lust. Sexual attraction. Base desires.

But this wanting was different. It was aching and desperate and all-consuming. He wanted *every* part of Audrey—her beautiful body, one of her rare vulnerable smiles, her truth. He wanted her innermost thoughts and dreams and fears. He wanted her trust.

But that was the thing about creating a perfect moment in a bubble...it would burst the second reality set in. And Kissing Creek was the big shiny pin waiting to shatter them.

Chapter Thirteen

On the drive back to Kissing Creek, Audrey couldn't help but fill the car with chatter. She'd only had two beers—certainly not enough to get her drunk—and yet she was babbling like someone who'd become intimate with tequila slammers.

She was...happy.

Genuinely happy. For someone who prided herself on being upbeat and a "get it done" kinda gal, it was strange that this feeling of happiness was so foreign to her. It was almost as if someone had replaced the blood in her veins with champagne, because that could be the only explanation for the all-over tingling she felt right now. She was giddy. Fizzy. Effervescent.

Her eyes darted over to Ronan as he drove them back home.

"Thanks for bringing me out tonight," she said. "I needed that like you would *not* believe."

"I would believe it." His eyes darted over to hers. "And you're very welcome. It was a really fun evening."

"It was, wasn't it? Even if I *did* hog all the trivia questions."

"Well, you got yourself a free dinner at the pub. I'd say it was worth it."

The prize felt like a carrot dangled out of reach—dinner to the value of two hundred dollars at the Falls Inn and Pub that Ronan insisted Audrey take, since she'd single-handedly earned it. Who would she invite? She could take her siblings out, but she wasn't sure they'd appreciate it. Perhaps, if she could find another night off soon, she'd treat Nicole to a meal out.

But even thinking about that was like wondering if she might buy herself a pet unicorn.

Another night out would be bliss, and yet she knew getting used to such things was a bad idea. Although not as bad as asking Ronan himself. Wouldn't that make it even harder to face reality every other day of the week?

Ronan pulled off the highway and followed the road through Kissing Creek toward the college parking lot, where Big Red was waiting for her. The local mechanic had gotten her working again, but every time she turned the engine over, she was worried it would be the last. Audrey glanced at her watch. It was just after eleven thirty—plenty of time to get home before her father even *thought* about wrapping up his poker game.

Ronan slowed down to turn in to the parking lot and pulled up beside Audrey's car. There were only a few vehicles scattered across the otherwise empty space, and when he killed the engine, it was deafeningly quiet. For a second, Audrey could have sworn her heartbeat was loud enough that Ronan could hear it. But if he did, he didn't say anything.

"I'm sorry I assumed your life was perfect before." She didn't even know where the thought had come from, but it popped out of her unbidden. A delay tactic, maybe? Because the second she got into Big Red, that would signal that Cinderella had to hang up her pretty dress and get back to scrubbing floors. "Sometimes things look one way from the outside, but I should know better than to take it at face value."

Ronan shifted in his seat, turning so that he faced her. Even in the dark night, with streetlamps casting light in yellow pools, his eyes were mesmerizingly bright. "I'm not even sure why I told you all that, to be honest. I don't usually talk about it."

For some reason, knowing that he'd chosen her to confide in made Audrey feel warm all over. It made her feel special... and that was *not* a word she ever associated with herself.

"I guess I felt like..." Ronan dragged his fingers through his hair. "Something told me you'd understand."

Did he feel that connection with her that she did with him? That little spark of magnetic attraction that told her they were cut from the same cloth? They were fighters. Doers. Survivors. Only he'd managed to climb out of the hole his parents had dug for him and move on to bigger and better things.

Audrey was still trying to find a ladder.

"We're not broken," she said softly. "Our parents' mistakes don't have to define us."

It was the thought she clung to on her darkest days, when she looked at her father and wondered why she didn't recognize him anymore. He was broken, and she was the strong one, even if it didn't always feel that way. If only she knew how to put him back together so they could be a real family again. So she could live her life.

"How are you so young and so wise?" He shook his head.

"I had to grow up fast." She shifted so her head was resting on the headrest, facing him. If there was a way to pause time so she could stay in this darkened car, staring into Ronan's eyes forever, then she would gladly do it. "I didn't have a choice. Either I grew up or my siblings would have been taken away."

That threat had loomed until Audrey was of legal age—when her father was repeatedly found washed up in some bar and she was home with the kids. She'd spent sleepless night after sleepless night wondering if Child Protection Services would show up and say her dad wasn't fit to care for them. The day Audrey turned eighteen, it was like a weight lifted off her...but she felt *far* older than her tender years, back then. She was an adult too soon.

"Don't you wonder what life might have been like?" he asked.

"No," she lied. Of course she wondered, but saying it aloud would be like opening Pandora's box. Wondering didn't help anybody.

"You're a better person than I am."

"I don't know about that." Her breath hitched. Energy crackled in the car, zipping between them like lightning bugs. The way he was looking at her had her under a spell—so intimate. So full of longing. "I think you're pretty wonderful."

Her words, though quietly spoken, were like taking a hammer to glass. It shattered the restraint, shattered the reasoning holding them back. Ronan leaned forward, sliding his hand along her jaw and around to cup the back of her head. He was closer now. Their noses brushed, and his lips parted, hers following in automatic, instinctual want.

They hovered there for a moment, ready to drown in anticipation, and Audrey let her eyes flutter shut, blotting out the light. She wanted only to feel.

Ronan's warm breath skated across her skin, and then the soft yet firm pressure of his lips melted her. Her hands reached out blindly, catching his shirt and curling so she could tug him closer. His tongue darted across the seam of her mouth, encouraging her to open to it. And she did. He tightened his fingers in her hair and tipped her back, sliding closer so he could kiss her more deeply.

His facial hair scratched against her skin, but in the most delicious way possible. The friction was fire in her blood, air in her lungs, electricity in her brain. His thumb brushed over her ear as he delved deeper into her mouth, and Audrey pressed against him even though something dug into her hip and thigh. She didn't want to stop.

Her whole body pulsed with sensation. Tightness gathered between her thighs, and liquid heat pooled lower in her belly. She felt her breathing come harder, like dragging air into her lungs was a second priority to the feel of his mouth on hers. A sigh rose up from deep inside her, and she leaned farther forward while Ronan's hands began to explore her body. He skimmed over her shoulders and down her arms, tracing the dip at her waist and the flare over her hips. It was so good to be touched. To be learned and understood.

Encouraged, Audrey slipped her hands down, too. Hard chest, flat stomach, the leather of his belt and soft denim over muscular thighs. And...oh. Her fingertips brushed the ridge of his erection lining his inner thigh, and Ronan groaned in response.

The loud squawk of the car horn made them jump apart, and Audrey clapped a hand to her chest. Her heart was thundering, though whether it was from the offensive sound or the kiss she wasn't sure. Outside, a couple walked hand in hand to their car, paying them no mind.

But anybody *could* have seen them. What if a college staff member had been walking past? Or a student who recognized them?

"I... We shouldn't..." Ronan scrubbed a hand over his face as he let out a breath. "Shit."

"Don't," Audrey said breathlessly. "Please don't ruin it."

She hadn't been kissed in forever. And while she knew it was wrong, she wanted to cradle that precious moment in her mind. It would be like a snow globe, a thought she could shake when she felt sad to watch it glitter and shine. And she refused to tar it with reality.

Ronan's eyes were hot like an open flame, but his jaw remained tense. Tight. "I can't be doing this with—"

"I know, I know." She nodded, holding up a hand. "It didn't happen."

Only it *did* happen, and Audrey wouldn't forget it anytime soon. For a moment she wanted to scream and pound her fist against the dashboard, because any time something good happened to her there seemed to be a catch. Why couldn't she have a night of fun without worrying about the consequences?

She wanted to say something more, but her throat was clogged with anger and frustration and...desperation. She pushed the door open and got out before he had a chance to respond.

Her hands trembled as she fished the car keys from her bag, her body still running on adrenaline from their kiss. But she had to get herself together. She slid into the driver's seat, started the engine, and drove out of the parking lot as though she were simply going about her business.

She didn't dare look to see if Ronan was behind her.

Audrey felt her armor slide back into place, as it always did when she returned home—shoulders straightened, eyes bright, smile painted on. She pumped the radio so loud it made her ears hurt and the bass rattled the shitty speakers in her dash. The second she pulled into the driveway, the night would be safely tucked into the back of her mind for safekeeping.

Audrey kept her mind blank as she navigated the empty streets of her hometown, until she made it home. She pulled Big Red to a stop in the driveway and killed the engine. The living room looked dark, but there was something flickering inside. The TV, probably. Maybe Deanna or the twins were watching a movie.

She got out and headed to the front door, keys jangling as she opened the lock. There was definitely a movie playing inside—something with explosions and gunfire. Audrey frowned. She didn't like Deanna watching those movies, as she was sensitive and prone to nightmares if something was too gory.

"Dee?" She flicked the lock on the door behind her, but there was no response. That's when she saw a figure sitting in the beat-up recliner facing the television...a figure that was far too large to be any of her siblings. "Dad?"

"And where have you been?"

"I thought you were at poker tonight." Uh oh. He wasn't supposed to be home yet; he *never* made it in before midnight. He flicked on the lights and stood, watching her with a dark stare. Her mind raced, trying to come up with a solution.

"Holton's missus came home early and kicked us all out," he said with a derisive grunt. "No matter. The cards weren't playing in my favor anyway. So where were you?"

"I was pulling an extra shift."

Her father's eyes flicked over her outfit. "At the café?"

Hmm, now she had a decision to make. It would be more plausible to say she was at her aunt's shop, given how she was dressed, but what if he'd spoken to her? Harriet sometimes called the house to check in on everyone.

"Yeah, uh... We were doing inventory."

"At ten o'clock at night?"

"We can't do it when the café is open."

Why did she even have to justify herself? The twins were old enough to look after the house for one night—she'd certainly done more at their age. And Deanna never made trouble. Her father expected her to not only hold the family up financially, but she had to do it all without having a life of her own?

Audrey's blood was almost boiling, and tears pricked the backs of her eyes, but she blinked them away. No way would she break. Not now, not ever.

Her father was looking worse for wear these days, with gray whiskers growing unchecked and his skin papery and dry. He wore a black T-shirt that clung to his broad shoulders and the potbelly that he'd steadily grown with beer and fried food since her mother died. He never ate the healthy stuff she prepared.

It was hard to look at him these days. In fact, some days she didn't—because she could still see the kind, crinkle-eyed man who'd tossed her in the air as a child and who'd read her bedtime stories, doing all the different voices. He was a good man then, a man who'd adored his family, and even though they'd always been strapped for cash, he'd done everything he could to make her childhood wonderful. They'd had picnics on the floor of the trailer, looked for fairies in the trees, and made up magical worlds together.

Why couldn't she have that man back?

"Can you explain this?" He came forward, a piece of paper folded up in his hand.

Audrey's breath caught in the back of her throat. What *was* that? She reached out, forcing her hand not to shake, and took it from him. Her stomach dropped as she caught sight of the Harrison Beech logo as she opened the paper. It was a letter, addressed to her, informing her that there had been an error with her payment. She'd been overcharged $50. It stated that there should be a check enclosed, but obviously her father had palmed that.

Letters from the college were supposed to go to her aunt's store. She'd requested that specifically, and previous mail had gone there, but of course the college had her home address for their official records.

"What do I need to explain, exactly?" Audrey tilted her

face up and met her father directly in the eye.

She was so done being worried that he would snap. So done with tiptoeing around him.

"You think money grows on trees, Audrey? How the fuck are you paying for this?"

"With money *I* earn." She didn't yell, didn't shout. Because she wasn't the emotional firework in this house—she was the calm, steady, level influence. "From my multiple jobs."

She decided to leave out the fact that her aunt supported her by paying half the tuition, since she knew it would make her father even angrier. Harriet *refused* to give him any money directly, since she didn't trust him to spend it wisely. The last time she'd done that, not long after Audrey quit school, he'd taken it all to the greyhound track in an attempt to "earn" more and lost all of it.

"Is that a dig at me? You're really giving your unemployed father a hard time because he hasn't been able to find work."

"It's difficult to find work when you don't look for it." The words came out colder than the depths of their freezer, and Audrey was almost shocked at the little bubble of hate that formed in her gut.

It's the kiss. It's...everything about tonight. You got a taste of what you can't have, and it's knocked you off-kilter.

"So instead of helping the family, you'd rather be selfish and spend that money on yourself?" Her father barreled on as though she hadn't called out the fact that he was willfully unemployed. "You'd rather force Deanna to wear shoes that are too small and the twins to have to share clothes so *you* can go off to college and pretend to be some smart-ass big shot? What are you going to do with that education, huh? Do you think you're going to leave us?"

Audrey caught sight of a door opening in the hallway and two faces poking out to see what was going on. Her sisters were mirror images of each other—wide-eyed, worried. Audrey swallowed down the desire to tell her father what she really thought—that he was selfish and useless and that he didn't deserve any of them—and instead she said something that was more for her siblings' benefit.

"I'm not going anywhere, Dad."

"The only reason people study is so they can get a decent job, and you think any of those exist in Kissing Creek? Do you really think I believe that you're spending all this money to go to college so you can keep working at that café?" He shook his head. "You should be ashamed of yourself, taking food out of your brother and sisters' mouths like that."

For a moment, Audrey *did* feel ashamed. Now her dirty little secret was out—she had spent money on herself for no real reason. Her father might be a deadbeat, but he knew his daughter well. Audrey wouldn't leave her family, and what kind of job would she ever get in Kissing Creek that needed a handful of mismatched college night classes?

That's not why you're doing this.

No, it was an even more selfish reason than that— pleasure. Personal enjoyment. Something she couldn't even claim had future benefit.

"That life is not something that people like us get to have," he said, his voice low so that only Audrey would be able to hear him. "We Millers don't have big, shiny degrees and fancy fucking houses and piles of money in the bank. We're not *those* people, so you need to stop pushing your stupid dreams on your brother and sisters, because you're only setting them up for disappointment."

But he was wrong. Jane was already at college on a scholarship and doing so well. She called every Thursday afternoon when she knew Audrey would be on break to tell her all about her week and how happy she was. That girl could easily have gone down the other path—the drinking and petty crimes and bad crowd path. Education had given her a future, and Audrey would do *everything* in her power to make sure it did the same for the others.

Even if it meant sacrificing herself.

"I'll go to the school tomorrow and get the money back," she said, not letting an ounce of her defeat show. As much as she hated her father's words, he was right...she *had* taken money that could have been better spent and used it on herself.

"You need to know your place, Audrey," he said, his eyes raking over her. "It's here at home, taking care of your family. It's what your mother would have wanted."

Would she have, though? Would her kind, sweet, caring mother have wanted invisible shackles around her daughter's wrists?

Sucking in a slow breath, Audrey turned away from her father and headed toward her room, her heart as heavy as if it were made of rocks.

Chapter Fourteen

There is a king penguin who holds a Norwegian army rank.

Ronan had been in his head all week, thinking about kissing Audrey on repeat, until he'd been asked by one of his students if he was high during a class. Not a good look. And no, he wasn't high, thank you very much. Smitten, more like it. Totally, utterly, and devastatingly smitten.

Which, obviously, he knew was not good for his job. Nor his reputation.

And when his Wednesday night class had rolled around, he'd planned to check in on Audrey in the hope that there wouldn't be any lingering weirdness between them. Only she hadn't shown. The class had ticked by slowly, his eyes catching on the door every few seconds, but she didn't appear.

Now he was here, standing outside Kisspresso Café's bright pink door, trying to muster up the courage to talk to a girl like he was fourteen instead of thirty-four. He caught a glimpse of himself in the reflection of the big windows— Kissing Creek had been kind to him. The persistent sun had taken away the pallor he'd developed from working all hours at Cambridge. His hair was slightly longer and the beard suited him, if he did say so himself.

"Go in there and talk to her," he muttered. But it took another moment and a few odd glances before Ronan got his feet moving.

Inside, the café was bustling. A line snaked from the counter past a few sets of tables and chairs. Despite his initial impression that this was some kind of Barbie Dreamhouse version of Starbucks, he'd grown to appreciate the quirky styling. In fact, he'd learned that all the "dine in" cups and plates were made by a local ceramist, and the cozy throw blankets strewn along the backs of the booth seating were knitted with yarn milled from local farms.

There was a strong sense of community pride here.

Ronan joined the line and slowly made his way to the front. He spied Audrey behind the espresso machine, working as she always did with a smile on her face and her motions fluid as a ballet dancer. There was a quiet grace about her. Well, as graceful as someone could look in a bright pink polo shirt with a kiss mark embroidered on her chest.

"Professor Walsh, good to see you." The young woman behind the cash register beamed up at him. "The usual? We've got chocolate-raspberry or cardamom-blackberry muffins today."

"I'll try the blackberry, and yes, the usual coffee. But I'll have it here."

"Day off?" she asked as she rang up his order.

"Kind of."

Ronan was on a mission—to get his ass into gear with his book. Settling into his home for the next year had taken longer than expected, and Ronan had found himself more distracted than ever, which was affecting his work. Figuring a change of scenery might help, he'd stashed his laptop into his satchel and come here.

Oh yeah, change of scenery. Riiiight.

More like if he didn't see Audrey, he was worried he might never concentrate again.

She continued making the coffees, calling out the orders and names in her usual cheerful tone. Pink passion mochas, cappuccinos, lattes, and cold brew flew out, and soon Ronan was at the front. When she looked up, ready to greet him like any other customer, her eyes widened.

"Ronan, hi."

"Hi." He leaned against the side of the bar. "We missed you yesterday in class."

"We?" Her movements halted for a moment, and she set the full force of her glorious olive-green eyes on him. "Or just you?"

His lip quirked. "I guess I shouldn't speak for everyone."

"Probably wise." She dumped an espresso shot into a large mug and topped it with hot water. A second later, his muffin appeared on a small pink plate with gold edging. "Here you go. Good call on the blackberry muffin, the cardamom is delicious."

"I don't suppose you want to join me for a few minutes?"

Audrey glanced toward the clock on the wall behind her. "I'm not supposed to go on break for another half hour."

"Take it now." The woman whom Ronan assumed was Audrey's boss was pottering around behind her, carrying a small wood crate filled with jugs of milk. "It's only going to get busier, so you may as well grab a bite to eat while you can. I'll cover you."

"Thanks, Jamie." Audrey untied her apron and motioned for Ronan to grab a seat. "I'll meet you there in a minute."

Ronan snagged an empty table that was tucked around the corner of the service counter and placed his food and drink down. Should he be worried about people seeing him and Audrey sit together? He shook off the thought. There was nothing wrong with a professor and a student grabbing coffee and talking. In fact, he was pretty sure he'd spotted one of his colleagues doing just that on the way in. The only reason he felt even mildly guilty about it was because he knew the thoughts he harbored for Audrey were less than professional...but nobody else had to know that.

"I have a question for you today," Ronan said as Audrey set down a coffee for herself and took the seat across from him. "I'm still determined to find something you don't know."

"Tell me." She took a sip of her coffee.

"There's an animal that holds a Norwegian army rank. What type of animal is it?"

"Oooh, good one." She looked stumped. "I know their national animal is the lion, but something tells me that isn't right."

Ronan tore a piece off his muffin and popped it into his mouth. "Final answer?"

"I don't know." She laughed. "You have actually stumped me."

"Finally!" Ronan pumped his fist into the air. "It's a king penguin."

"I doubt he's served."

"Uh, no. Brigadier Sir Nils Olav III currently resides in the Edinburgh Zoo. It's a fascinating story. You should read up on it."

"Deanna will *love* this. You don't mind if I repurpose this quiz question for my morning fact tomorrow?"

"Be my guest."

"She's obsessed with penguins." Something about the way she said it sounded almost...sad.

It was then Ronan noticed a hint of blue and purple under Audrey's eyes, as though she hadn't slept much. In fact, while Audrey didn't usually wear a lot of makeup, she always had this air of being fresh and put together. Today, she seemed worn out.

"Is everything okay?" he asked.

"Of course." She nodded and cradled her coffee cup between both hands. The ceramic was a swirling mix of pale pink and white, giving an almost tie-dyed effect. There was an imperfection in the glaze, a tiny bubble that Audrey rubbed her thumb over as though it soothed her. "Actually, I'm glad you came in today."

Ronan suddenly felt something heavy in his gut, like he'd swallowed a boulder. His intuition was never wrong. "What's going on?"

"I, um...well, the reason I missed class..." She licked her lips, stalling. "I won't be coming anymore."

The breath rushed out of his lungs. Shit. How could he have been so stupid as to kiss her? He *knew* it was dangerous. He *knew* she was off-limits. And she felt so uncomfortable that she didn't even want to attend his class anymore. God, he could kick himself.

"Audrey, I'm *so* sorry about—"

"It's not that." She cut him off, her eyes darting over his shoulder. "Trust me. I have no regrets. None at all."

He frowned. "Then why? I thought you were enjoying the class."

"I am...I mean, I was." She shook her head. "But I can't keep doing it."

"Why?" He felt like a toddler, but it pained him to see Audrey struggling with something. She clearly loved learning, and she was a brilliant student, from all he'd seen of her work thus far.

"I can't afford it." She sighed. "My family situation is... tough. I'm supporting my brother and sisters, and my father isn't working. Spending money on a night class is a frivolous expense."

Were those her words or someone else's? Because they sounded hollow. Rehearsed.

"Learning isn't frivolous."

She let a soft smile drift across her lips. "Of course the professor would say that."

"I'm not talking as a professor now. I'm talking as a friend." That was a stretch, wasn't it? He'd only known Audrey a few weeks, and one shared trivia victory did not a friendship make. Still, there was something between them. He knew that much.

"I appreciate the concern, but that doesn't change anything, unfortunately. I've withdrawn my enrollment, and I'm no longer a student at Harrison Beech."

There was a weight to her words—she was no longer a student. No longer *his* student. The words lodged in his brain, circling like vultures.

"You deserve to be here," he said stubbornly.

"Yeah, I do." She nodded. "But realities must be faced, and that means that I have to spend the money I earn more practically."

"What if I paid for you?"

She shook her head. "One, I don't even know if that's allowed. It could be a huge ethics breach. Secondly, I don't take charity."

She was right; it was probably an *enormous* breach. But the words had skated out of him without triggering a single sensible thought in his head—all he wanted was to help her have what she deserved.

She deserves more than taking a night class here and there. She deserves to take her life and her education as far as she wants.

But that wasn't going to happen. Audrey had dropped out of high school to care for her family, and now she'd dropped out of her college night class. It made his gut twist. How many other sacrifices had she made? How much of herself had she carved up and handed out to her family?

And all while keeping her shoulders square and her head high and a smile on her face...

What had given her so much strength?

It made him think of himself and Keira and their grandmother, how tough they all were and yet how separate. They each had their own lives, and they held survival and achievement in the highest regard—higher, even, than being together as a group.

"I'll be fine," Audrey reassured him. "I'm sad, but it's what's best for my family."

"What about your father?"

Something changed in her eyes, like a light being flicked off. "What about him?"

"Doesn't he want you to better yourself?"

"No," she said bluntly. "He'd rather I support the family. But I'm not doing it for him. I'm doing it for Deanna and the twins."

He stared at her across the table, brows knitted. "At what cost?"

"At any cost." Her gaze dropped. "I know you probably don't understand, but when my mom died, it fell to me to keep the family together. Nobody else could do it, and that's the mantle I've taken up. I can't afford to be selfish."

"When is it your turn, Audrey? Surely there's a way for you to study *while* you take care of your family. I've had plenty of parents and caretakers in my classes."

"Until my siblings are all out on their own, my studies aren't a priority."

Her tenacity was admirable, but Ronan wondered what would happen in the future. It was easy to say that she'd do what she wanted once her siblings were all gone, but would she be able to leave her father behind? Or would she let herself be trapped forever?

"What if we make a deal?" Ronan said. "I can take you through the lessons I'm teaching outside the classroom, and in exchange, you can help me with my book."

"How on earth would I help you, Ronan? What skills could I possibly offer?"

"All books need a second set of eyes to make sure concepts are clear and the flow makes sense. And it's actually better that you're not in the field, because I want this book to reach beyond the academic community. You can be my beta reader. I'll pay you for your time."

"No." She shook her head. "I can't do that."

"Why not?"

"I don't want you to be my boss." There was an air of passionate defiance about her, a swelling of some feeling that had Ronan ensnared.

What did she mean by that? She didn't want him to be her boss, but for what reason? Was it because she viewed it as charity or something else? A tangle of anticipation knotted itself in his stomach.

"I don't want to work for you," she said. "But I'd be happy to work *with* you."

She wanted to be equal. Ronan nodded. "An exchange, then. You offer your keen eye, and I'll share my lectures with you."

"An exchange." She bit down on her lower lip, but her eyes were sparkling and alight. "I like that idea."

"Me, too."

Her gaze drifted over to the big clock on the wall, and she drained the rest of her coffee. "I have to get back to it, but if you text me the times we can meet up, I'll check my schedule."

"Deal."

She stood, still cradling her mug. "Thank you."

"No thanks required," he said. "You're the one who's helping me."

She looked as though she might say something else, but Audrey simply put her game face back on and headed toward the little gate at the service counter. In a few seconds, she was back at her station, smile in place and moving like a well-oiled cog in a machine.

Suddenly inspired, Ronan pulled out his laptop and opened up the document where he was keeping notes for his book. He'd never met anyone like Audrey. She faced some very difficult life circumstances, and yet he'd never heard her complain once. She never pouted or said anything bad about her siblings or seemed to resent her lot in life.

Motivation.

He typed the word in bold font. What were people capable of if presented with the right motivation? Did it make people more positive, or was positivity a component in connecting motivation and action?

Ronan leaned back in his chair and watched Audrey for a moment. She was special, even if she didn't see it herself. She was sharp and hardworking and deserving.

And she was no longer his student.

• • •

Audrey had a "date" with Ronan to meet at the Harrison Beech campus library at six thirty p.m. on Monday. He was going to take her through the class she'd missed the previous week due to canceling her enrollment, and they were going to talk about his book.

But first she had to finish her shift.

"Audrey, darling, can you come here?" Harriet called from the back.

Audrey left the Game of Stones front counter to see what

her aunt needed. She found the older woman high up on a ladder, a long velvet skirt embroidered with silver stars and moons covering her feet.

"Don't move," Audrey said. "Why on earth are you climbing a ladder in a skirt like that? It's all tucked under your feet!"

"Who's the boss here?" her aunt said peevishly. "Now, take this."

She handed Audrey a box which had "oracle cards" written across the top in black Sharpie. Hefting the heavy box with one arm, Audrey held out her other hand to help Harriet down.

"You're going to give me a heart attack one day," Audrey muttered. "You have no sense of occupational health and safety."

Harriet eyed her sharply. "And *you're* going to give me a heart attack one day, young lady. I know you pulled out of that class."

Audrey's head snapped up as her aunt walked past her into the front of the store without so much as a sideways glance. "How do you know?"

"I called the house yesterday. I was hoping to chat with Georgie but your father answered."

Audrey carried the box out to the front counter and set it down, fetching the box cutter and dragging it along the seam. "What did he have to say?"

"That you're an ungrateful so-and-so and that education is a waste of money." Harriet's eyes narrowed, and Audrey caught a rare glimpse of her aunt's true feelings about her father. Usually, she tried to hide it. "I told my sister not to marry him, you know."

"Why?" Audrey's attention was ensnared. Harriet didn't talk about her sister much, since it was so painful, and therefore Audrey had been starved of many details of her mother's life before she had kids. "I thought he was a good man before."

"He always had a streak of something...selfish inside him. He had a single-mindedness for his own desires." She slid the box along the glass counter toward herself and pulled the flaps open. Inside were dozens of identical, ornately decorated card boxes. "He was a good man before because he had what he wanted, and it's easy to be a good person when the universe is singing your song."

Audrey leaned against the counter and reached for one of the decks. She'd seen her aunt use these decks before, whenever she was having trouble with a decision or life event. "I guess that's true."

"It's how I know you're a truly good person," her aunt said. "With everything life has thrown at you, it would be hard to judge you for being angry or spiteful or selfish. But you're none of those things."

Selfish. Isn't that what her father had called her? Isn't that the fear she'd cradled in her mind as she crawled into bed that night with Deanna tucked in beside her? She wouldn't stop crying because she thought Audrey wanted to leave them.

Wasn't she being selfish worrying about her own needs and spending money they didn't have?

"Don't you *dare* listen to him." Harriet cupped Audrey's face. Up close, she smelled sweet and familiar, like incense and sandalwood and fresh-cut roses. Her aunt's crystal bracelets brushed her cheek, cool and comforting. "Your father wouldn't know goodness if it smacked him upside the head with a wet fish."

Audrey laughed. "That's quite an image."

"I mean it. I heard his vitriol on the phone, so I can only imagine what he said to you." Harriet closed her eyes, and for a moment Audrey wondered if she was in actual, physical pain. It's certainly how it looked. "You can still come and live with me, you know. Bring the kids."

"I can't." She shook her head. "Your place is tiny, and the twins are struggling enough as it is, barely having any privacy. At least Oliver has his own room at Dad's."

"Well...when they go off to college, then, and it's only you and Deanna." Her aunt's gaze bored into her. "You can come then."

"I'll think about it."

"Promise me."

Audrey nodded. "I promise."

But in her heart of hearts, she knew it wouldn't make a difference—her father would still refuse to find work, and therefore he'd need money. Which meant he'd be hassling her aunt more, coming around to collect what he could. Was she supposed to let him starve?

She couldn't do that. He was still her dad.

Why do you cling to who he used to be instead of realizing who he is? The man you loved is gone.

"I'm disappointed you dropped out of that class," Harriet said, going back to unpacking the box of oracle decks. "I know you don't want to hear it, but I am."

"You're right—I don't want to hear it. Anyway, I've come up with an alternative solution." Technically, it was Ronan's idea, not hers, but Audrey had decided to fully embrace it. "I'm helping the professor with the book he's writing, and, in exchange, he'll give me the rundown on the classes he's teaching."

"He's allowed to do that?"

"I don't see why not. I won't be doing assignments or getting grades or using college resources or anything like that. It'll be more like a...discussion group."

"This is the professor who came into my store that day?" Harriet didn't lift her head up as she worked. "The one with the sexy name."

"You think his name is sexy? I can ask if he's interested in going on a date with you," she teased.

Harriet snorted. "I'm old enough to be his mother. Besides, I think the man is already smitten."

Audrey opened the deck of oracle cards and admired the pretty, almost watercolor-like designs. They had uplifting names like hope, adventure, and resilience. She started shuffling them, focusing on the repetitive motion and whispering sounds of the cards sliding against one another. "You think?"

"I did not come down in the last shower," she replied. "I know when a man has a crush."

Audrey focused on the cards, shuffling them so they became a blur of pink and blue and sparkling gold in her hands. It was easier to do that than to think about Ronan crushing on her—sure, she knew he was attracted to her. Well, unless he went around kissing anyone like that.

Nobody kisses like that unless they feel something.

Heat bloomed in her cheeks. "What we have is more of a business relationship."

Bullshit. You specifically didn't want him to pay you so there's no more power imbalance.

"Maybe business is a strong word," she self-corrected. "Maybe more like...mutual respect and admiration from an academic standpoint."

Except that wasn't right, either. How could he have mutual respect for her academically when she was the furthest thing from an academic one could get?

"Or maybe it's whatever two people are when a friendship is starting to form." Yeah, that sounded about right.

"So you're smitten, too? Interesting." Harriet picked up the empty box, and Audrey watched as she disappeared out the back with a smug expression firmly in place, her long skirt swishing around her feet.

"Maybe a little," Audrey admitted under her breath.

Her hands stilled, the deck of oracle cards feeling heavier than when she was shuffling them. She peeled the top card off the deck and placed it faceup on the glass, the way she'd watched her aunt do time and time again. The card showed a blond woman in white robes striding forward, the title and subtitle in intricate gold font.

Action. Go forth and stop sitting on the side lines.

A bubble of excitement expanded in her stomach. Maybe this *was* her time to stop sitting on the sidelines of her own life. Maybe her father's cutting words had actually steered her in the right direction.

Because this evening, when she went to see Ronan, things would be very different.

Chapter Fifteen

There are 25,000 possible combinations for coffee orders at Dunkin' Donuts.

Ronan leaned back in his chair, arching his back so that the muscles protested. He was stiff after sitting for so many hours, painstakingly going through the results of an experiment he wanted to reference in his book. The general structure was starting to take shape, and rather than blobs of data and academic papers and journal articles, he was finally seeing the "story" it all told.

His mentor, an experienced and acclaimed professor who'd been like a father to Ronan at Cambridge, had read through a draft of his latest chapter. It had come back covered in changes marked in red, comments and questions littering the margins like debris. Not one to be discouraged, Ronan had steadily worked through each and every one and could now see exactly how he needed to tighten his ideas.

But his brain was officially mush.

"Long day?" A feminine voice caught his attention.

Audrey.

He sat up and motioned for her to take a seat. Collecting his notebooks and the scraps of paper covered in his barely legible handwriting, he made some space for her. "You could say that. I was up late last night going over the first assignment submissions for the Wednesday class, and then I had an early meeting this morning."

"You work hard," she said with a nod. She lowered herself into the seat next to him, long blond hair trailing over her shoulders. It was loose today, lightly curling at the ends and gleaming like champagne-colored silk. In her hands were two coffee cups bearing the Kisspresso logo, and she placed one in front of him.

"How did you know?" He reached for it as though it was a pitcher of water and he was a man who'd crawled through the desert.

"Coffee is *always* required, especially when there's study involved." She grinned. "Did you know there's twenty-five thousand possible combinations when ordering your coffee at Dunkin'?"

"Don't you mean Dunkies?" Ronan winked and took a long drink of his coffee.

"Is that a Boston thing?"

"Maybe. Didn't they drop the 'donuts' part anyway? Maybe we Bostonians are ahead of the curve."

Audrey made a snorting sound. "That's *exactly* something a city person would say."

"Why do I get the impression you say 'city person' like it's a bad thing?" He narrowed his eyes at her. "I'm quite proud of my heritage."

"As am I. I find cities so…" She wrinkled her nose, but not like she'd smelled something bad. More like she was trying to figure out the right words to say. "Intimidating. I mean, I'd like to travel more, but something tells me I'll always be a small-town girl at heart."

"They're not intimidating. They're just faster, more aggressive, and filled with bad drivers who swear a lot," he said with a laugh.

"Sounds delightful."

"You should go some time. Boston is a great city. There's so much history and culture. The architecture is amazing, and then there are all the parks and great restaurants and so many things to do."

"Do you miss it?" Audrey asked.

"I miss my family, mostly, but I miss the city, too." He glanced at his phone, which was sitting facedown against the table. He'd been deep in work when it had rung earlier, and he'd let it go to voicemail. When he'd taken a moment to listen back, his mother's voice had shocked him so badly he'd hung up without listening to the rest of the message.

What could she possibly want?

"Will you go back there when you're finished with your contract here?" Audrey asked.

"Maybe. I'm still trying to figure out where I'm going. Anything is possible." He shrugged. "But it *would* be nice to be close to Gram and my sister. I've got a nephew now, and..."

For some reason, Lukas had been stuck in his head. When he'd gone to visit his sister at her home, he'd spent a few hours playing with the bright little boy and found himself wondering what it might be like to be a father himself. These kinds of thoughts had never entered his head before— because having a family wasn't part of his plans. Yet there was something about holding a small child with familiar eyes and a smile that was basically a family heirloom that had hit him deep in the chest.

The love he felt—so unconditional it was almost illogical— was like nothing he'd ever experienced before.

"I want to be part of his life," Ronan finished. "I don't want to be an absent figure to him, you know?"

"That's really sweet." Audrey reached out and touched his arm. "He's lucky to have an uncle who cares about him so much."

"Like your aunt cares about you?"

"Exactly." She let out a breath and shook her head. "Some days I don't know what I would have done if it wasn't for her. She's my rock. There are days that I feel bad about depending on her, because I know she always had plans to leave this place. But after my mother died, she decided to stay a while to make sure me and my siblings were okay..."

"And then she never left?"

"Yeah. It's part of what makes me so sure I have to take care of my siblings. I can't let her sacrifice mean nothing. She gives me strength when sometimes I feel like it's all too much."

Ronan thought back to the last time he and Audrey had coffee at Kisspresso, where his mind had circled on the idea of motivation and how it allowed people to persevere through difficult circumstances.

"Do you think about the future?" he asked.

For a moment, Audrey said nothing. Her gaze traveled beyond him, into the quiet college campus library. There were a few study groups dotted around, and people talked in quiet murmurs. A row of single-person study nooks were tucked in a line against one wall. It was quite a modern building, considering some areas of the campus were in need of a facelift.

"I think about achieving my goal of ensuring all my siblings get out of Kissing Creek and make something of themselves."

"I mean *your* future."

"I don't know." She shrugged and took a sip of her coffee,

shaking her head as though he was asking her a silly question. "Anyway, I came here to learn. Not give you my life story."

"Ah, but this week's class was all about how striving alters brain chemistry. I got the class to journal about a goal they really want to achieve in the future—a component of their ideal life."

For most people, thinking about something like that would encourage a big smile or an expression of deep thought. For Audrey, though, the question made her look like a deer in headlights.

Curious. For someone who was so positive and upbeat and self-sacrificing, why did the thought of the future frighten her? Maybe she didn't know herself beyond the role she played caring for her siblings and working herself to the bone. Maybe she was worried that she couldn't achieve anything else.

Stop psychoanalyzing her.

But Audrey was a puzzle he wanted to understand until every last piece clicked into place. She was a riddle he wanted to solve. A surprise gift he wanted to unwrap.

And this wasn't a normal behavior for Ronan. Ask his ex. She had claimed that he was chronically disinterested in their relationship—that he was only ever excited by some shiny new idea in his head, never in people.

Yet Audrey interested him. She *intrigued* him. She captivated him.

"My ideal life?" Audrey nodded and sipped her coffee, stalling. "That's very...deep."

"Doesn't have to be. Maybe you want a Scrooge McDuck–style vault filled with Doritos that you can swan dive into." Ronan bobbed his head. "And yes, that was an actual answer I received in my class once."

"But that would be so...sharp and crunchy. It doesn't sound pleasant at all." Her posture eased a little, her shoulders pulling away from her ears as she sank further back into the chair and tilted her face up to the ceiling.

"One man's nightmare is another man's Doritos dust."

Audrey snorted. "Amen to that."

"Visualization is actually very helpful to the brain," he said. "It's critical that we tell our brains what to focus on, because as we are bombarded with information every second of every day, the only way to survive is to filter."

"That makes sense." Audrey dug her notebook out of her bag and started taking notes.

"So, if we have to filter information, perception becomes reality, right? What we focus on and what we filter out shape the way we view the world." He watched her neat handwriting flow across the page of her notebook. "There's something called the reticular activating system that helps this process. The RAS is a network of neurons that ensures our brain isn't overloaded with more information than it can possibly handle. It sorts information into what we notice and what we don't."

"So it's like the brain's sieve?"

"Exactly. The RAS and how we utilize it is actually a big part of the book I'm writing—because I believe that if we understand how to adjust our filter to see the world more positively, then we will naturally find more opportunity, more creativity, and more innovation in our lives."

"Huh." Audrey nodded, tapping her pen against the page.

"And if we understand what our ideal 'end state' looks like—although I don't believe there is ever a *true* end state with life—then we can wire our brain to make sure we don't filter out things that will help us along that journey. The RAS can act like an internal GPS system, guiding us toward what we want by noticing more opportunities and making it easier for us to make decisions in alignment with our goals."

"Like stockpiling Doritos when they're on sale?"

Ronan laughed. "Exactly."

"Gosh, it's…maybe I'm horribly unimaginative. I would never come up with something like that."

"Close your eyes."

She raised an eyebrow at him.

"I'm serious." He reached over and gently removed the coffee cup from her hands, then placed it down on the table. "Close your eyes, and I'm going to guide you."

With a reluctant sigh, Audrey did as he requested. He noticed there was something subtle and shimmery on her eyelids, like someone had sprinkled stardust there. It was pretty, and it made him smile for some stupid reason.

"Okay, let's start with the basics. We're going forward ten years into the future."

"So I'll be old like you?" she teased, a cheeky expression crinkling her nose and making her cheeks pop. But she kept her eyes closed.

"Excuse me. In ten years' time, you'll be *older* than I am now by two years, and not a day more," Ronan said drily. "Shall we continue, smarty-pants?"

She nodded, sucking on her lower lip as if trying to stifle an amused smile. "Uh-huh."

"Ten years into the future. I'm going to ask some questions, and you have to say the first thing that pops into your head, no filtering."

"Okay."

"Are you still in Kissing Creek?"

"No." Something shifted in Audrey's expression, as if she was surprised by her response. But she kept her eyes closed.

"Are you in the United States?"

"No."

"What can you see?"

"Blue water," she replied. "The beach. It looks…tropical."

"Are you on vacation?"

"Yes, I think so." She nodded. "I'm standing on a balcony."

"What does it feel like?"

"It's warm; there's a breeze." Her voice was more relaxed now, as though the visual soothed her. "I can see palm trees moving, and the tiles are cold under my feet. I'm not wearing any shoes."

"What can you smell?"

"Salt water. Something vanilla, like ice cream."

"Why are you on vacation?"

"Because I want to see what else exists in the world. I want to experience other places and…have time off."

Her words, so sincere and so heartfelt, struck him in the chest. "Okay, when you come home from your vacation, what can you see? You've gotten off the plane, and you've caught a cab home. Is it a big house, an apartment?"

"It's an apartment. I'm in a city, I think. There are people noises and music and lights twinkling."

"Walk through the front door. Tell me what you see."

"It's pretty—the place is tidy, and there's a pink couch. I've always wanted a pink couch with loads of cushions. There's a big bookshelf that's overflowing with books." Audrey sighed. "It's beautiful."

"What else do you see?"

"Textbooks on the coffee table. A laptop. Someone works there."

"Is that someone you?"

"I think so."

Ronan studied her closely. "Keep walking through the house. Is anyone else there?"

"Yes." She sucked in a breath. "I walk into the bedroom…"

Her eyes flew open, her cheeks suddenly warm and colorful. Her pupils had grown, and she blinked against the bright lights of the college library, her hand coming to her chest.

"What did you see?" Ronan frowned.

Audrey reached for her coffee and took a long gulp. "A man."

"Your husband or boyfriend?"

"Husband," she whispered, and her eyes were locked on his. "I never thought I wanted to get married. Ever."

"How come?"

She shook her head. "I...I saw what losing my mom did to my dad, and I don't ever want to go through that. I don't want grief to turn me into a monster."

"But maybe you do want to have a relationship. These exercises are designed to allow what's already in your brain to bubble to the surface, so we can view our desires in a safe and nonjudgmental way."

"But I *am* judging it." Audrey looked affronted, as though her own desires had offended her. "I know logically that relationships are dangerous. When you open up to another person, you're handing them power to hurt you."

Ronan nodded. He couldn't argue there—his own views on love and relationships were pretty much aligned. "Unfortunately, logic and desire don't always line up."

"Humans are poorly designed," Audrey muttered.

"I agree. But it's important to know what you want, because constantly suppressing those desires can leave you feeling unsatisfied or disconnected from your own life. You saw textbooks and a full bookshelf—those things are there for a reason."

"But that doesn't mean it can happen."

"Maybe not now. But you have a whole long life ahead of you that can be filled with those things. Understanding desire doesn't mean we get what we want right away, but it *does* mean we have the opportunity to put plans in place and pave a road toward it."

She eyed him warily, as though he was a fortune-teller promising security and she was certain she knew it couldn't possibly exist. "No one is guaranteed a long life."

"Exactly. We have to enjoy what we have."

"Ah, so you're one of *those* people." She cocked her head. "Personal desire trumps responsibility, because *carpe diem* or insert other meaningless Instagram quote here."

"Wow, was that some actual cynicism from Little Miss Sunshine?"

Audrey blinked. "I'm not cynical at all. Quite the contrary—and I believe in the importance of what I do and the sacrifices I make. Which is all the more reason to avoid selfishness thinly veiled as a motivational quote."

"You're very motivated by the present."

"Isn't the here and now the only thing we know for sure?" she asked. "I understand the whole brain-filter GPS thing, but surely focusing too much on the future isn't productive."

"It has to be a balance," Ronan admitted. "But understanding where you want to go will give you a much higher chance of getting there in the future. There's nothing selfish about wanting, Audrey. It's a fundamentally human thing."

"Isn't it dangerous to want things you can't have?" Her lashes lowered for a moment, exposing the shimmery particles on her lids once more. They glimmered when she blinked, luring him closer.

"I guess it comes down to the reason you think you can't have it," he said. Were they even talking about brain filters and visualization anymore? Ronan had no idea.

All he wanted to know was what Audrey saw in the bedroom...or rather, *who*?

"Sometimes there's a barrier to what you want. But then the barrier is removed, and I guess it's unclear if there are more barriers or not," she said quietly.

Ronan's breath stilled in his lungs. Audrey had been

on his mind from the second he'd walked into her café, and her hold on him had only grown stronger. It was like a fist continuing to tighten around him, the pressure building and building.

The library was quieter now. It was verging on dinnertime, and many of the students who lived on campus would be heading toward the main hall for their meal. Or maybe they'd ventured out into the town, seeking out something different. Only the most die-hard students remained, dotting the space so quietly you'd be forgiven for thinking there was no one there at all.

"What possible barriers might there still be?" he asked. He was leaning one arm on the table, his body craned toward her, and she faced him, legs tucked under her chair and hair tumbling over one shoulder.

She had on a pretty tank top thing with lace around the bottom and thin straps that left most of her shoulders free. One of the straps had veered toward the edge of her shoulder, the delicate piece of fabric less than an inch away from sliding down her arm.

"Personal barriers," she said. Her voice was barely a whisper.

"Such as?"

She sucked on the inside of her cheek for a moment. "Mutual attraction."

"That's not a barrier, trust me." His nostrils flared for a second. God, how could she even question that? With all the reasons in the world not to touch her, he still kissed her like his life depended on it that night in the car. "That's squarely in the pro column."

"Age?"

"Is that a barrier for you?" To him, eight years didn't mean anything.

She shook her head. "No, it's not."

"What else have you got?"

Were they really doing this? Negotiating. Maybe it wasn't that; maybe it was more like due diligence. Sexy, hot-under-the-collar, fueled-by-tension due diligence.

"Reputation?"

"You're no longer my student," he said huskily. "And you're not my employee, either. You made that clear."

She nodded her head. "I wouldn't want to do anything that might upset your career."

"People will talk, though. Isn't that the way of small-town life?"

"Not if we keep it under wraps." She looked at him hopefully. "I mean, this isn't…"

Real? To him it felt real, in a way. After all, if he only wanted sex, then that wasn't too hard to acquire. It certainly wasn't something that warranted a discussion about reputation and barriers and whatnot. But that's because Ronan wasn't simply after sex. He wanted Audrey, specifically. Completely.

"I'm not looking for forever," she said with a nod. "No matter what the visualization showed me."

He wasn't going to push it, partially because that wasn't what he wanted, either. He'd come to Kissing Creek with a goal—be closer to his family, write his book, spend the year figuring out the next step. Audrey was tied to this place. He didn't want to be tied to anything.

"That's not what I want, either."

"What *do* you want, Ronan?" Her lips parted, and he had to restrain himself from leaning forward to kiss her. "Because you're very good at talking about internal GPS systems and guiding other people through their wants and desires, but you never talk about yourself."

"I've told you more about my life than anybody else in this town." Or Cambridge. Or Harvard. Or before all that. In fact, if there was a career in being a closed book, Ronan would be an industry leader.

"More doesn't necessarily mean a lot," she said.

"Maybe there are other things I'd rather be doing than talking about myself."

They were dancing around it, neither one willing to pull the trigger. But Audrey had made her desires clear, even if she didn't quite agree with whatever was lurking in her dream apartment.

But she needed to be the one who gave the go-ahead. Because even if he wasn't her professor or her boss or anything else, the last thing Audrey needed was one more person dictating her destiny.

"If you want this, then I'm all yours," he said. "I will walk you out of this library right now and take you back to my place. We've been trying to avoid this for weeks, and I'd like very much to see where it goes. But I'm not moving a damn inch unless you say so."

Her breath came quicker, her eyes wide and cheeks and neck flushed pink. She ran her tongue along her lower lip. "You want me to be the boss, huh?"

"I want you to be in control of what happens next."

She nodded, her breath hitching as she reached out to touch his hand. "This isn't some game you're playing, is it? You're not trying to teach me a lesson about the future?"

"I wouldn't be here unless I absolutely wanted this for myself."

"I'm not looking for someone to fix me, okay?"

"Audrey..." He let out a breath. "You *don't* need fixing. You don't need a white knight. Which is good, because that's not what I am. I'm just a man."

"That's all I want," she said, her eyes sparkling. "Just a man. Just you. No promises or lies or games. Just you."

Ronan got to his feet and held out his hand, and Audrey slid her palm against his. "Then let's go."

Chapter Sixteen

A person can be 3 times more likely to have a heart attack during or immediately after sex.

Audrey felt like they were a pair of thieves in the night, walking quickly and quietly; the only sounds they made were of quickened breath and the whisper of shoes over wet grass. The campus was quiet, but it was still warm. Muggy. The aftermath of summer rain and the chirrup of insects made it seem even more romantic somehow.

Even more real.

Was she really going to do this?

Ronan's hand gripped hers as they headed to his place. There was a building way back behind the newer portion of the college's campus. It was a small apartment complex, with only three stories and a single entrance at the front.

Ronan pulled the keys from his pocket, and Audrey stayed close to him, her cheek tucked against his arm even though they had nothing to hide. But there was something about coming here with Ronan that felt...fraught. Not because she was worried about him being a professor, but because she knew people would look at him, then look at her, and be confused.

Why on earth would a man like him—a smart man with a future tinged with gold—want a going-nowhere small-town lifer like her?

Ronan might not know exactly what his future held, but it was full of possibility. Audrey, on the other hand, knew *exactly* what the next five years held for her. Beyond that, well… it wasn't like she'd be able to move to a big city, no matter how the lights had shined in her fantasy. Putting her lack of savings and education aside, she didn't even have marketable skills. No gold stars on her résumé beyond making a wicked coffee.

But it hadn't stopped her from imagining it…and him. When she'd walked through the fantasy bedroom door to see a man lying on her bed, no shirt, muscles rippling and a smile sexier than sin… *Lordy.* The fact that it had been Ronan had shaken her to her core.

But not as much as the gold band on his finger and the diamond perched on hers.

Ronan pushed the door open and tugged her inside, sweeping his blue eyes down to hers for the briefest second. That one glance blanked any and all worries from her mind. Tonight wasn't about the future; it was about *now.*

The present. The glorious, decadent, rebellious present.

"You still with me?" he whispered in a husky tone as he closed the door softly behind her. His apartment was on the second floor, and they made their way up with careful footsteps.

"Of course."

The landing held a single potted plant and twin doors. Ronan walked to the left one, still holding her hand as though he was worried she might vanish like a puff of smoke. They stepped into his apartment, and he shut the door behind them with a soft *snick*.

Ronan released her for a moment to hang his keys on a hook and to dump his wallet and phone out of his jeans into a small ceramic bowl. She got the feeling this "unloading" was how he separated himself from the world.

"You're very quiet," he said.

She lowered her gaze. "I don't want to say something that might risk where this is going."

"Where do you want it to go, Audrey?"

How long had it been since she was with a man? One year...more? No, it had to have been two. At least. She'd forgotten how this was supposed to work. Her eyes flicked around the darkened apartment. Neither of them had turned the lights on, and the only glow came from a lamp outside, shining in through a window and reflecting on the raindrops still smattered on the glass.

It was like being in their own private bubble. For once, she could voice her desires without fear of repercussion.

"I hope it's going to the bedroom." She offered up a tentative smile, which bloomed into something more when she saw that Ronan was coming closer still, seemingly undeterred by her awkwardness. "Or maybe the couch...or a countertop somewhere. I'm open to suggestions."

"Really?" He was in front of her now, one hand coming up to brush a strand of hair from her cheek, curling it around her ear with such tenderness that it was a miracle she didn't melt on the spot. "I've always been a fan of up against a wall."

"Good suggestion." She nodded, her breath hitching when his lips came down to her neck and he slowly backed her up. "Although, not to be a stickler for details, but this is a door."

Ronan laughed and nipped at her neck. He braced one palm against the door and used his free hand to explore the hem of her camisole. The brush of his knuckles as he toyed with the soft fabric sent a shower of energy through her. She felt like one of those sparklers they'd saved for the Fourth of July, ready to light up the night.

"Sorry, I…" She gasped as his hand slid against her bare skin, finding its way under her top and up over the softness of her belly. "I never know what to say, especially with this stuff. I'm not…I'm not smooth."

"Smooth is overrated." Ronan cupped her breast, catching her nipple between his thumb and forefinger and pinching her.

Audrey bit down on her lip and let her head roll back. Hard wood met the back of her skull with a *thunk*, and she let her eyes flutter shut. The sound of the rain starting up outside was a cocoon around them. She shifted on the spot, widening her legs as Ronan pushed against her. His jeans and belt rasped against her where her camisole was pulled up, and the hard ridge of his cock dug into her belly. The evidence that he wanted her as much as she wanted him filled Audrey with warmth.

She looped her arms around his neck and dragged his head down to hers, opening her mouth for him. He tasted sweet and earthy, and the scratch of his facial hair against her tender skin was like flint sparking against flint.

Ronan's hand found its way between her legs, and his kiss swallowed her moan.

After a glorious minute, he pressed his forehead to hers. "So what's the verdict? Bedroom, couch, countertop, or wall?"

"Can I be greedy and say all four? In any order. Maybe twice through."

Ronan let out a strangled sound. "You're going to kill me, Audrey. You're going to kill me in the best way possible."

"Actually, you can be three times more likely to have a

heart attack during or immediately after sex than when not having sex."

"Of *course* you have a fact for that." Ronan cupped her face and planted a sweet kiss against her lips.

"Although to be fair, I think that was referring to a man in his fifties."

Shut. The. Hell. Up.

"If I could live in your brain for just a day…"

"I'm sure you'd find it very boring."

"I definitely would not." He took both her hands in his and started walking backward, bringing her along with him. In the dim light, his eyes looked strangely ethereal, and the lines of his face were sharper. More exaggerated. "You're far more interesting than you give yourself credit for."

"I'd rather be…"

Beautiful. Successful. Formidable. Powerful.

Free.

"Something else," she said.

"You can be anything and everything you want." They were in his bedroom now, and he tugged her back toward the spacious bed dominating the room. But he didn't immediately pull her down or start stripping her.

Instead, Ronan stared right into her eyes as if forcing her to focus and let her mind slow down. He was so beautiful she wanted to pinch herself.

Yeah, because that won't make you seem like a born-again virgin.

But it was hard for someone like her to accept that good things wouldn't come with a hefty price tag. Life had taught her that any time she wanted something for herself…well, it always turned out to be out of her budget.

Why wouldn't Ronan be the same?

So long as you're not paying with your heart, you'll be fine.

"Like I said before, I don't like Instagram wisdom," she said eventually, her hands coming to the ties holding the keyhole neckline of her camisole together. She tugged on the bow until it loosened, and then she slowly pulled one end to release the knot. "If anyone can do anything, then no level of success has meaning."

Ronan's eyes were fixed on the bow as she slowly undid it, opening the neckline of her top more to expose the press of her cleavage. She'd worn her favorite bra—the one with turquoise lace and hints of gold that she saved for when she needed an extra boost of confidence. And it appeared to work its magic on Ronan as well.

"I'm not saying that anyone can do anything; I'm saying *you* can do anything. Because you're not average, Audrey."

Her breath stuttered in the back of her throat. "You don't have to flatter me, Ronan. I'm already here."

"I want you to see even a *sliver* of the potential you have. I want you to see a speck of what *I* see when I look at you." He fingered the lengths of her bow, which now hung loose and useless. "I don't know whether you're afraid or if you really are blind to it, but I see, Audrey. I see all of you."

This wasn't what she came here for. She didn't want Ronan touching her soul as well as her body, because that was a path that she couldn't go down. *Feeling* something for him would be her undoing. Emotions would be her undoing.

This was about sex. Pleasure. Release.

Nothing more.

Even as she drew the lines in her mind, there was a niggling voice in the back of her brain—a whisper of discontent, telling her she was lying to herself. But sometimes lies were necessary for survival, right? Because Audrey told herself that everything would turn out okay on a daily basis, even though she knew that at any moment it could all come crumbling down.

Please don't make me crumble.

"You can see more of me," she whispered as she drew the hem of her top up and over her head. "Every last inch."

Her hands then went to her jeans, and she popped the button slowly. In the quiet, almost blotted out by the soft drumming of rain, was Ronan's breath. His eyes looked dark, his jaw tight, as he watched her undress. She toed off her sneakers, and then her jeans hit the floor. Stepping out of the pile, she brought her hands behind her back and released the clasp on her bra.

It felt good to shed everything. To take it back to the physical.

She didn't feel worried about being naked in front of Ronan—curves and dimples and jiggles and all. He'd never made her feel anything but beautiful. Audrey dropped her bra to the ground and then hooked her fingers into the waistband of her panties, pulling them down, down, down.

"Turn for me," he said with a husky voice.

Audrey did as she was told, taking her time to give him access to every angle. Then she ran her fingers through her hair, letting it filter down over her shoulders and her breasts and back.

"Touch me, Ronan," she said. Her mouth was dry, anticipation making her heart thump like a marching band drum in her chest. "I want your hands on me."

He stalked forward, wrapping his arms around her and lowering her to the bed. His clothes rubbed against her skin, reminding her that she was totally naked and he wasn't. That she was at his mercy.

His lips found hers, and she drove her fingers through his hair, sliding her tongue eagerly into his mouth and kissing him with all she had. The weight of him pressed her into the bed, his knee easing her thighs open.

"You drive me wild," he rasped, his hand sliding up the

inside of her thigh. "You drive me so fucking wild that I have no idea what's going to happen once this is over."

"Don't think about that." She cupped his face, letting her gaze bore into his. "Just be here with me now."

His hand found her sex. Letting out a harsh groan, he ran his fingertips through her wetness, finding her entrance and pressing forward. Audrey gasped as he slipped one finger inside, then two, and she arched against his hand. If she didn't shatter into a million pieces tonight, then it would be a miracle.

"Feels good?"

"So good." Her head pressed back against the soft duvet, shadows dancing on the roof from the trees swaying in the wind outside.

"Can I taste you?" The words were whispered against her ear, his facial hair tickling her while his fingers worked in and out.

Audrey felt the breath leave her lungs, and she nodded, eyes locked onto Ronan's. He pressed his lips against hers—such a sweet, almost chaste, brush that in the midst of everything else they were doing felt like him reassuring her. Or maybe he was seeking reassurance for himself. But she didn't have time to wonder, because the second his lips started moving down her body she was lost to sensation.

He kissed her breasts again, then down the side of her ribs, around her belly button, and lower, lower, lower. When his tongue brushed softly over her sex, parting her, she let out a deep sound that came from somewhere long-buried. It was primal and human, because that's how he made her feel—like a woman who deserved life's pleasures. Like someone who had every right to be here.

Ronan set his mouth on her, nuzzling her sex and seeking out the tight bundle of nerves at its apex. Her clit throbbed. And when he concentrated his tongue there, flicking back and forth...*Lord.* Audrey flung her arm across her eyes and arched, tremors ripping through her. He kept his fingers working inside her, all the while drawing her closer to the edge of release with his tongue. The scratch of his beard against her sensitive area made it even better.

"Ronan," she gasped, her hand finding his head and her fingers tightening in his hair. "Oh God."

The ripples of pleasure grew closer together until she couldn't tell them apart anymore. It was like one continuous, shimmering stream of sensation.

"I'm—" Her words were cut short as her orgasm hit for real, making her thighs quake and her sex clench. Suddenly aware that she was probably alerting every single one of Ronan's neighbors to their nighttime activities, she grabbed one of his pillows and held it over her face, letting the down and cotton absorb the sound of her cries until she had nothing left to give.

For a moment, there was a void, sound and light and feeling all blotted out by the wave a rightness and release that ebbed through her. She discarded the pillow and looked down into the dim light to see Ronan resting his cheek against her inner thigh. His eyes were like fire. The light shifted as the rain swelled outside, showing Audrey the details of him in flashes—the lips that had brought her to the brink, the eyes that she wanted to drown in, the hand he rested on her leg.

"Good?" he asked quietly.

Audrey's lips tilted up into a smile. "You have no idea."

"I have *some* idea."

"Your neighbors might, too." She cringed.

He crawled up onto the bed beside her and drew her against him so that her back lined his front. The soft cotton of his T-shirt was pleasant against her skin, and the way he hooked his arm around her waist was both comforting and possessive.

How could it feel like they'd been doing this forever when it was only the first time?

"I love that you're vocal," he said.

She rocked back against him, teasing the hard ridge of his erection with her butt. "Are you noisy, too?"

He laughed, and the sound was deliciously raspy. "You'll have to wait and see."

"I hope you don't make me wait too much longer," she said, twisting so she could look at him over her shoulder. "I've been thinking about this since long before I should have."

• • •

Audrey felt like heaven in his arms—her curvy body the perfect proportions for him. He loved the sensual shape of her—the curves and dips and how strong she felt, and yet how soft.

"I thought about it…shit," he muttered. "Way too much. Way, *way* too much."

There'd been a period where every night, the second he closed his eyes, she was there. But the frequent self-love didn't do anything to dull the edges of his desire. In many ways, it only made it worse, because he could see how difficult it was to banish her from his mind, and *that* was highly unusual.

"And yet you tried so hard to convince me to be your student again," she said.

"I wanted what was best for you. Not what was best for me."

"Is this what's best for you?"

Taking a gorgeous woman to bed was never a hardship. But being with Audrey wasn't simply about the physical, though he appreciated that very much. He also found her complex and interesting, and he loved the qualities of who she was as a person.

"I would never want something I desired to come at a cost for you," he said, choosing his words carefully. "But if you ask me whether I've wanted this from the second you walked into my classroom, even though I knew it was wrong…then yes."

"Is this the first time you've…"

He raised an eyebrow. "Are you asking if I'm a virgin?"

She rolled over so she could face him, her eyes alight with mischief. "I'm pretty sure oral sex isn't that good without a little practice. But I really hope you have some condoms here."

Shit. He hadn't even thought about that when he'd invited Audrey back to his place—his mind had been too focused on the fantastical. Not the practical. He was pretty sure he had an emergency one stashed in his wallet, though.

"I think so," he said. "Otherwise it'll be an, uh… interesting trip to the store."

Her lips curved into a wicked smile. "Welcome to small-town life, professor, where everybody knows your business."

Not wanting to let his imagination wander toward something that awkward, his lips found the curve of her hip, his hand smoothing over her thighs and stomach as if he could use his touch to commit her to memory. Everything about her was smooth, soft, and yet Audrey had an inner strength and conviction that he found utterly irresistible.

She was a woman who did things on her own terms.

She scooted closer to him and smoothed one hand up along his jaw, leaning in so her lips brushed his ear. "You should get undressed."

"You want to see what I'm hiding under here?"

"Very much so."

Ronan rose off the bed and took a step back. Audrey looked like a goddess spread out on his bed, hair fanned out behind her and her lips parted in anticipation. He tore his T-shirt off without any finesse or teasing because, as far as he was concerned, they'd waited long enough already. The sound of his belt cut through the quiet room, and soon it joined the floor, along with his shoes, socks, and jeans. He stood in his underwear for a moment, enjoying the way her eyes roamed his body, eagerly sucking in every detail.

He drew the last item down over his hips, feeling his cock spring out and bob against his stomach. God, he was hard. So hard it was almost as if he hadn't gotten himself off nightly for the last few weeks like some horny teenager. He went to find his wallet and prayed that he hadn't thrown the spare condom away at some point. *Victory.* With a relieved release of breath, he returned to the bedroom and tore it open.

"Wait." Audrey's eyes were almost black now, and she reached out to him in silent invitation. "I want to touch you first."

When he came down over her, his weight pressing her into the soft mattress, she hummed and closed her eyes. He dipped his head to kiss her, and, cupping the back of her head, he slid his tongue across hers, opening her. Allowing her to taste herself.

Audrey's hands trembled as she ran her palms over him, brushing the dusting of hair on his chest and following the flat plane of his stomach, dipping lower.

Ronan sucked in a breath to steady himself. He *never* lost his wits, ever. Not with a woman in his arms or in his bed. Not with anyone. But Audrey did crazy things to him. Her hand moved lower, tentative, and her fingertips brushed the sensitive head of his cock. It was so brief and fleeting that he wanted to growl in frustration.

Heat flushed across her neck and cheeks, and she hesitated before wrapping her hand around him. The guttural noise that came from the back of his throat was almost... animalistic. He urged her on, and she slid her hand up and down, stroking him.

"Audrey," he moaned and pushed his hips forward into her grip. He knew that it would be a fight to hang on. "That's so damn good."

As if emboldened by his praise, she pushed him so that he was lying flat on the bed and she was leaning over him. Seeing Audrey take charge...*shit*. Her lips brushed his cock. Every muscle in his body was coiled. She drew him in, sliding him along her tongue while her hand ran up and down his thigh, nails scraping against his skin.

"That's enough." His voice came out strangled. Edgy. He tangled his fingers in her hair, ready to pull her back, but she eased him out of her mouth and swirled her tongue over the tip of him.

"I'm enjoying this."

"So am I." He grunted, sweeping the hair over her shoulder and easing her back. "Too much."

He tore the foil packet open and rolled the condom down on himself. Then he pulled Audrey toward him, encouraging her to straddle him. She hesitated at first, but after a second, she squared her shoulders and slid one thigh over him.

"You look incredible from this angle," he said, running his palms up and down her thighs. Her hair trailed over her body. "From every angle."

His cock rubbed at her entrance, sliding between her slickness as he coated himself in her. Then she reached down between her legs and guided him into her. He pushed up, and, in one fluid movement, the shock of how tight she was enveloped him.

"Give me a second." She came forward, bracing one palm against his chest and squeezing her eyes shut. After a brief respite, she left out a soft moan and started to move her hips, rocking back and forth. "Oh yes."

Watching her take control was everything. He gripped her hips and thrust up to meet the rhythm she'd set, letting her dictate the pace. Audrey didn't hold back. She angled herself so that one palm came down on either side of his head and her breasts brushed against his chest with each stroke. He reached around and grabbed her ass, sinking his fingers into her flesh.

"Yes, Ronan." She came down lower, pressing her face into his neck and rocking her hips in a frenzied motion.

"Don't hold back," he said. "I want to feel you shake."

She grabbed his face in her hands and pressed her mouth down to his, meeting him thrust for thrust. Then he plunged deep, his body pulsing as he came, and she tipped over the edge a few seconds after, his name falling from her lips.

Chapter Seventeen

There are chili peppers so hot they can kill you.

Audrey had crept back home at the crack of dawn the previous night, parking on the street instead of risking the sound of Big Red's engine waking anybody up. But what she'd shared with Ronan was *well* worth a little subterfuge. And thankfully the house had been completely quiet. Not even Georgie, who was a light sleeper, had stirred when Audrey slipped into their bedroom.

Morning had come too soon, but Audrey didn't feel as though she was surviving on barely four hours of sleep. Instead she felt as though a fluffy cloud was helping her float through her day, and a dreamy smile had been stuck permanently on her lips. Now it was afternoon, and Audrey had gone to pick up Deanna from school.

"I'm so glad I didn't have to get a ride home," Deanna chirped as she slid into the passenger seat. "I was worried Big Red wasn't going to make it back."

"She *was* grumbly this morning." Audrey patted the

steering wheel affectionately, but when she started the engine, a deep, shuddering rattle made her cringe. "I'm worried she's on her last legs. Joe said we can only keep patching her for so long."

Deanna giggled. "Sounds like she needs to stop smoking cigarettes."

"She does."

"So...does this mean I get another fact, since you're driving us home?"

Audrey glanced at her sister. "Seriously? I'm not a machine."

"Pleeeeeeeeease."

Audrey laughed. Deanna had been extra clingy since Audrey's fight with her dad, and even this morning she'd hovered around like a bad smell. To the point that Audrey had asked her little sister to give her a moment of peace while she'd been washing her face, because her head was too full to deal with memories of Ronan *and* a barrage of questions about nothing in particular.

"Okay, how about this... There are chili peppers so hot they can kill you."

"Really?" Deanna's eyes widened.

"I was reading an article about one called the Dragon's Breath," Audrey said. "And it's supposed to be seven times hotter than a habanero and fifty percent hotter than the average Carolina Reaper."

"But how does it kill you?" Deanna asked.

"Well, the capsaicin concentration can trigger anaphylactic shock, which can cause a person's airways to close. Even if it doesn't kill you, something that hot will cause blisters in your mouth, and your body would likely immediately reject the pepper."

"You mean you'd vomit it up? Gross." Deanna pulled an icky face. "Spicy vomit would *not* be good."

"No," Audrey said with a chuckle. "It definitely wouldn't."

Deanna chatted happily the entire way home. She'd stayed late at school rehearsing her audition for the school play, so Audrey had been able to pick her up after work. It was a little after six, and the sky was still light and golden. The neat little rows of houses rolled by as they drove. Eventually, the scenery started to change, and Audrey felt the pit form in the depths of her stomach.

Coming home was often giving her this feeling lately. But she had a fun evening ahead—it was taco night, her personal favorite. Afterward, she'd clean up from dinner, put the washing on, tidy the house, and take the trash out, and *then* she would settle in and do some reading for Ronan. He'd emailed her a copy of the first chapter of his book, and she couldn't wait to dive in. It would be the first time she'd actively used her brain today.

She pulled Big Red into the driveway and killed the engine. But before she'd even had the chance to get out of the car, Georgie flew out of the house, letting the front door bang behind her. The look on her face made the blood in Audrey's veins run cold.

She pushed open the door and got out. "What's wrong?"

Georgie's face was streaked with tears, her eyes red-rimmed and her lashes stuck together in little spikes. For a young woman who was usually meticulous about her hair, it was currently in disarray, falling out of her ponytail in chunks. She tried to speak but hiccupped instead.

"Georgie, calm down." Audrey grabbed her younger sister by the shoulders and rubbed her hands up and down her arms. "What's going on?"

"Oliver." She hiccupped again. "He had a fight...with dad...about his graphic design stuff...Dad said he needed to...stop fucking around...and get a real job..."

That was rich, coming from the man who was chronically

unemployed. Audrey shook her head; she wasn't going to focus on the fact that Georgie was cursing when she knew she shouldn't—a hard thing to uphold when any time one needed to quote their father it involved dropping the F-bomb.

"Slow down," Audrey said. Then she shot a look at Deanna, who was standing beside them, eyes big and round and brimming with worry. "You, get inside and start your homework."

Deanna shook her head. "But—"

"Now." Audrey stared her down until Deanna's shoulders sagged and she went into the house, her backpack slung heavily over one shoulder. "Okay, what happened after the fight?"

"Oliver left, and Dad said 'good riddance' and called him a selfish little..." She bit down on her lip. "It was bad. I wanted to follow Oliver, but then Dad started storming around the house, and then he left, too. I figured I should stay here in case Deanna came home, because I couldn't remember who was picking her up and I didn't want her to come home to an empty house."

Audrey pulled Georgie into a hug. "You're a good big sister. Do you have any idea where Oliver went?"

"No. I tried to call him, but...then I heard his phone buzzing in his bedroom. He didn't take his wallet, either." She shook her head, another tear spilling out of her eye. "I know they fight sometimes, but this was different. Oliver said he was going to leave because he hates living here and he hates our family and he wants to be alone."

"You know he doesn't mean that, right? He was just upset."

"I hate Dad sometimes." Hurt glimmered in Georgie's eyes. "He's always angry and mean, and...I think you should be able to take a college class if you want."

Audrey let out a long sigh and released her sister,

scrubbing a hand over her face. "I don't want to get into that now. Let's focus on Oliver, okay?"

"I looked out the window after he left, and…" Georgie dropped her eyes to the ground as though she really didn't want to say what was coming next.

"Tell me."

"I think he stole Mrs. March's car."

"What?" Audrey let out a groan. "Why didn't you lead with that, G?"

"I don't want to get him in trouble, and…" She blinked tearfully. "I saw him sitting in the front seat, and there were wires."

"He hot-wired her car? How does he even know how to do that?" Audrey felt herself spiraling, panic seizing hold of her lungs and airways. But she couldn't fall in a heap now. She had to find Oliver and bring him back with the car before it got out of hand. An arrest on his record could ruin everything. "You know what—I don't care. Take twenty dollars out of the envelope under my mattress and order pizza for you and your sister. Make sure she does her homework. I'll find Oliver."

Audrey got back into her car and pulled out of the driveway, having no idea where the hell she was going to find her brother. But Mrs. March would have to come outside her house eventually. The fact that nobody had called the police was a lucky break…unless they had? What if Oliver was already down at the local station?

A sick feeling swished in her stomach. "Think, dammit."

One thing in her favor was that Mrs. March's car was the approximate color of Big Bird. They always joked about it: Big Red and Big Yellow. It stood out. Audrey drove past a few of Oliver's friends' houses, but there was no sign of the car. She circled Kissing Creek, going past the high school and the rec center and the library and the main strip. Nothing.

She called her aunt, but he wasn't with her, either. Would

he have left town? Audrey wanted to scream at the top of her lungs until her voice box gave out. When she saw her father again, she was going to rain fire and brimstone down on him. *She* could take the brunt of her father's assholery...but the others were sensitive. Oliver possibly the most sensitive. He'd been increasingly withdrawn lately, curling in on himself like an armadillo.

"You should have done more about this," she scolded herself as she drove, her heart thumping at twice its normal speed. "You should have kept a closer eye on him, and instead you're too busy screwing around with Ronan and classes and shit that doesn't matter. What Oliver needs is a mother figure."

Then it hit her like a bolt of lightning. She *knew* exactly where he was...the one place Audrey avoided at all costs.

When she pulled Big Red into the parking lot of the Kissing Creek cemetery, Audrey felt a wave of something black and oppressive slide over her. There was only one other car in the parking lot—an old, bright-yellow sedan.

Audrey sat for a moment, the past playing out as clear as if it were laid out in front of her. She could feel the chubby grip of Georgie and Oliver's hands, one on either side of her, and hear baby Deanna wail as though she somehow knew what had been lost. She remembered the scratchy feel of the black polyester dress her aunt had made her wear, even though Audrey hated black. But everyone wore black. It was like the world had been drained of color that day. And every day since.

Drawing in a long breath, Audrey filled her lungs until her chest started to ache. There was no getting around this. She had to put her own feelings aside and help her brother.

Even though she hadn't been back to the cemetery since the day of the funeral, Audrey knew the way without hesitation. Left at the little fountain, right at the rosebushes.

She saw a lanky figure sitting cross-legged on the ground and heard the sound of her brother's deep voice on the breeze. He was chatting away, almost as if a fight hadn't happened. He seemed...happy.

Audrey approached quietly, her footsteps silenced by the spongy grass, and it wasn't until her shadow cut into Oliver's vision that he looked up. Their mother's grave was well-tended. Fresh flowers sat in a squat green plastic vase, and the twigs and other natural debris had been brushed to the side.

Mary Patricia Miller, in loving memory. Always smiling.

Her mother had always told her that a smile was her best defense against life's obstacles, and it was something she practiced herself.

"What are you doing?" Audrey asked her brother, shaking her head. She held back the desire to shake him and yell, because that wouldn't get her anywhere, even if it might be a good release for her own bubbling emotions. "You stole a car?"

Oliver had the good sense to look ashamed. "I had to get out of there."

"Committing a crime will certainly do that."

"Mrs. March said I could borrow the car any time." Oliver clearly knew the response was BS, because there wasn't an ounce of confidence in his tone.

"Borrow, buddy. Not steal. *Big* difference." Audrey crouched down beside him, keeping her eyes clear of her mother's grave. She couldn't bear to look at it right now—not with the sorry state her family was in. Their mother would be devastated. "We need to get you home and return the car."

"I'm not going back there." He crossed his arms over his chest.

"Oh, you're going to sleep overnight in a cemetery, huh? Great decision. Literally no horror movies have ever started like that." Audrey rolled her eyes. "I'll see you later, zombie boy."

Oliver snorted. "Don't make me laugh."

"Someone has to." She wrapped her arms around him and rested her cheek against his head, ignoring how gross it felt from all the hair product he used. Ugh, why did teenage boys do that? "I know things have been tough at home."

"Don't you want to leave, too? You get the worst of it more than any of us."

She did. She'd fortified her armor so she could absorb the verbal blows her father dealt them, shielding her siblings as best she could. That was her lot in life. "I'm not leaving you kids, ever."

"Couldn't we all go somewhere else? Together?" Oliver sighed. "I wish Mom was still here."

"Well, she's not. It's just us."

"Are you angry at her for dying? Is that why you never come here?"

Audrey swallowed against the lump in her throat. It felt like he was reaching right into her chest and ripping her heart out with those questions. "There's no point being angry. Nobody wants to die."

"That's true."

"Please come home. I know it's been tough, but you're so close to finishing school, and the second you've graduated, we'll get you out of here. I promise."

Oliver looked at her warily. "How are we going to do that if I don't want to go to college? You might want that, but I don't. So how else am I going to get out? I...I can't be stuck here forever."

They'd been dancing around this decision for a year—with Audrey telling him a course in graphics would help his chances of finding a job and Oliver pushing back. Even if he didn't, Oliver's grades might not be enough to get him the scholarship he'd need to get an education somewhere with room and board included. Because his fears were right. Without college, how else would she protect him?

"I don't know," she said softly. "I wish I had all the answers. But I promise we'll talk about it and figure something out. Maybe we can look at moving you in with Aunt Harriet? She keeps offering, and while I hate to separate you from the rest of us, if that's what it takes to stop you from running away…"

Oliver looked up at her, eyes full of hope. "Really?"

"We can talk about it," she repeated. "I can't promise anything, but I'm hearing you loud and clear, and we'll find a solution."

"Do you want to say goodbye to Mom before we go?"

Audrey still couldn't even force herself to look at the grave. She was hanging on by a thread now, her positive facade so cracked and crumbling she was worried it might slip off for good. "We should get you home as quickly as possible, and then you're going to give Mrs. March an apology."

Oliver sighed and nodded. "Will you come with me?"

"Of course."

She helped her brother to his feet and tried to sling an arm around his shoulders, but he was way too tall, so instead, Oliver put his arm around Audrey. He was barely a boy anymore. A young man on the verge of adulthood who wouldn't be forced to stay at home much longer. She needed to help him figure out what was next and make sure he didn't end up like their dad.

"Do you come here a lot?" she asked as they reached the parking lot, her eyes still turned away from her mother's grave.

"Every week," he said with a nod. "I don't actually study at the library on Wednesdays."

"You come here?" She looked up at her brother, fighting the tears that wanted to prick the backs of her eyes.

"Well, Mom always liked keeping the house tidy, and

I figure she'd feel bad if her grave was messy. I change the flowers and brush all the leaves away." He shrugged like it was the simplest thing in the world. "I miss her a lot."

"I miss her, too, bud." Audrey squeezed her brother. "I miss her, too."

• • •

Ronan dropped onto the small couch in his temporary apartment and raked a hand through his hair. Rich, golden sunlight poured through the windows, tinting everything orange as the sun set outside. It made the small place look more alive—glossing over the fact that the appliances were old and that Ronan hadn't given any care to decorating the walls or surfaces.

Part of what had stopped him from filling the space with anything personal was his indecision about the future. He'd made no commitment to stay in Kissing Creek beyond his contract...so what was the point of decorating? But for some reason, having Audrey in his space last night had made him suddenly aware of how he was living like a nomad. His place in the UK had looked much the same—bare walls and sterile-looking furniture and a sense that he was going to flee at any moment.

It was as if he couldn't bear the thought of setting down roots. Or making commitments.

Or opening himself up to anything more than *now*.

Luckily, work kept him busy enough that he didn't have to think about it *too* much. Today, he'd taught two classes, had three hours of "open office" with students, and spent the afternoon going over his mentor's feedback on another chapter for his book...which basically meant starting that section from scratch. After that, he'd attempted to have a quiet few moments at Kisspresso, only to have some PhD students want to ask him questions.

By the time he'd gotten home, his brain felt like mashed potatoes. Maybe he could stare into space for long enough that he'd reach a respectable amount of time before he could slide into bed.

At that moment, his phone buzzed. His mother was calling him—again. She'd started trying yesterday around noon, and the calls would come through every few hours. But she never left another voicemail. Never texted, either. He'd called his grandmother to make sure she was okay and then followed up with Keira. Both of them were fine. No family emergencies.

After his mother ignored him most of his life, what could *possibly* be so urgent now?

It was clear she wasn't going to stop calling until he picked up. Frustrated, Ronan thought very seriously about dropping his phone into the toilet bowl and flushing it. But sticking his head in the sand wasn't going to accomplish anything.

He swiped his thumb across the screen. "Hello?"

"Hi, Ro."

His mother's soft voice was always a punch to the chest. She sounded the same as he remembered from his childhood—this quiet, almost girlish voice with a faraway quality to it. Everything about her had a dreamlike element, as if she might vanish in a puff of smoke at any moment.

"What's wrong?" he asked, scrubbing a hand over his face.

"Why do you assume something is wrong?"

Oh, I don't know. Maybe because I called you a dozen times after I first moved to England and you never got back to me. Not once.

He stood and paced the length of the apartment. "You don't usually call, so I assumed something had prompted it."

For a moment, there was nothing but silence on the other

end of the line. "Well...that's precisely why I'm calling. I know I haven't been attentive."

Understatement of the last thirty-four years.

"I realized when I saw you at the hospital that maybe I've done some damage over the years," she added. "And it's time to fix that."

Maybe she'd done some damage? *Maybe?* Like there was a chance that abandoning her kids to live on their own before they were even legal might result in the creation of well-adjusted adults. Seriously?

"I'm glad you feel ready," Ronan said stiffly. "But I've got a lot on my plate at the moment, and I don't really have the headspace to sift through the past."

"Oh." His mother had the audacity to sound surprised. "I thought you wanted to hear from me."

"When I called...six years ago." He let out a rush of air. This was a bad idea; he should never have picked up the phone. "Look, I'm sorry, but I'm too busy now. I'll call when things have calmed down."

He jabbed at the end button, missing several times before he made a connection. Growling, he raked a hand through his hair. No wonder he couldn't seem to set down roots—he'd been untethered since he was a child. Settling down didn't come naturally to him.

Commitment didn't come naturally to him.

Maybe that's why he studied human behavior. It had always been a mystery. Why did people behave the way they did? What motivated them to hurt or love others? Studying data was much easier than trying to engage in an *actual* relationship.

But the second that thought popped into his mind, something inside him disagreed. Being with Audrey didn't feel difficult or fraught or dangerous—at least not anymore. The two of them clicked, and their connection was natural and easy.

He turned his phone over and over in his hand. Audrey was the only person who'd ever made him feel like maybe being with someone *was* worth risking all the things he avoided in life—vulnerability, connection. Trust.

She made him feel...safe.

He unlocked his phone and brought up the chain of texts between them. They were innocent—definitely nothing that would hint at a night of sweat-drenched sheets and the deepest, most lingering kiss against the side of her car as he'd seen her off in the dead of early morning.

As if she knew he was thinking about her all the way across Kissing Creek, three little dots appeared to show she was typing a message. If that wasn't a weird twist of kismet, then he didn't know *what* was.

AUDREY: *I need to see you.*

RONAN: *It's like you're reading my mind.*

AUDREY: *Your place okay?*

RONAN: *Get here as fast as you can.*

Chapter Eighteen

A group of lemurs is called a conspiracy of lemurs.

Audrey did something she had *never* done before—left the house in complete disarray. She'd followed Oliver home so he could return Mrs. March's car and promise that he'd clean her gutters as payment. Then she'd forced him, Georgie, and Deanna to pack up their things so she could drop them off at various places to spend the night. Georgie went to a girlfriend's house, and Oliver and Deanna went to stay with Aunt Harriet.

The house itself was a disaster—pizza boxes open, dishes in the sink, laundry needing to be hung up. Audrey left all of it. It was tough luck if her father came home and found them all gone. Maybe he needed to see the consequences of his actions.

There'd be hell to pay tomorrow; she knew that. But for once in her life, Audrey couldn't find it in herself to care. She'd tossed a change of clothes into her backpack, including a fresh polo shirt for her shift at Kisspresso in the morning, and had messaged Ronan. Maybe it was a bit presumptuous to assume he'd be okay with her staying the night.

But she had nowhere else to go.

That wasn't true. She could have shared the pull-out couch at Harriet's. Or crashed at Nicole's. So it would be more accurate to say there was nowhere else she *wanted* to go.

One night, and he's already your safe harbor?

Audrey parked her car and hurried across the grass to Ronan's apartment. It was getting dark outside now, and the sky had a serene purplish tinge to it. Her heart thumped with each quick step, and the anticipation of being in Ronan's arms drowned the stress of her day. It was like the closer she got to him, the more faded her worries became. Tonight, she wanted nothing more than to forget—to forget that she still had grief over her mother's death, to forget that her family was falling apart, to forget that some days she had nothing but the fake smile plastered to her lips.

All of it.

By the time she got to the door, she needed his touch more than she needed air to breathe and blood in her veins. She needed *him* more than anything.

When Ronan pulled the door open, she walked straight into his arms. Not caring if she should play it safe, not caring if maybe there was some weird dating etiquette that said she shouldn't wear her heart on her sleeve. Mercifully, he met her with equal enthusiasm, yanking her inside and shoving her up against the door with one hand, flicking the lock with the other.

"I told you I liked it up against the wall," he said, his voice rough and gravelly.

"Door," she corrected, pulling his head back down to hers. "For such a smart guy, I'm surprised you can't tell the difference."

"When it comes to you, as long as it's a flat surface, I don't care *what* you call it," he said. "Although I feel like you're questioning my intelligence again."

"Never." She laughed.

"I had another question for you today. I was going to text you."

"Ask me." Warmth bubbled in her chest. The game she shared with her siblings had become something of a staple for herself and Ronan. They quizzed each other relentlessly, going for one more round and one more round with random facts until one of them was victorious. It was such a silly thing, and yet it made her feel connected to him. Like they shared something unique and special.

"What's the collective noun for lemurs?"

"Lemurs? Hmm." Audrey traced her hands down Ronan's chest, smoothing them over his flat stomach and down to the buckle of his belt.

"Don't try to distract me, temptress."

"I know it's got to be one of those funny names, or else you wouldn't have asked." She ran her fingertip over the front of his zipper, feeling him twitch in response.

His mouth was at her jaw, her neck, her ear. Hot breath skated over her skin, mimicking the smooth glide of his hands under her top and around her back. "Answer the question."

"Well, lemurs are primates, so maybe they share a name with one of the other primate groups. I know gorillas are a troop. Or a *whoop*, which is my personal favorite." She looped her arms around his neck and arched into him, her breasts plastered to his chest. Her entire body pulsed with wanting. "Am I close?"

"Way off."

She thought for a moment more. "Well, I think the word lemur is derived from the Latin word for ghost. Or was it spirit? Maybe something to do with that?"

Ronan kissed along her jaw and neck, his hands exploring her body. "Nope."

"Tell me."

"A group of lemurs is called a conspiracy of lemurs, because of the way they conspire to outwit predators." He grinned.

"Smart little things."

"Just like you." He lowered his head to hers and kissed her deeply, appearing more than a little smug that his questions were getting the best of her.

For a second, playing that game with him, she'd felt free of the stress from her family. Free of the stress from watching her brother implode and her father destroy everything around him. But there was still emotion bubbling inside her—anger and fear and resentment. Ugly emotions that she tried to avoid. Ronan stilled as though he sensed the swirling beneath the surface. He pulled back and looked at her, skimming a thumb over her cheek.

"What's going on?" he asked.

"Nothing."

"Don't lie." There wasn't any accusation in his tone, only a sense of acknowledgment. Understanding. "You can talk to me."

"Honestly..." She looked up at him. "I don't want to talk right now. I didn't come here to talk."

He frowned. "I won't settle for being a distraction."

The words made her smile. Because they were a sign that he *did* feel something more for her. If sex was all he cared about, then her motivations wouldn't matter.

"You're not a distraction. I..." The afternoon was still fresh in her mind—the panic, the dread. The sadness. "You make me feel good, and right now I really need to feel good."

He lowered his head and kissed her. His lips were soft yet firm, coaxing and encouraging and wanting. It was slow and romantic, and she sighed into him, fists curling into his T-shirt.

"Is that all you want from me?" He brushed a strand of hair from her forehead.

Wow. He was really laying it all out on the line, wasn't he? Audrey had been prepared to shove any questions about the future to one side like she usually did—because it was hard to see them ending up anywhere good. If she looked at the facts...well, she wasn't stupid enough to believe that they were a good long-term match.

"I don't know," she whispered. "I'm not used to having the luxury of wanting. It's scary."

That was all she could say without cleaving her heart out in front of him. She knew the answer that echoed in her head. Yes, she wanted more. Yes, she wanted all of him.

But Audrey had a history of disappointments shackling her wrists.

"So you *do* know." He brushed the hair from her forehead. "You're not just a warm body to me, Audrey."

How she wanted to believe that he saw something special in her, because everything about her life was so relentlessly *not* special.

"If it wasn't you here..." He touched his forehead to hers. "This apartment would be empty. My bed would be empty. I don't want anyone else here with me, and I need you to know that."

She swallowed against the desperate temptation to believe him. "I don't want anyone else, either."

He's still going to leave. You're not enough.

Audrey knew that. But being with Ronan was the only bright spot in her life at the moment. Because as much as she loved her siblings, caring for them was still attached to some difficult emotions. The only time she ever felt truly free as an individual was when she'd gone to class. And now, when she was here for no other reason than because she wanted to be.

Because she liked Ronan. A hell of a lot.

"You promise you're okay?" he asked.

Audrey traced the curve of his biceps, hugged by soft cotton. Then she moved her hand across his chest, hard muscle twitching beneath her fingertip. He caught her hand and kissed the underside of her wrist, making her pulse skyrocket.

"Yeah." She nodded, lowering her eyes for a moment. "I'm always okay."

"No person is an island."

Sometimes it felt that way—like she was adrift in a stormy sea, battling the waves and trying to keep from drowning with no one to help her. But in his arms, she felt grounded. Safe.

The memory of last night swirled in her mind. The taste of him. The scent of faded cologne and the barest hint of sweat on his skin. The confident hands roaming her body, melting her.

What's going to happen when this falls apart?

He had a golden life in front of him. Opportunities. Extended hands. People respected and admired him, and whatever path he wanted would be available. Eventually, Kissing Creek would have nothing else to offer.

She would have nothing else to offer.

"Touch me," she said, sinking into the pink haze of need. Blood pounded in her ears, and red flags waved in her mind, flapping and frantic.

Ronan *could* ruin her. But that was a risk she was willing to take, because nothing else in her life had ever felt this good. And right now, for a taste of something so perfect, she was willing to risk it all. Her body and her heart.

His hands coasted over her hips, tracing the dip at her waist, then back up over her breasts. The soft, flowing touch soothed her. How could something that already felt so good be bad for her?

When his thumbs brushed under the hem of her T-shirt, grazing her bare stomach, a gasp escaped her lips. She was still pressed against his door, palms flattened to the wood behind her as he explored her body.

"I've been thinking about you nonstop for the past twenty-four hours," he said, sliding a hand under her T-shirt. "You're in my head."

"You're in mine, too." She sucked in a breath as he cupped her breast, finding her nipple between his thumb and forefinger. The bra she'd worn today had a soft lace cup, and his hands were hot through the flimsy fabric.

"Tell me what you were thinking?"

Oh God, could she really say it out loud? Audrey had lost herself daydreaming earlier today, her mind wandering when she should have been concentrating on her work. "I wish we'd had time to…"

"Tell me," he growled. He pressed his body against hers, the hard length of him rubbing against her thigh. His hand continued to palm her breast, and it was difficult to form words while he touched her like that.

"I want you to take me in the shower," she whispered. The image had been stuck in her head all day—bare skin, water running in rivulets across his hard body. Steam and soap and open-mouthed kisses. Tiles against her back.

The moan that escaped Ronan's lips was like a rocket of wanting through Audrey's body. He stepped back, slipping his hand into hers and tugging her farther into the apartment. She allowed herself to be led, the relief of not having to be the leader was a weight lifted that she didn't even know she carried. She *was* strong. And it was exhausting to always be the one in charge, to always be making decisions and looking after people.

Right now, all she wanted was for Ronan to take care of

her.

They made it to the bathroom, and he wrenched the shower faucet on. While the water warmed, he took her face in his palms and kissed her again. Their breath came hard and fast, mingling with the building steam. Hot water started to fog the shower's glass door, and the gentle slide of Ronan's tongue stole the breath right from her lungs.

His fingers slipped between her legs, sliding up the inside of her thigh until the heel of his palm found her center. Her knees almost buckled. Yes, this was exactly what she wanted. Not to think or decide or consider or determine.

Only to feel.

She kissed him back, her hands coming down to the buckle at his waist, and she yanked at the leather strap. The metal clinked, and then she worked on the button. Then the zipper. Denim slipped over his hips as she pushed his jeans down. Water drummed an incessant beat behind her, echoing the hammering of her heart.

Ronan drew his T-shirt up, stepping out of his jeans at the same time so that the only thing remaining was a pair of black underwear. Beneath the stretchy fabric, his erection bulged, and Audrey's hand brushed tentatively over it. Knowing she turned him on like this, knowing that what she felt was absolutely reciprocated…it made her feel desirable. Wanted.

New.

"Undress me," she whispered.

Ronan's eyes never left hers as his hands came to the hem of her top. Gently, he eased the fabric over her head and dropped it to the floor. His eyes were almost black now—black like the edge of a cliff at night.

His hands drifted to the waistband of her jeans, and he hooked a finger underneath the fabric and tugged her closer. "I want you like nothing else, Audrey."

He popped the button and drew her zipper down,

dropping to his knees as he slid the fabric down over her hips and thighs. Her underwear was nothing fancy—that *wasn't* something she'd ever spent much money on—but the bubblegum-pink shade made her feel good, and with Ronan, none of that stuff mattered.

He pressed a kiss to the apex of her sex through the thin cotton, and Audrey gasped. "Everything about you is perfect."

Audrey glanced at herself in the mirror above the sink. Perfect was not a word she'd use to describe herself. Ever. Her stomach stuck out, and her thighs rubbed together when she walked. But with Ronan, she felt something...pure. Something that went *far* beyond the physical.

He tugged her panties down her legs and helped her step out of the pile of clothing that had gathered there.

"We're going to run out of water," she said, a teasing smile on her lips.

"So be it." Ronan stood and shoved his own underwear down, standing naked before her.

Audrey reached behind herself and unhooked her bra, and the second she was finally naked, he lowered his head to her breast, taking one hardened nipple in his mouth. He rolled it against his tongue, and her hand fisted in his hair, tugging sharply.

"Oh my," she gasped, but she pulled his head to her other breast. He worshipped her body, leaving pink marks against her skin with his teeth. "Shower. Now."

He stepped into the shower before her and tested the temperature of the water, adjusting the knobs before pulling her in with him. The steam made everything feel so much more intimate. So much more...everything.

Reaching out, she brushed the tip of him, and his whole body tensed, the muscles in his shoulders bunching up around his neck. Audrey wrapped her fingers around Ronan's erection, and he grunted as she squeezed him. Feeling how hard he was—how thick—lit a fire inside her.

"What you do to me..." Stepping out of her reach, he lowered himself to his knees in front of her. His facial hair was prickly against her thigh—the opposite of how soft his fingers felt, spreading her legs and finding her damp and ready. A soft sigh came from her lips, and the gentle pressure of her hand against his head told him what she wanted.

"Please." Her voice trembled as he brushed his lips over her. "I need..."

"Tell me."

She barely had an ounce of control left—little more than the finest thread—and she wanted to see it shatter into a million pieces. She wanted him to do that to her. To bring her undone. She cried his name. Softly at first. Then louder, not caring one iota if the neighbors heard them. Let them listen. Audrey was high on the feelings gathering inside her, on the delicious pressure building like a storm.

She was close, and he slipped a finger inside her. Oh yes. Yes, yes, *yes.* The shaking started, and without any restraint at all, she came hard against his mouth.

She barely had a moment to catch her breath as she came down, and he was standing in front of her. "Wait right here."

The running water masked the sound of him in the bathroom, but he was back in an instant, rolling a condom down his length. Then he grabbed her hands and slid them up the tile until they were pinned above her head. Audrey's eyes fluttered shut. She held her hands in place, suspended above her, even when he released her to use his hands elsewhere. He found the crook of her knee and lifted her leg up, opening her.

"Ready?" he whispered, lips brushing over her ear.

"Yes." Her leg came around his waist, and he rubbed against her, shifting into position.

When Ronan pushed inside her, Audrey gasped, her eyes flying open and catching his unwavering blue stare. She felt so *seen*. So treasured. Her body melted as he buried himself, and in that moment, Audrey felt completely whole.

A woman reborn. A woman with a life that was her own.

"Oh, Ronan," she sighed.

His lips pressed against hers, and she urged him on by rocking her hips. Matching him. Finding a rhythm between them. They clung to each other—fingers digging into flesh and muscles tightening. She could feel his orgasm gathering in the way his movements became jerkier, more desperate. His eyes never left hers, and his palm came to cup her face. He didn't shy away from connection, and she loved that about him.

This isn't love.

But it *was* something. More than like. More than sex. More than basic instincts.

When Ronan pushed into her for the last time, seating himself deep, the sound he made rocked Audrey to her core. It echoed in her head as she held him close, eyes closed and face pressed against his chest, wishing she could stay with him, here, forever.

Chapter Nineteen

Ronan and Audrey fell into a routine over the course of the next few weeks. He'd visit her most mornings at Kisspresso, and she'd leave messages on his takeout coffee cup. Sometimes it was a word she found interesting or a quote she liked. If she had time, she wrote out a question to test his knowledge.

Twice a week, she stayed late at his place, always creeping out at some obscene hour to make sure she was home when her siblings woke. He worried about her driving so late at night, but Audrey had made it clear she wouldn't stay. It was a boundary between them, but he respected it and her devotion to her family. Those nights kept him going through long hours of classes, reading academic papers, and toiling over his book. She brought her notes with him, and he shared his lessons with her.

No woman he'd ever dated previously had ever been so interested in the same things as him, but Audrey was a sponge for information.

And it killed Ronan that she wasn't taking classes at the college anymore, even if that *did* make it a hell of a lot easier—

and less risky—for them to be together. She deserved to do what she wanted with her life, and it was clear that study and learning were the things that excited her most in the world.

He wanted to help her with that.

A knock at the front door snagged his attention, and he gave his pasta sauce a quick stir before setting the heat down low. Audrey wasn't supposed to be here for another fifteen minutes, since she was finishing her shift at Game of Stones on the hour. And the last time she'd come to visit him, he'd surprised her by giving her a key.

Maybe it seemed crazy. They'd barely been together a month.

Perhaps he'd spooked her. Ronan's brow furrowed as he went to the door. She'd *seemed* delighted at the time, but—

As he yanked the front door open, his muscles turned to stone.

"Hi, Ronan." It wasn't Audrey at all.

"Merrin." He couldn't help the remote tone.

Ronan's mother stood on the landing outside his apartment, wearing her trademark "artsy" clothing—long, billowy pants and sandals, a linen tunic, beads around her neck, and a resin bangle on her arm. But her hair was slicked back into a bun. It made her look older. More serious.

"Can I come in?" she asked, her hands interlaced behind her.

He glanced around and caught the eye of one of the other residents—another visiting professor from the English Literature department—unlocking her front door. She waved, and Ronan nodded in return. He could hardly stand out here and argue with his mother for everyone to hear. This might be his home for the moment, but it was still connected to his workplace.

"I've got someone coming over shortly," he said, stepping back and holding the door for Merrin. "So you can't stay long."

"I only need a moment." She stepped into his apartment, and her gaze swept across the room.

It wasn't quite as barren now, since Audrey had added a few personal touches. She'd brought some flowers over a few days ago, commandeering a mason jar that had previously contained some fancy granola to use as a vase. She'd also brought over a strange rock thing from her aunt's store and an extra blanket that she'd been gifted by her friend. The pops of color made the place feel more like a home and less like a temporary parking spot.

"You haven't returned my calls," Merrin said.

"Doesn't feel great, does it?" The words shot out before Ronan had a chance to compose himself. It frustrated him, because getting angry at his mother was pointless. He'd tried so many times to connect, and now it felt like when he'd finally given up hope, *she* decided it was time to try and rebuild their relationship.

What about what *he* wanted?

What do *you want?*

That question used to be easy to answer—academic domination. A book that students would study in the future. A career that people would remember.

But now? Those things only felt like part of the equation. The long hours he'd spent over the course of his twenties and half of his thirties, working and working and working...the empty walls and solitary nights and the "next step" always hovering in front of him, had started to feel like a weight holding him back instead of a path leading him forward.

The nights he spent with Audrey, discussing ideas and sharing food and joining their bodies...*that* felt like something real.

Merrin regarded him with raw hurt simmering in her eyes. "That was unkind."

"The truth hurts." He couldn't find it in himself to pretend. Decades of baggage and resentment were not so easily shrugged off.

"This isn't how I raised you, Ro."

"That's because you *didn't* raise me." Dammit he was angry. He'd had a *long* day grading his students' assignments, and his brain wasn't as agile as it normally was, which meant his emotions bubbled even closer to the surface than normal. "You can't turn up on my doorstep, complaining that I haven't returned your calls, when you never showed me the same courtesy."

"I've made mistakes," she admitted, shaking her head. "I know I wasn't the best mother. But I'm still a human being, Ronan. I deserve respect."

She would never understand what she'd done to him. His mother was self-centered. She was the sun in her own universe, the heroine of the only story she knew how to tell.

He raked a hand through his hair. "Why did you come here?"

"I'm not well."

The words sucked the life out of the room. She wasn't saying "not well" like she had a cold or the flu or something that popping a few Tylenol might fix. It was more saying sick like...

"I have Alzheimer's," Merrin clarified.

Fuck.

"That's serious." Ronan didn't know what to think—his mind spun and spun and didn't gain traction. It was like he couldn't catch a single thought, and they all whizzed around his head, bumping into one another. "*Really* serious."

"Yes." Merrin nodded. "I've always been forgetful and in my own world, so I was able to explain the symptoms away for a while. But then I started randomly forgetting people's names and my birth date. I got the diagnosis the day you came home. That's why I missed your dinner."

"Oh."

She bobbed her head. "I, uh…I wasn't sure how to tell everyone, and so I stayed home."

Her fingers tucked a stray strand of wiry gray-tinged hair behind her ears, and Ronan was socked in the chest with a memory—being a little boy, her sitting on his bed and reading to him. She used to trace the outside of his ear to help him fall asleep, repeatedly tucking his unruly hair away over and over and over until his eyes fluttered shut.

"What happens now?" he asked.

"I'm taking part in a study, actually. They'll see me every few months until…" She swallowed. "Well, until I can't anymore. But I want to do what I can."

He shook his head, almost like his body was rejecting the information. He simply stared at his mother, unable to form words or do anything more than the automatic functions that kept him standing and breathing.

"The doctors have said it's not a good idea for me to be living in an isolated place, and with all the appointments I'll have, being so far away from the city will be tough."

"You're moving back to Boston?"

Merrin nodded. "Yeah. I'm moving in with Mom."

He wasn't sure if he was more surprised by the announcement or that she'd called Orna "Mom." But his grandmother and mother living under one roof wouldn't exactly be a piece of cake—that was a lot of personality for one house. "How does Gram feel about that?"

"To be honest, I think she's happy to have someone at home with her. Not that she'd *ever* admit it." Merrin rolled her eyes. "We're a stubborn bunch, aren't we?"

In spite of his mixed feelings and the heavy weight of the conversation, Ronan laughed. "It seems to be a defining family feature."

"I wanted you to hear all of this from me," Merrin said. "I told Keira a few weeks back, but I asked her not to say anything, so don't be angry at her."

Keira, unlike him, had probably answered her phone instead of avoiding the calls as they came up. Guilt flashed through him. Sure, he felt justified in his anger toward his mother, and he couldn't give up the memories and hurt so easily. But knowing she'd been trying to reach him with such awful news...

"I'm sorry," he said. Whether it was for not picking up the phone, or holding a grudge, or for the news itself, he wasn't sure.

Merrin opened her mouth to respond, but the sound of metal on metal drew his eyes to the front door. The lock flicked, and it swung open. Audrey was carrying a big box in front of her, so big she could barely see over the top.

"Hey Ro!" she singsonged as she walked in, bumping the door with her hip to close it.

Ronan went over to Audrey to help her with the box, and as they lowered it to the ground, Audrey looked up and caught Merrin's eye. "Oh, I'm so sorry, I didn't realize you had someone over."

"It's okay." Hmm. He had *not* expected to make this kind of introduction. Ever. "Audrey, this is my mother, Merrin. Merrin, this is...my girlfriend, Audrey."

Both his mother's and Audrey's eyes shot up. Girlfriend? Ugh. They hadn't even talked about putting a label on it. First he jumped in with the house key, and now he was using the G-word before knowing if it was the right time.

What are you doing, man? It's like you've never dated a woman before.

"So nice to meet you." Audrey stuck her hand out and flashed her trademark beaming smile.

"Likewise." His mother returned the gesture, and then

everyone stood around awkwardly for a moment. "Well, I should get going. I don't want to interrupt your plans."

"We're only having dinner," Audrey said. "You're welcome to join us."

"That's very sweet, but I have to get on the road. I've got a long drive back home." Merrin looked at Ronan like she wanted to say something more, but the moment of truth they shared earlier had evaporated like a puff of smoke. "I'll call you soon, Ronan."

He nodded and watched his mother leave, hands hanging uselessly by his sides. Audrey's gaze flicked to him as the door shut, her sunny expression morphing into one of concern. "Everything okay? Should I not have asked her to stay? Sorry, I... It's an automatic thing."

Automatic, because Audrey was wired to care about others. And he was wired to keep people out. If Audrey knew he'd ghosted his own mother these past few weeks, she'd probably be disgusted. Here she was, caring for her brother and sisters and even the father who treated her like shit.

She wouldn't walk away from a family member, no matter how bad things got.

He raked a hand through his hair and went to the stove, grabbing the wooden spoon and stirring the sauce, jabbing at the bits that had started to stick to the bottom because he'd left it unattended too long.

"Ro?" She came up beside him, hands knotted and olive-green eyes wide. "Is everything okay?"

"My mother has Alzheimer's." His voice sounded stiff. Unemotional. He could already feel the layers sliding over him, locking into place. Protecting him.

"Oh my God, I'm so sorry." She slid her arms around his waist from behind and pressed her face against his back.

Ronan stood there for a moment, stirring the sauce as though he was a robot programmed only to do that action.

He wasn't sure how to feel, what to say. Audrey didn't try to get him to talk. Instead, she stood there, holding him while the minutes ticked on, letting her care seep into him one breath and one heartbeat at a time.

Eventually, she broke away. "Why don't you let me cook the pasta and put everything together? You can pour us a drink, and I'll call you when it's done."

What had he done to deserve such an angel?

Nothing. You don't *deserve someone like her.*

He nodded, numbly moving away from the stove while Audrey took over. His feet carried him past the dining table to where the box Audrey had been carrying was laid. Curious and desperate for a distraction, he peered inside. It was a box of books. He spied novels by Ruth Rendell, Patricia Highsmith, Sue Grafton and Agatha Christie, to name a few.

"My aunt was clearing out her garage, and she found some boxes of old books," Audrey said, watching him as she waited for the pasta water to boil. "She's a big mystery reader, so you might find something for your grandmother."

She remembered. That trip to the bookstore, he'd been looking for Agatha Christie first editions, and even though he'd never mentioned it again, she'd catalogued that item away in her brain.

"Are you real?" He looked up at her and shook his head. "Or is someone listening to me talk to myself right now?"

She cocked her head, a confused smile on her lips. "Huh?"

He abandoned the books and went to her, drawing her right to him. She had a dot of sauce on the edge of her lip from where she'd tasted it a second ago. "You're too perfect."

"There's no such thing as perfect," she whispered.

"Oh, but there is. And I keep wondering what's going to trip this up—what thing is going to jump out and make me realize that there was a giant problem all along that I couldn't see."

Something flickered in her eyes, something like worry and confusion and...fear? "You think there's a problem we can't see?"

"I don't know." He shook his head. "All I know is that I'm not sure how, when I wasn't looking for anything at all, I found someone who fits me so perfectly. I had no idea I wanted you until you showed up, and then I realized you were exactly the thing I'd been missing."

Audrey's lip trembled. "Don't put me on a pedestal, Ronan. I don't belong there."

"Yes, you do." He touched his lips to hers, and she melted into his kiss. Something clattered to the floor—possibly the wooden spoon she'd been holding—but it wasn't enough to break them away.

He swept his tongue into her mouth, lips punishing and demanding. His hands glided around her waist and down her back, cupping her round ass. Fire pumped through his veins, need and want roaring like a lion in his head. *Yes*. It drowned everything out—quieted his self-criticisms and doubts, shooing away the fear that he was broken and unlovable and unfixable.

He filled himself with her taste and her scent and her curves. There was no better antidote to his pain than this.

"Ronan," she moaned, winding her arms around his neck and meeting him with passion and force. "Shit, Ronan!"

A hissing sound broke them apart as the water bubbled up over the edge of the pot, sizzling as it hit the hot stove top. Audrey scrambled for the dial, turning the heat down and shooting him a saucy look.

"Dinner first."

He held up his hands and laughed, already feeling soothed by her. Audrey was that presence in his life now— his sunshine, his balm. In three and a half short weeks, she'd become the best part of his day and the last thing on his mind before he went to sleep. Maybe that's why the whole "girlfriend" thing popped out so easily. Shaking his head, he went to fetch a bottle of wine and two glasses from the cabinet.

"So, about before." He unscrewed the lid off the bottle and poured them both a glass. Rich, red liquid flowed, and the scent of it mingled with the bubbling pasta sauce. "I didn't know she was coming by."

"It's fine. I was glad to meet her." Audrey dumped the pasta into the hot water and waded a clean wooden spoon through.

"I meant more that I hadn't thought about how...about what we..." He let out an aggravated huff. "I know we haven't discussed what this is, and I was put on the spot when I had to introduce you."

"Oh." Audrey nodded knowingly, a hint of a smile on her lips. "The G-word thing."

Why was this so hard for him? Any time he'd dated someone in the past, he'd avoided this topic of conversation like it might infect him. Now he was rushing into things without giving it any thought first. He *never* jumped forward in commitment. Ever.

"It popped out, and I couldn't simply call you a friend when that's not what you are."

"And 'fuck buddy' was probably too much info for your mom, huh?" She laughed.

He looked up. Is that what she thought this was? But before he could open his mouth to clarify, Audrey winked at him in such a way that it was clear she was trying to add some levity to the conversation.

"I wanted to bring it up," she said, her tone turning serious. "But I wasn't sure how. We were having such a good time these past few weeks, I didn't want to ruin it."

He carried the two glasses of wine over to the kitchen and handed her one.

"I like that you called me your girlfriend," she added, sipping her wine and lowering her lashes as her cheeks went a little pink. "I certainly don't want anyone else in my life."

"Me neither." He couldn't even imagine being with someone else now. It shocked him how quickly that had changed.

When something feels right...

Did that make it right? What *actually* changed? Ronan's time in Kissing Creek would still end with the school year, and he wasn't ready to commit to what came next. Audrey would have to stay with her family. She was still a gentle, caring soul, and Ronan...

Ronan was the guy wondering if he could forgive his sick mother.

If that didn't make him a capital-B bastard, then he didn't know *what* would.

This was all too much to process at once. Ronan was quite happy studying other people's behavior, but he was finding it increasingly confronting to study his own. All he knew was that Audrey meant something to him—she was important. Special.

It was everything else that had a giant question mark hovering over it.

Chapter Twenty

Ironically, hippopotomonstrosesquippedaliophobia is the fear of long words.

Later that night, Audrey wasn't quite sure what to make of her evening with Ronan. Clearly he was dealing with some big things. Scary things. He hadn't really talked about his parents much. All Audrey knew was that his relationship with his mother was strained. That she'd hurt him. A lot.

And then there was the whole "girlfriend" thing. The putting-her-on-a-pedestal thing.

Now they were laying on his couch, having made love after a delicious meal and a bottle of wine. He was stretched out, one arm above his head and the other curled protectively around her shoulders. She lay with her cheek against his chest, legs tangled with his. He'd pulled the blanket over them and only a single lamp lit the room, leaving them in a dim, cozy glow.

She was seriously considering not going home until the next morning.

"Tell me something," he said, stroking her hair. "My brain won't shut off."

"Even after what we just did?" Audrey looked up at him disbelievingly. "Clearly I didn't do my job properly."

He laughed, and the sound was gravelly and sexy and sinful. "Zero complaints there, trust me. You're a firecracker in bed."

Audrey blushed. "And on the couch."

"And up against the wall."

"Door," she corrected, as was now their running joke. "You want a question?"

"Yeah. Something silly."

"Okay." She traced patterns on his skin, feeling the dusting of hair on his chest under her fingertip. "What's the word that represents the fear of long words?"

"It's going to be a long word, isn't it?"

Audrey laughed. "No hints allowed. You know the rules."

"The longest word I know is antidisestablishmentarianism, twenty-eight letters."

"That's not it."

"Tell me."

"Hippopotomonstrosesquippedaliophobia is the fear of long words." She grinned. "Thirty-six letters. But it's not the longest word. The longest word in English is the chemical name for the titin protein, which has almost one hundred and ninety thousand letters and takes three and a half hours to say."

"Of *course* you know that." Ronan shook his head. "Although one might argue the technical terms for compounds are a verbal formula rather than a word."

"Spoilsport." She snuggled against his chest.

It rose and fell with a deep breath. Ronan was a bit of a closed book when it came to his life—he seemed more than happy to listen to her talk for hours on end about her family.

He knew all about her siblings and the trouble with their dad—she'd opened up to him more than anyone. Ever. He always listened with the same serious, thoughtful expression, not trying to force solutions on her. He asked after her aunt and Nicole and showed an interest in all the people who worked in Kisspresso, and it dawned on Audrey that nobody knew a damn thing about him.

He was a mystery to Kissing Creek. In many ways, he was a mystery to her.

"Are you doing okay? I know your mom's diagnosis must have been a blow." She propped herself up so she could look at him.

Ronan's blue eyes struck her with such intensity that it almost stole Audrey's breath. "It was a shock...but I don't know how to feel about it."

"How come?"

"Because..." He sighed. "We don't have a relationship. I tried for years, to no avail. I'd given up on her. Now she's got this awful diagnosis, and I feel like an asshole because all I can think about is how it doesn't erase what she did to Keira and me."

"That *doesn't* make you an asshole, Ronan." Audrey frowned. "Someone getting sick doesn't automatically make them a saint. It certainly doesn't excuse the past."

"It's complicated."

"Life's complicated. But you *can* sympathize with her situation while still being hurt. It's possible to do both."

"Is that how you deal with your dad?" he asked.

"Yeah, I guess it is." Audrey twisted the length of her hair around and around while she sorted through her thoughts. "Although I wonder if I've gone too far in the other direction."

"How so?"

"For a long time, I was fueled by the hope that he'd

change back into who he was before my mom died. That I'd get the old version of him back." She swallowed and found a small lump in the back of her throat. "But if I'm being honest, I know he's not going to change unless there's a catalyst of some kind."

"What can you do about it?"

"It's not my responsibility to change him," she replied. "My responsibility is to my siblings—to make sure they have a good life and that they become independent and successful. If after that point, he still wants to sit around and do nothing, then that's on him."

"You think you'll be able to walk away?"

She kept telling herself she would. But there was a little voice in the back of her mind that said if she was going to walk away, she would have done it already. So many people offered to help them, and yet…she stayed. She kept the family together.

"I find it hard to think about the future beyond that point," she admitted. "It's like my brain shuts down because it all seems so far away, and I've spent my whole life taking one step at a time."

She looked up at him and narrowed her eyes.

"What?" he asked.

"We were supposed to be talking about you, not me." She jabbed a finger softly into his chest. "You're very good at that."

"Misdirecting?"

"Hiding."

"I'm an observer, a studier. I don't like being the subject of anyone's attention."

"You're the subject of my attention," she said, leaning forward to brush a kiss over his lips. "And I wouldn't have it any other way."

"What would you do?" he asked. "I don't know if I can

forgive and forget so easily."

"You don't have to. You can support her and give her a chance to hear your side of things while knowing that she might not have changed. But these things *do* change people, and..." Audrey pressed a hand to his chest. "It could be the last chance you have."

"I've never wanted *anything* from my father. He was never around, and so I never expected things. But she would come back in just long enough that I'd start to hope, and then she'd leave again." He let out a long breath. "Anyway, I need to think. I'm not very good company tonight."

"I don't expect you to be a robot."

"Did you not call me a sex robot the very first time we met?" A sly grin pulled his lips upward.

"No, I did *not.*"

"Liar, liar, panties on fire." He pulled her down to him and tugged the elastic of her underwear down her hip. "Look, they're practically melting right off your body."

"You do seem to have that effect on me."

His eyes became dark as his hands roamed her body, slipping underneath her underwear and finding her still achy and damp. "I want you again, Audrey."

"Who's using sex as a distraction now?"

"Never. My want for you overrides everything else. Some days, it's the only thing I'm sure of."

"Me too," she whispered against his lips, savoring the magnetic pull between them. She couldn't resist Ronan. She didn't *want* to resist him.

And that was a dangerous thing, because he represented the life she couldn't have. The future that scared her too much to think about. He might put *her* on a pedestal, but that's where she had him. He was the one with the life of his own making, the freedom and ability to go wherever he wanted. And what if one day he wasn't content to wait for her anymore? What if she wasn't enough anymore?

He could leave...but she couldn't follow.

• • •

The following morning, Audrey woke with a start. Lilac light streamed in through the windows of Ronan's apartment, and the man himself slept soundly on the other side of the bed. After they'd gotten hot and heavy on the couch for the second time, they'd ventured into his bedroom to finish the night with more kissing, cuddling, and talking.

Satisfied to a totally new level, Audrey must have drifted off and slept the night away.

"Shit." She scrambled out of the bed, not even waking Ronan. The man slept like a log, heavy and unmoving and totally peaceful.

Audrey couldn't help the stupid grin on her face, even if this was a disaster. She'd never make her shift on time at this rate. Not since it was a school day and the kids were probably wondering where the hell she was.

She gathered up her clothes, no easy feat with them scattered through the apartment. There was a grumble from the bedroom and the sound of bedsprings squeaking, then silence. Audrey located her phone in the depths of her bag. There were missed calls from both Georgie and Oliver, and she hurriedly dialed her sister back.

"Hey, sorry I'm not home—"

"It's fine. Dad's still asleep, so Mrs. March is taking us to school," Georgie said in a totally nonchalant way. There wasn't a hint of worry in her voice—not even curiosity.

"You weren't wondering where I was?"

"We figured you'd gone to work early and forgotten to tell us."

Audrey laughed and shook her head. Teenagers. Their

self-absorption wasn't often of benefit, but she'd take it on this one occasion. "Is Deanna okay?"

"Don't worry, I looked up a fact to share with her on the ride."

Tears unexpectedly sprung to Audrey's eyes—seeing her siblings take care of one another always struck her in the chest. And sullen as the twins might be, they really *did* care about one another. "So everyone's fine?"

"Yes, Audrey. Everyone is fine." Georgie sighed. "Can I go now? I was texting Bianca."

"Sure. I'll see you tonight."

She ended the call and quickly pulled on her clothes from yesterday. Luckily, this morning she was working at Game of Stones. She could turn up in her regular clothes and then wrap one of her aunt's beaded shawls around her so she didn't look like she'd just rolled out of someone's bed.

"You stayed the night." A sleepy voice behind Audrey caught her attention. When she turned, Ronan was leaning against the bedroom doorframe, wearing only his underwear.

What a sight. He was lean and muscled and delightfully mussed. His brown hair stuck out in all directions, and his blue eyes were hooded, as if slumber still had its dreamy hold on him.

"Yeah, I stayed." She jammed her phone into the back pocket of her jeans. "Not on purpose, I might add."

Ronan smirked. "Did I wear you out?"

"Thoroughly."

He stalked forward, gaze pinning her to the spot like a butterfly on a specimen board. "Thoroughly?"

"Completely." She sucked in a breath. "I'm surprised I have the use of my legs after what you did to me."

His chuckle had the sexy edges of sleep still clinging to it. She could listen to that sound forever. "I should be the one chastising you. After all, I was sleeping rather peacefully when I felt you back that ass up on me in the middle of the night."

"I rolled over. That's all." But her cheeks warmed at the memory—she knew he loved when she rocked back against him like that. She encouraged his arms around her waist, knowing he'd take her from behind, slow and dreamy, almost like they weren't quite awake. "You're the one who decided to turn it into round three."

"I'm a simple man." He cupped her face and planted a kiss on the tip of her nose. "You put that delicious ass in my vicinity, I'm going to have a physical reaction."

She made a scoffing sound, but there was no stopping the delighted smile that broke through whenever they teased each other like this. "Such a caveman."

"Such a great ass."

She swatted him, laughing. "Is that all I am to you?"

"No." He looked affronted. "I'm quite partial to your legs, too."

"Ro!" She squealed when he hauled her toward him, a feeling of rightness bubbling like champagne inside her. Audrey couldn't remember the last time she'd felt so relaxed. So herself. "You're an animal."

"You love it. Don't try to pretend otherwise."

"I don't have to rush home this morning, because my neighbor is taking the kids to school."

Ronan's eyes lit up. "What time do you have to be at work?"

"Not until eight thirty."

"Can I take you to breakfast?"

Her heart did a silly little flip. Joke as he might about wanting her for her body, she knew that Ronan enjoyed *all* the time they spent together. "You can take me anywhere there's coffee."

"Give me five minutes to have a quick shower, and then

we'll go."

She knew that her never staying the night was a disappointment to him—but not once had he pushed her. Truthfully, it was a disappointment to her, too. Of *course* she wanted to wake up in his arms and get croissants and revel in that post-lovemaking bliss as long as possible. But her life didn't have time for reveling, unfortunately.

This morning was a rare treat, and she would enjoy every moment of it.

Ronan disappeared into the bathroom, and a second later the sound of running water floated into the apartment's main area. Audrey gathered up the rest of her things, including the laptop she'd brought over. On the table, where they'd sat and discussed her feedback on Ronan's latest chapter until well past ten p.m., were the remains of his work.

Audrey decided to gather it up for him, since they'd left the table a bit of a mess, distracted by each other's lips and hands. He had a box that he kept everything in, since he wrote most of his notes and first concepts by hand—something delightfully old-fashioned that Audrey loved about him. As she went to place the paper she'd scribbled on with red pen from the previous night in the box, something caught her eye. A few pieces of paper stapled together.

High school completion program vs GED.

It was an article with the pros and cons of completing a high school diploma versus taking the equivalency tests. Frowning, Audrey pulled the sheaf of papers out of the box. In the stack was a form to enroll in a high school completion program with an organization based out of Boston. Behind that was information about scholarships for several top universities and colleges. Written in pen with Ronan's telltale angular script were a phone number and name and the words *appointment for Audrey.*

Her blood ran cold.

Ronan had been looking into options for her finishing high school and going back to college...after everything she'd told him about her situation. He *understood* why she stayed in Kissing Creek. Why she'd made sacrifices and why she couldn't simply disappear off to Boston for something as frivolous as getting her high school diploma.

This wasn't a simple internet search. This was *research*.

Of course it was. That's what Ronan did best. He found something that interested him, and he studied it. Instead of wanting to be happy, like most people, Ronan made it his job. Instead of trying to figure out why people behaved the way they did, Ronan made it his life's mission. Instead of accepting that Audrey had chosen to sacrifice something for the greater good of her family, he pursued the issue behind her back.

Did he see it as a fault? Was she a project? A fixer-upper?

How could a respected professor with a pedigree like his be confident enough to show off a girlfriend who hadn't even finished high school?

Her mind flicked back to the meet and greet and how he'd cut in with a lie to stop her from confessing her lack of education to that nosy professor. Her stomach rocked. Was he ashamed of her? From the moment they'd met, he'd made her feel like she was special. Important. And yet there was this piece of evidence, this red flag, showing her that maybe he didn't think she was enough.

That maybe he viewed her education status as a flaw. Something to correct. Something that needed to be addressed in order for their relationship to work.

The water shut off in the bathroom and Audrey dropped the pages back into the box as if they were burning her. It was ridiculous to think that she and Ronan had a future. Despite their chemistry and compatibility, their lives were *very* different. Ronan followed his own path. Hell, he'd left his grandmother and sister behind to follow an opportunity to the other side of the world.

And Audrey...well, she was stuck here. More importantly, she would never "unstick" herself at the expense of her brother and sisters.

Letting herself play house with Ronan was dangerous, because it would only make it hurt more when he left. And he *would* leave. He said he didn't know what was next, but it was obvious he wanted a life bigger and more exciting than the one she had laid out in front of her. Why would he put everything on hold and miss out on opportunities to stay in Kissing Creek?

Shaking her head and refusing to indulge the tears threatening to fall, she slung her bag over one shoulder and headed for the front door. Her hand wrapped around the handle as Ronan walked out of the bathroom.

"Audrey?" He had a white towel around his waist. "Where are you going?"

For a moment, Audrey couldn't respond. Her throat was tighter than a pair of non-stretch jeans after a Thanksgiving turkey. She released the doorknob and sucked in a deep breath.

"This isn't working for me," she said evenly. "I have to go."

Confusion splashed across his face like red paint. "A few minutes ago, you were smiling about us going to breakfast. What happened?"

Audrey's eyes betrayed her by darting over to the kitchen table and the box of Ronan's notebooks and research materials. Knowing that even after she'd poured her heart out to him, confessed things about her family she'd never told another living soul...that he still didn't respect her decision enough *not* to try to "fix" her.

Or worse, "complete" her.

Wasn't she enough as she was? Couldn't she ever be enough with what she had? Why did it feel like everybody questioned her decisions? Her dad wanted a say in everything she did; her aunt kept trying to convince Audrey to move in with her; Nicole pushed her to visit her mother's grave.

"I need to make my own choices," she said, pressing her palm against the doorframe. But that's when she realized he couldn't hear the swirling tornado of thoughts in her head.

"We don't have to go to breakfast if you don't want to," Ronan said, bewildered.

"I saw the research, Ronan, about the high school diploma. And don't insult me by trying to pretend it's for someone else."

Ronan scrubbed a hand over his face. "I looked into it for you."

"Why?"

"Because…" He threw his hands up, and for a moment Audrey was concerned they were going to have a wardrobe malfunction in the middle of their breakup.

Breakup. You already know it's happening.

"Because you deserve it," he finished.

"So?"

"So…" He let out a huff. "You should have it."

"How nice it must be to get things simply because you deserve them," she said, shaking her head. "My life doesn't work like that."

"That's because you lock yourself away in a bubble." He let out a breath. "You cut yourself off from exploring opportunities."

"I know what I can and can't have."

"Audrey." Ronan came forward, his hands up. "Let's take a minute to talk this through."

"I don't have time for this. I don't have time for someone who thinks he can swoop in and solve my problems like I haven't thought a hundred million times about how I could change things to have *everything* I want." Her lips pulled into a flat line.

"But you *can* have what you want. What's to stop you from finishing your diploma and then enrolling in a course here? You could stay in town, be close to your brother and sisters—"

"I'd still need money for all this. Not to mention time. It's one thing to take a casual night class where the grades don't mean a damn thing and entirely another to have even *more* pressure heaped on me when they do count." Her heart pounded in her chest, the vibrations rattling all the way through her body and setting her on edge. "How can I work enough to feed my brother and sisters *and* get a degree at the same time?"

"There are options."

"Theoretical options," she argued. "But not real ones. Not ones that work in practice."

He shook his head. "You're frightened."

"I'm *not* frightened. I simply know my limitations."

"No, you're frightened. You're frightened of the future because it's not defined by the clear boundaries you have now. You're worried that if you aim for something and miss, then you'll have wasted the opportunity, whereas sacrificing it all is safer because there's no risk."

"How *dare* you tell me how I feel." Audrey balled her hands into fists. "And how dare you psychoanalyze me, Ronan. I'm not your test subject."

"No, you're not." He raked a hand through his hair, sending a fine mist of water into the air around him. "You're a person who deserves more than being a servant in her own house. You're not Cinderella."

"No, because Cinderella had to rely on other people to save her, and I am *not* doing that."

"Is it so wrong that I want more for you? That I think you're holding yourself back from achieving great things?" He came forward again, but she held her hand up, halting him. Touching him now would be a mistake.

Well, more of a mistake than she'd already made by thinking her relationship with Ronan wouldn't go down in flames. Because the fire had already started, and there was no putting it out.

Chapter Twenty-One

Ronan wasn't sure what to do—yes, he knew that Audrey thought it wasn't possible for her to have it all. She'd created this divide between her and her dreams that didn't allow for looking to the future or even considering what she could achieve. She didn't believe that it was possible to care for her family *and* start working toward her dreams at the same time.

Audrey was at her best and brightest when she was learning. When she was sharing knowledge. Last night, when she'd gone over his chapter, pointing things out and giving him insights that he hadn't seen coming...damn. She was magnificent.

Corny as it sounded, he was as much attracted to her brain as he was to her body.

But the second he even tried to talk about how things might be different, it was like a power switch flipped. The light in her eyes dimmed, and she became wooden. Remote.

She flat-out refused to even consider other options.

"I can't ignore the reality of my situation," she said, her olive-green eyes locked intently on him. She wasn't shying away from this argument, but she wasn't budging, either. "And it's not your job to save me."

"I don't *want* to save you. But I *do* want you to see yourself as worthy and deserving, because you absolutely are."

For a moment, she didn't reply. He could see the thoughts swirling around in her head, her eyes flicking in a way that told him her brain was racing a million miles a minute.

"Talk to me, Audrey." He sighed. "I've clearly overstepped, and I'm sorry. But I can't apologize for wanting you to have everything life has to offer."

"So it has *nothing* to do with how you feel about dating someone uneducated?"

She may as well have slapped him across the face for how much those words stung. He could practically feel the burning imprint on his cheek. After all the nights they'd shared, the vulnerable stories that had passed between them, the fact that Ronan finally let someone in...

"I can't believe you asked me that," he said, his voice rough with hurt. Five minutes ago, he would have said that Audrey knew him better than anyone. But the fact that she could even ask such an insulting thing made Ronan question everything.

Maybe she didn't know him at all.

"What about the meet and greet?" Her lip trembled, but she drew her shoulders back as if reinforcing her inner strength.

"That I invited you?"

"No, that you *lied* to your colleague so I wouldn't have to admit that I hadn't finished high school."

"God, Audrey. I already said I was sorry for that." He threw his hands up in the air. "You looked uncomfortable, and I know that guy can be a real pain in the ass."

"You basically hauled me out of there." She shook her head. "And then I find out you've been requesting GED paperwork and making appointments on my behalf, *after* we'd already discussed why it's not a good time for me now."

"You put everyone else ahead of you. When is it *your* time?"

"When my brother and sisters are safe and have a future."

"And then what? You'll magically slot back into life as though you hadn't been on hiatus for more than a decade?"

He wanted to snatch the words back the second they left his mouth. The fear that flashed across Audrey's face made his gut churn, but it also reinforced his concerns. She *was* scared of the future. And she was avoiding it.

She sighed. "If you're ashamed of my lack of—"

"Stop." He held up his hand, fury burning a path through him. "Don't even finish that sentence, because it's the most insulting thing you could possibly say to me."

Audrey folded her arms across her chest. "It's a fair assumption. You're the one who wrote a whole damn chapter of your book on motivation—so if I, the person you supposedly care about, am not able to go back to school, what's motivating you to force the issue?"

"I looked into a few things so we could discuss it. That's not forcing the issue."

"You spoke to someone else about it. About *me*." That's when he saw the armor crack more fully—the shimmer in her eyes, the tautness in her full lips. "Behind my back."

"It was a hypothetical conversation. I called an old friend, and I didn't give them your name or anything," he said.

"Why didn't you tell me first?"

"Because you would have told me not to do it."

"Exactly!" She tipped her eyes skyward. "So why did you do it anyway?"

"Because I thought if you could see how things might be...then maybe you'd consider not letting the next five years blow by you."

"How things might be?" She bobbed her head slowly. "You mean like leaving my family behind."

Of course Ronan hadn't said those words, but he'd be lying if he said he hadn't allowed himself the little fantasy of him and Audrey somewhere else, in a big city, doing great things. Chasing their dreams together. Yeah, he'd thought about that...a lot.

More than he should have for a relationship that only recently had a label attached to it.

"I'll take that silence as your confirmation," she said.

"I don't expect you to follow me. But have I thought about where this relationship might go beyond my contract? Yeah. I *have*. I've thought about you and me and what a life might look like."

Just saying those words was like taking a steak knife and carving his chest open. For a kid who'd grown up on a steady diet of rejection from his own parents, he avoided being vulnerable wherever possible. It was easier to chase success with unemotional things—like school and work—because *that*, he could control. But Audrey had snuck into his life and under his skin and deep, deep into his heart.

"What a life might look like so long as it isn't here, you mean?" There was something raw in her words, like a trace of hope that he might give her the answer she wanted.

"My job is going to take me to different places," Ronan said. "You knew that from the start."

"Then why do you care what I do with my life?" she asked. True to form, Audrey wasn't yelling or getting angry. She had too much of a wall around her for that—too much of a tight fist around her emotions to let them run away with her. For a woman who could be so passionate, seeing her like this was like seeing a poor imitation of a work of art. The thing that made the original so special was totally erased.

"Because I care about *you*," he said. "Haven't I made

that clear?"

"If you cared, you'd let me do what I need to do instead of tempting me with things I can't have. It's cruel!" She sucked in a ragged breath. "Kissing Creek is my home, my family is the thing that's most important to me in this world, and I am doing everything I can to be the kind of woman who would make my mother proud."

Her conviction was like an old tree root—it went down so deep it could hold anything in place. Even a brilliant, shining beacon of a woman like her.

"If that's not enough for you, I'm sorry. I don't see the point of dragging this out toward its inevitable conclusion." She yanked the door open and walked out onto the landing, letting it swing shut behind her. The noise triggered something in him, like a chain yanked deep in his brain, dragging to the surface a memory he'd long tried to keep buried.

He could practically feel the cold floorboards beneath his bare feet and the warmth of the blanket clutched in his hand. Voices had woken him, the sound of muted anger and hushed pleas and simmering resentment coaxing him from his bed. He'd crept on small feet down the stairs in time to see the front door slam, and the only remaining part of his mother was the lingering of patchouli perfume like a scented ghost.

He remembered watching his grandmother stand there, head bowed, shoulders slumped. It was so foreign to see her in such a position that Ronan had actually gasped, making the older woman's eyes swing toward him. His mother had left...again. Without saying goodbye, without offering her children a say in it, without seeing if they wanted to come with her.

He'd grown up on the toxic ideal that "boys don't cry," and he remembered the flood of shame at how his cheeks were suddenly wet and hot. He remembered the tremble in his lower lip and the flickering question in his mind: *What did*

I do wrong? Most of all, he remembered how his little heart had hardened that day, like scar tissue knitting over a wound. Every time she left, another scar was created, until there were more scars than soft tissue. Until he was certain that the only person who could be trusted was himself.

Why the hell would people *ever* put themselves in a position to be staring at a closed door, abandoned and unloved? Discarded.

Because having her in your life is worth it.

The little whisper was so soft he almost didn't hear it. It was more like the expelling of breath than spoken word. Ronan couldn't remember a time in his life when he'd felt so happy, so content. When he actually looked forward to the end of the workday, because there was something else waiting for him. On the nights when Audrey would be coming over, he'd almost itch with anticipation—seeing her was the highlight of his day. Being with her gave him joy and reason.

It dawned on him…people were at the heart of motivation and happiness. Not things, not achievements, not accolades.

Relationships.

The very thing he'd used his work and success to avoid was at the heart of what he was studying. It was like coming full circle. He'd been training not to let himself get close to people, but in order for him to be happy now, he had to put himself on the line.

Without thinking, Ronan yanked the door open and started down the stairs, calling Audrey's name. It wasn't until a crisp breeze hit him in a place that cool breezes didn't usually hit that he remembered he was still wearing only a towel. But he only had two options: miss catching Audrey or make himself vulnerable in *every* way possible.

Swearing under his breath, he bounded down the stairs and prayed that none of his neighbors would come out of their apartments. He was one gust of a breeze away from a public indecency violation.

Ronan made it down in record time. "Audrey, stop!"

She was strides ahead of him and powering forward like the hounds of hell were nipping at her heels.

How far are you willing to let this go?

All the way. He didn't even need to think about it. He would parade his bare ass down Main Street if that's what it took to get Audrey to stop and hear him out. Because they might not see eye to eye, they might disagree, and they might do things differently, but he cared about her. A lot. So much it felt like letting her walk away now would be the biggest mistake of his life.

"Audrey!"

She stiffened and turned, eyes widening as she caught sight of him on the outskirts of the college campus, bare-chested and the breeze tickling his nether regions beneath the towel wrapped precariously around his waist. He gripped the fabric tightly with one hand.

"Ronan, for God's sake…" She shook her head. "You're practically naked."

"I don't care." He took several long strides toward her.

"But the college might." She scrubbed a hand over her face. "I can't… This is ridiculous."

"No, it's not. I couldn't let you walk away without making something crystal clear." He sucked in a breath and braced himself as a couple walked past, their eyes almost popping out of their heads. He ignored the giggling and focused his attention on Audrey. "I like you a lot. I…I care about you."

"I care about you, too, Ronan," she said, her expression so sincere and so serious his heart squeezed. "But that doesn't make us compatible. It doesn't make our *lives* compatible."

"We *are* compatible," he said stubbornly. "As for our lives, we have time to figure it out. It's not like I'm leaving next week."

She shut her eyes for a moment, as if gathering her strength. "But you *will* leave."

"How can you know that when I don't even know what's going to happen next?"

"Because people like you always leave places like this." She shook her head. "And if you left next week, it would hurt like crazy. How is it going to be in a year's time? If it hurts now, it's going to decimate me in a year. I can't risk that. I can't risk more loss."

But there was already loss.

He was losing her. He could feel it as clearly as if water was running through his fingers.

"I know it hasn't been long, but being with you has changed me," he said. "I never wanted a relationship. I never wanted to have someone in my life because I couldn't understand why anybody would hand over power to another person like that. Hell, not only did I not want it, I didn't think I was *capable* of it."

"Of course you're capable of it," Audrey said softly.

"My ex told me I wasn't." He'd never told anyone about that breakup, about the shame he felt in being called the same things he'd accused his mother of: unfeeling, selfish, self-absorbed. "She said that loving me was like trying to coax affection from an inanimate object and it required someone with more persistence than I deserved."

Audrey's jaw twitched. In spite of their argument, he could see the words affected her. "That's not true."

"I thought it was. I thought I was exactly like my mother—that I was created in her image to be a loner who hurt anyone who tried to get close. So I kept to myself. I worked myself into the ground because that was my safe space...until you."

Audrey's eyes glimmered, and she shook her head. "You're making this harder."

"I need you to know that you've affected me. You've

fundamentally changed my perspective on the world. I never understood the purpose of personal sacrifice before you. And even though I think you *can* have everything you want, I respect the love and devotion you have for your family."

She sucked on the inside of her cheek and looked skyward as if she might find answers there. It was obvious she was trying her hardest to keep control—because that's what Audrey did. She kept things on an even keel, never letting things tip out of balance. Never pushing the boundaries. Maintaining equilibrium at all costs…and there *were* costs. He wouldn't apologize for believing she could have more, that she deserved more.

Because she did.

"Then I need you to also respect the decision I'm making now," she said softly. "I think you're an incredible person, Ronan. I think you're smart and ambitious and impossibly attractive. And I think you deserve more than what my life will entail. I won't feel bad for the choices I've made to stand by my family, but I also don't want those choices to limit you in any way. I like you too much for that. And I know I can't be enough. So even if we have time now…"

She drew in a shaky breath, and it took everything in Ronan's power not to haul Audrey against him.

"If we keep going along this path, when the time comes, I don't know if I'll be able to handle you leaving." Her voice trembled. "And I won't ask you to slow down your life. To stunt your possibilities."

"You *are* enough, Audrey. The education thing… I don't care that you didn't finish high school. It doesn't change anything between us. I only care that you're holding yourself back from what *you* want. It has nothing to do with my criteria for a partner, because I never had any criteria for that. Hell, until you came along, I didn't want a relationship at all."

She looked at him long and hard, and Ronan's heart

thundered in his chest. His brain roared out at him to hold her tight and never let her go.

"I'm not walking away because I misunderstand why you're trying to help me. But…" She sucked in a breath. "It also made me see that it takes more than two people sharing interests and physical chemistry to be together. Our approaches to life aren't compatible. I'm *not* a lone wolf, like you. I can't walk away from my family the way you did."

Oof.

The comment struck him in the chest like the sharp poke of a cattle prod.

"My life *isn't* my own. Not yet, and I'm okay with that. I know that's not how you live…and that's an irreconcilable difference. I won't hold you back, and you can't drag me out of this situation." She bobbed her head. "So, that's it. A dead end."

"You won't even talk about this anymore?" His head pounded, and he raked a hand through his hair. More people trickled onto the college grounds now, as one of the parking areas was close by, and everyone who walked past stared at them. "Can't we hash this out?"

"We're not going to see eye to eye on this." She blinked, and he caught the glimmer of tears being held back. "And it's too painful."

But the pain was worth it to him. What they had was worth the emotional cuts and bruises from fighting their way to a solution. But they could only do that together, as a team.

"I'm sorry." For a moment, it looked as though she might lean in and touch him, but then she turned and walked away.

He stood there, the air cooling his skin and the breeze reminding him that he was *way* too underdressed to be out in the open. But none of that mattered. He was numb. Frozen. At a total and utter loss.

Because the only woman to ever stir his heart was gone.

Chapter Twenty-Two

For the rest of the week, Audrey was in a fog. Which, for someone who needed to juggle adult tasks like a master Cirque du Soleil performer, was *not* a good thing. Audrey's brain was, as her aunt would say, more useless than a pen with no ink.

But she would persevere. Push on. Do the things. Be strong.

Make adulting her bitch.

At least, that was the plan. The plan, however, came crashing down when a perfect storm of things collided like bumper cars driven by an army of drunk toddlers. It started with a very unwelcome customer entering the Kisspresso Café.

Holly, one of the new trainees, looked up from the cash register. "What the—?"

Her surprise was cut off by an angry bleating sound and the stamp of hooves, which caused one of the customers waiting in line to shriek in surprise.

"Dammit, Lily! What are you doing in here?" Audrey

put the jug of milk that she was frothing down and motioned for Holly to take over. Digging her phone out of the pocket in her apron, she hit call.

At this point, the whole town of Kissing Creek had Devon Huxley's number on speed dial. No matter what he did to keep Lily in her paddock, that damn llama figured out an escape route.

Audrey's call was answered with a gruff, "Yeah?"

"Your llama is out again," she said with a frustrated sigh. "Kisspresso Café."

"I'm coming now. Keep her there."

Audrey ended the call and shoved her phone back into her apron with a grunt. "How the heck is it our job to wrangle his misbehaving llama?"

Customers had backed away from the grumpy animal, who was swinging her head back and forth as if trying to figure out who her next target was. But Audrey had a secret weapon—a secret llama-disarming weapon. She crouched down behind the glass pastry display counter and found the leftovers of yesterday's stock. This stock didn't get served to customers, obviously, but ever since they discovered the llama had a taste for day-old bran muffins, they kept one or two whenever possible…just in case.

"Here, Lily-girl," Audrey said, making a kissy noise. "I've got your hard-as-a-rock, disgusting day-old muffin."

She held it up in front of her, and the llama's head immediately swung in her direction. Maybe this was a bad idea. While the muffins worked to get Lily out of the store, Audrey was convinced she now knew that Kisspresso was the place to go for treats.

Lily's black lash-fringed eyes locked onto the muffin.

"If you spit on anyone, then no muffin for you." Audrey waggled a finger at her. "Now get your furry butt outside."

The llama stood stubbornly in front of the counter. Okay,

so it was going to be one of *those* days. They seemed to be happening more frequently of late. Or maybe it was that Audrey was struggling to see the good in the world anymore. Since the day she left Ronan Walsh standing in a towel on the Harrison Beech campus grounds…well, her world had been a lot less vibrant.

"I seriously don't have time for this, Lily. Can you not be an asshole for *one* day? Please?" She sighed, and the llama stared at her intently. "Okay, fine. Have it your way. Excuse me? Person in the red shirt, can you open the door and hold it for a sec?"

The student standing by the door looked on in bewildered silence, nodding mutely and inching along the wall so she could pull the door open. Audrey drew her arm back, remembering everything her school sports teacher had instilled in her during her time playing second base on the high school softball team.

"Get out of the way, everyone," she said. "One, two, three…"

She released the muffin, and it hurtled through the café, straight on target to where the door was open. Lily's head whipped around, and just as she was about to bolt through the door to chase her snack—

"Oof!" Devon Huxley stepped right into the path of the flying muffin, and it hit him smack between the eyes, knocking him backward out of the doorway.

Lily stamped her feet and chased after the muffin, which had bounced on the ground outside.

"Oh my God." Audrey pushed through the swinging door separating the dining area of the café from the staff area and jogged outside. "I am *so* sorry!"

Devon was on the ground, pushing himself up into a sitting position and shaking his head. "What part of Kisspresso's mission involves throwing food at customers?"

he said peevishly.

"Technically, you're not a customer, and neither is Lily." Audrey reached down to help him up, but he waved her hand away. Typical. Devon thought he could do everything himself—except keep his damn llama in check. "She's a menace."

"She comes here because you all keep feedin' her." He stood and dusted his hands down the front of his jeans. Lily munched happily on the muffin beside them. "Now that she knows where to get muffins, she's going to keep coming back."

"What am I supposed to do, let her terrorize my customers? She spit in someone's latte last time."

He grunted and didn't respond. For some reason, and even though Audrey had *never* gotten pissy with Devon before, something snapped inside her. Maybe she'd officially reached her capacity for dealing with other people's crap. Maybe after a week of trying to ignore the yawning ache inside her, she didn't have anything left over to keep her emotions in check.

"I am *sick* and tired of people not taking responsibility in this place! She's your llama. Figure out a way to keep her locked up." She jabbed Devon in the chest.

Which was a mistake, just like throwing a muffin like she was trying to get a double play was a mistake. Lily took the motion as a slight against her owner and immediately trotted over to defend him. She nudged Audrey with her head, startling her and knocking her off-balance. The ground was slippery from the rain overnight, and the worn tread on Audrey's sneakers was no match for muddy ground.

She slipped straight back and landed on her butt right in a puddle. Immediately, the water soaked through her jeans and the strings on her apron, splashing Devon's boots in the process. Like a gentleman, even though she probably didn't deserve it, he leaned down and offered her a hand and helped her up.

"She's mighty protective, this one." Devon patted Lily's neck. "Come on, girl. You got your muffin, so let's go home and stop causing people trouble."

Audrey watched him lead the llama away, and when she looked down at her legs, she knew there was no way she was going to be able to finish her shift. Shoulders slumped, she headed back toward the café's door to organize a replacement. Then she'd go home and change.

Twenty minutes later, Audrey found herself driving around in circles, unable to head home. Her boss had given her the rest of the day off, but the thought of having to head home and face her father... She didn't have the mental fortitude for that right now.

There was something pent-up inside her—a frustration that had burrowed deep into her bones. A sense of sadness and loss and anger, like a gross mélange of all the emotions she despised most. Useless emotions. Defeating emotions.

Poisonous, hard-to-shake, scary emotions.

She never allowed herself to feel these things, because they would only stop her from achieving what she wanted to achieve.

But right now they bubbled close to the surface, hot and raw. Strong. Stronger than she'd ever felt those things before. Why? Losing Ronan had been like slicing open a part of herself that she kept locked away. Because he was the one person who made her feel like life had something more to offer than sacrifice and duty. Like *she* could be more than a barista and caretaker.

Like her dreams didn't have to be corralled and kept under lock and key.

Audrey turned a corner, driving aimlessly, her hands white-knuckling the steering wheel. Tears pricked the backs of her eyes, which only stoked the fire inside her. Crying was of no use. But nothing would scrub the memories of Ronan from her mind. Every time her mind went quiet, she thought of him. Of his touch and his kiss and the passion and belief he had for her.

Of the sinking feeling in her stomach when she'd found his handwritten note.

Just as Audrey was about to turn the car around and head back toward home, Big Red made an awful clunking sound. Then it shuddered and lurched.

"Oh, not now," Audrey groaned. "Come on, girl. You can do it."

But Big Red *couldn't* do it. Audrey managed to get the car mostly to the side of the quiet street, so that it wouldn't block any oncoming vehicles. But the engine sputtered once more, and then it died. She let out a long sigh and rested her forehead on the steering wheel, counting to twenty before she tried to turn the engine over again.

It whined, wheezing like a lifelong smoker. Then nothing. This time, when she turned the key, there was nothing at all. No spark of life. Nada.

Big Red had finally kicked the bucket.

"*Damn* it!" Audrey let out a growl and slammed her fist down onto the steering wheel.

Where the hell was she? She'd taken one turn after another after another without really taking note of where she was going. All she knew was that it wasn't close to home. When she looked up, a stone settled in the pit of her stomach. The street was quiet, peaceful, and leafy…and she knew *exactly* where she was.

The Kissing Creek cemetery stretched out alongside the road, a sprawling green lawn with vibrant blades of grass and tall trees shuddering in the breeze. Dappled light flickered across her windshield, and a leaf drifted down, landing on the glass and sliding until it settled against her wipers.

Audrey stared for a moment, her gaze catching on the elegant wrought iron fence that ringed the cemetery and the lines of neat standard roses and rows of plaques. For some reason, it felt like Big Red had brought her here on purpose. Pushing the door open, Audrey got out of her car and slammed the door shut, not even bothering to lock it.

Her feet carried her toward the entrance, almost as if of their own volition. The scent of flowers and wet grass and dirt hit her nostrils, and memories kicked up like ocean sediment disturbed by a strong wave. Shaking her head, she pulled out her phone and texted Nicole.

AUDREY: *I'm having the day from hell, and Big Red finally gave up the ghost. I'm stranded at the cemetery. Can someone come get me?*

Nicole immediately texted back that she'd be there in fifteen. What would she do without her? Guilt struck Audrey for the fact that she hadn't seen Nicole much lately. She'd skipped their last hike to pick up an extra shift at Kisspresso, and she'd been slow responding to texts.

Fifteen minutes. Audrey shifted on the spot, not sure how to kill the time. There was nothing much in this part of town, just houses. Getting to Main Street would take half an hour on foot, so that wasn't an option.

She ventured into the cemetery, her throat immediately tightening. A memory floated up in her mind—Georgie crying because she accidentally spilled the can of Coke Audrey had bought her while they waited for their dad to meet with the funeral director. The brown fizzing liquid had splattered all over the ground and left spots on Georgie's favorite sneakers. Her tears had come fierce and free in only the way a small child's can. Oliver had looked on, scowling, silent. He'd already started turning in on himself then, tragedy snuffing out the last of his childhood joy and wonder.

Audrey drifted toward the flower shop, eyes unfocused. The florist recognized her right away—she was a regular at Kisspresso. That connection was how she ended up with a fistful of peonies in a glass jar with a pink ribbon tied around the neck. Audrey hovered at the edge of the path that would take her to her mother's plot.

"You don't have to do this," she said to herself. There was a trash can a few feet away—she could dump the flowers and head back outside to wait for Nicole. Or she could donate the flowers to another grave.

But something inside Audrey drew her up the path, operating her arms and legs like she was a puppet on strings. Her mind flicked between past and present until she reached her mother's plot. She brushed her hands over the plaque, clearing the little twigs and other natural debris that the wind had blown across it. Her fingers caught on the raised lettering of her mother's full name: *Mary Patricia Miller.*

Nobody had called her Mary. For some reason, she'd always been known as May. Maybe it was because she had that kind of personality—sunny, hopeful. Like a spring day.

Audrey's knees sank into the wet grass, and she didn't care one little bit about getting stains since her pants were already dirty. The flowers trembled in the glass, and Audrey realized she was shaking. It felt like there was a storm inside her, angry and thrashing.

"This is why I didn't want to come here." She shook her head, but the grief was too strong. It wrapped a hand around her throat and squeezed, cutting off her air. Her words. Her blood.

Her chest heaved as she drew a deep breath, fighting against the boulder clogging her throat. She wanted to scream, but nothing came out. The breeze caught her cheeks, and they were cold. No, wet. Tears rolled unchecked down her face. Audrey's hands tightened around the glass jar, the blood draining out of her joints, and she applied so much pressure it was a wonder the damn thing didn't shatter.

"Why?" She dragged the word in through tight lungfuls of air. "Why didn't they save you?"

Her chest was so tight she was worried her rib cage might crack from the pressure, but she couldn't move. Everything poured out of her—everything she'd bottled up and swallowed down and tucked into a safe corner of her mind all came roaring out of her. It felt like she was being exorcised, that the ugliness of her emotions wasn't really her.

Only it was.

"I hate you for leaving me," she said, swiping at her cheek with the back of one hand. "I miss you so much."

She placed the jar of flowers down and pressed her palm to the grave's plaque and felt...something. It was like a vibration, so small it was barely perceptible—or maybe it was simply her imagination desperately searching for meaning—that rippled through Audrey's body. She could almost feel her mother's presence wrapping around her like a warm blanket.

"My life would have been so different if you were here."

Ronan was right. She had a fear of living. A fear of the future. Because at fifteen, Audrey had thought she'd figured it out—top marks at her high school, acceptance into one of her dream universities, travelling around the world, a husband who loved and respected her, giving her parents some grandbabies to snuggle. But that had all been ripped from her grasp.

What was the point of planning for the future when life might take everything you wanted and rip it to shreds?

I've thought about you and me and what a life might look like.

Ronan's words circled in her brain—he thought about their future. Thought about them together. Any time Audrey's mind had wandered to what could be, she'd shut it down. Forced herself to think about something else.

The present was the only thing she could control—not what came before or what might come next. But now. Tomorrow was unknown. Next month was a blank page. Ten years from now…nothing. It was like her brain had been rebooted.

Wanting was pointless. Trusting was pointless.

"Audrey!"

At the sound of her name, she turned. Nicole rushed over to her, worry splashed across her face. She was wearing a pencil skirt and a pale blue top, and her long, dark hair swirled around her shoulders with the breeze.

"I was so worried." Nicole all but skidded to a stop and dropped down next to her, wrapping her arms around Audrey's shoulders. "I saw Big Red, and then I couldn't find you, and you weren't answering your phone…"

Audrey hadn't even noticed it vibrating. "I'm sorry."

"It's okay."

The two of them stayed like that, glued together, for what felt like an eternity. Nicole kept her arm like a vise around Audrey's neck. But Audrey's storm of emotions had started to quiet down, and for a second she almost felt…peaceful.

She hadn't expected that. But there was something surprisingly cathartic about crying your eyes out, even if she did feel snottier than a toddler with a cold. When she snuffled, Nicole fished a tissue out of her handbag and handed it over.

"You okay?" she asked.

Audrey nodded. "I don't know why I came here. I… The car broke down right outside, and it felt like…"

"Providence?" Nicole offered.

"Kinda." Audrey sighed and toyed with the stem of one of

the peonies. She had no idea if they were her mom's favorite or not. After spending the last fourteen years so focused on putting one foot in front of the other, it was like her mind had erased some things that were too painful to remember.

But now she wished she'd hung onto those memories a little tighter. "Maybe it was time. Everything's going to shit now anyway, so what's one more thing to deal with?"

Nicole frowned but didn't say anything.

"I broke up with Ronan," Audrey explained.

"What happened?" Nicole placed a hand on Audrey's arm.

"He..." She sighed. What the hell was she supposed to say?

He tried to help me, so I dumped him. He gave a shit about my future, so I dumped him. He treated me like he thought I could do anything, so I dumped him.

It didn't make sense anywhere except in her head.

"He overstepped a boundary," Audrey said eventually, biting down on her lip. "I told him that I hadn't finished high school, and he took it upon himself to look into how I could get my diploma so I could be eligible for a college scholarship."

"Okay." Nicole bobbed her head. "And that's a bad thing because...?"

"I told him I can't do that."

Audrey touched her fingertip to her mother's grave, stroking and tracing the letters and numbers. Their birthdays were only one day apart, and her mother had always said Audrey was the best birthday present. Her mother had told her over and over as a kid that she could do great things. She'd *wanted* her to get good grades and set her sights high and dream big.

"What if I try, and my life gets better, and suddenly a terrible thing takes it all away again?" The words rushed out of Audrey like a freight train. There; she said it. Her greatest fear.

If life was good, she had too much to lose.

Loss equaled pain—she knew that already. Losing Ronan had hurt like having a limb carved off with a rusty spoon. Losing her mother had…ruined her.

"So it's better to live an unsatisfying life because at least you have nothing to lose?" Nicole asked. "That's a slippery slope, babe."

"What if next time I end up like him?" She sucked in a shaky breath. "My dad was broken after my mom died, and he *hasn't* recovered. I…I can't be like him."

"You *won't* be like him. Ever," Nicole said fiercely. "Because you're stronger than he is. You're smarter, and you have a bigger heart, and you care about others."

Audrey swallowed and nodded. That all sounded true.

"Here's the thing," Nicole continued. "I'm going to sound real cynical for a minute, but hear me out. Things can *always* be worse. Having a shitty situation now doesn't protect you from having an even more shitty situation in the future. Therefore, this approach to not visiting your mom's grave before today and not doing anything for yourself doesn't guarantee protection. You could still be hit by a bus tomorrow."

"Morbid much?" Audrey muttered.

"What I'm saying is, choosing not to live a satisfying life doesn't protect you. So, if there is *no* way to protect yourself from bad things in the future…why not try to improve your situation?"

Like Ronan. Like the things she was passionate about in life.

"But I have to look after my family," Audrey said.

"Yeah, you do. But you also have to look after yourself, because otherwise…what are you teaching Deanna? Would you want her to be in your shoes?"

"No." The answer was so true the resonance of it rang through her body like a church bell. "I would never want her to do this."

"I'm sure your mom would say the same for you," Nicole said softly. "She wouldn't have expected you to shoulder the burden of the whole family by yourself."

"But if I don't do it…" She shook her head.

"You have people who want to help you," Nicole said. "Your aunt is always offering. And hell, maybe if you stopped supporting your dad, he might actually get off his ass and do something. He's your parent, *not* the other way around."

She was right. Her aunt was right. And Ronan was right.

"I think I've been hiding behind it all," Audrey admitted. "Because nobody can argue with me if I say I need to care for my family. It's a certified conversation stopper. But I've been using it as a shield to avoid…well, everything."

It was easier to avoid. Easier to soldier on with the day-to-day.

"Do you really think Ronan overstepped by looking into some options for you?" Nicole asked. "If you think he did, then that's totally fine. But maybe he really believes he has your best interests at heart."

"At first I felt like he was saying I wasn't good enough because I didn't finish high school," she said, cringing at how she'd reacted. It was nothing but a projection of her own fears and criticisms. "But I think that was me judging myself."

"We all do it," Nicole said, resting her head against Audrey's shoulder. "You deserve an amazing life with a hot guy and loads of incredible sex and as many boring textbooks as your heart desires. Your mom would want all of those things for you, too."

Audrey looked down at her mom's grave. Her heart was achy and full and so very scarred, but coming here today hadn't been the breaking point she thought it would be. It hurt, sure. But it also fueled her, and *that* was a hope-inducing surprise.

Audrey swallowed against the lump in her throat from all the crying. She couldn't keep going on like she had been—because she *was* miserable. She'd been miserable for years, even though she tried her hardest not to let anyone see. She had obligations—more than most. But maybe that didn't have to define her.

Maybe she didn't have to be scared of the future...or of love.

Chapter Twenty-Three

Ronan walked up his grandmother's street, trepidation in each step and the book in his hand heavy enough to sink the *Titanic*. After Audrey had left his apartment, he'd let the box of books sit untouched for almost three weeks. Then, after deciding he was sick of looking at the damn thing, he'd started to sort through it.

Lo and behold, there *was* a first edition inside, from the 1970s. It was a little beat-up, but the design was beautiful—a black hardback with gold details, including a depiction of the ever-present Poirot and his infamous mustache. The title had felt appropriate. *Curtain: Poirot's Last Case*.

That's what Ronan got for not believing in fate—a dark joke from the universe.

It seemed even more appropriate now, given coming here would mean facing his mother again. And any time he visited in the future.

He paused at the front door of the townhouse he'd lived in right up until he left for Harvard without a backward glance. Charlestown was as he remembered. The street was almost impossibly narrow, with cars jammed along one side and colorful clapboard houses sitting like rows of book spines on a shelf. The Bunker Hill Monument wasn't far away, and there were younger families walking along the street, hand in hand. Some tourists, too, who'd probably wandered from the Freedom Trail to look at the historic neighborhood.

Ronan steeled himself and raised his hand to the front door. He knocked three times and waited, clutching the book. A second later, the door swung open, and his mother stood there, a dressing gown wrapped around her body and bags under her eyes.

"Hi, Mom."

To his total surprise, his mother threw her arms around him and pulled him close. His body stiffened at first, unused to such open affection from her—it had been decades since she'd hugged him. But the second her familiar scent hit his nostrils, Ronan's tough exterior was challenged. For how many years as a child had he begged for this moment?

There was so much baggage to sift through. But Audrey's words echoed in his head: *you can sympathize with her situation while still being hurt.*

He wrapped his arms around his mother's small frame. He wasn't sure how long it would take to fully forgive her for what she'd done to him and Keira when they were children, but he only had one opportunity for closure. If he decided not to allow her into his life, then at some point that decision would be forever.

He thought about Audrey and all she'd done for her family, about how big her heart was and the goodness she brought to the world. Deep down, *that* was the kind of person Ronan wanted to be—someone who had a positive impact on others. Someone who made the world a better place.

Someone who didn't abandon his family.

But he hadn't been that person. Instead, he'd lived an

isolated life, knee-deep in research so he didn't have to risk himself by having a real relationship. Chasing his career around the globe because constant movement made it easier to remain alone. And safe.

When Merrin pulled back, Ronan caught sight of his grandmother watching from deeper within the house. Her expression was hard to read, as always.

"I guess you came to see your grandmother," Merrin said. Her eyes were watery, as if she'd held back tears.

"I came to see you both," Ronan said. He might not be able to forget what his mother had done, but he *could* forgive. Eventually. He could allow them both to have closure while it was still an option.

Audrey had shown him that those things were important— family, forgiveness. Love.

Love?

What else could he call what he and Audrey had shared?

"Don't stand there in the doorway," Orna said with a wave of her hand. "If you're going to visit, then come into the damn house."

Merrin shot him a look. For the first time in as long as Ronan could remember, they shared a moment of amusement. Stepping into the house was like being thrown back in time— the floorboards still squeaked in exactly the same places, and he avoided stepping on the board with the crack in it, like he had as a kid. Old superstition.

Ronan followed his grandmother and mother into the kitchen tucked down the back of the long, narrow building. There was already a stove kettle boiling and two mugs with teabag tags dangling over the edge.

"I brought you something," Ronan said, holding the book out toward his grandmother.

Orna's face lit up. There wasn't much that brought her a moment of pure joy, and it always warmed Ronan's heart.

So far the only thing they'd found was her beloved Agatha Christie novels, ginger chocolates, and her great-grandson.

"Where did you get this treasure?" she asked, turning the book over as though it was the most precious thing in the world. "I have this, but not a first edition."

"I know."

She looked up, her brow crinkled.

"I keep a list on my phone," he explained. "Every time Keira or I buy you one, we make a note of it."

For a moment, the old woman didn't say anything. This might be the first time that Ronan had seen his grandmother officially at a loss for words. She blinked, looked at the book, then up at Ronan, then back down.

"You're a good boy," she said, her Irish accent more pronounced than usual. It got thicker with emotion, which didn't happen too often. "We raised you well."

"*You* raised him well," Merrin corrected softly.

Ronan looked at his mother, surprised to hear her acknowledge it. Sometimes it took a drastic thing for people to come together.

"We're still a family," Orna said stubbornly. "No matter what happens. No matter how many mistakes we make. You don't get to abandon people simply because you don't like something they did."

A heavy silence settled over the room, like snow falling. Where did they go from here? Ronan wasn't sure—his experience in rebuilding relationships was absolutely zero. All he knew was that he wanted to keep trying.

And he'd never wanted that before. Because it was easier to let people walk away. To stay rooted to the ground and hold his tongue and not fight. It was easier to distract himself with work and commit himself to career success instead of people.

The day Audrey had walked out of his apartment, he

knew he didn't want to lose her. He'd tried to convince her to give them a chance...and the old Ronan wouldn't put himself in the firing line again. Just like how he'd stopped trying with his mother, he would have stopped trying with her.

But it felt wrong. Not being with Audrey felt wrong.

I love her.

He felt it down to the core of him. Down to the deepest, most protected part of his soul. An emotion he was never sure he'd willingly feel ever again.

"Did that book come from the box your girlfriend dropped over?" Merrin asked as if reading his mind.

Orna's eyebrows rose so quickly Ronan was surprised they didn't shoot right off her head and launch themselves into space. "Girlfriend? Why is this the first time I'm hearing anything about a girlfriend?"

"It's...complicated." He held up his hands as if that might stop the questions. It wouldn't. His grandmother was a steamroller when she wanted information. "And no, I don't want any advice."

Orna made a huffing sound. "What did you do, Ronan?"

"Why do you assume I've done something wrong?"

"Because I know men," she replied sagely. "And I know you're all difficult bastards."

Ronan shoved his hands into his pockets. He wanted to argue with his grandmother, but...what could he say in his own defense? *Yes*, he'd wanted to help Audrey. *Yes*, his intentions were golden.

But the issue of him researching completion methods for her high school diploma wasn't really the crux of the issue. The more he thought about it, the more he realized that he'd expected *her* to take risks and make sacrifices. He'd expected her to change and grow and realize her potential, and what growing had he been willing to do in return?

He'd remained noncommittal about where he was going

to be next year. He'd turned the focus of their relationship on how she could be her best self, and yet he was…doing the same old thing he always did: holding himself at arm's length. Keeping one foot out, ready for a speedy exit if things turned sour.

"I didn't want her to leave," he said. But even as he said the words, he knew he was focusing on the wrong thing again.

This wasn't about Audrey leaving. It was about whether or not he would *stay*.

He wouldn't have the same opportunities at Harrison Beech as he would at a place like Harvard or Yale or Dartmouth or any of the other elite institutions he'd set his sights on earlier in his career. Choosing to remain in Kissing Creek would mean a totally different life.

You mean a life where work is only one component of what you do? Where you have a real home? Where you have a woman in your arms who makes you feel like a better man…a man who has everything?

It was the kind of life that had never appealed to him in the past. The kind of life he assumed was nothing more than smoke and mirrors—because real relationships weren't happy on the inside, right?

But the more he thought about it, the more he saw why Audrey walked away. She didn't want to feel like a project to be completed. A broken doll to be fixed. She wanted to be his equal…and that meant *he* had to change, too.

"I'm going to stay there," he said. "In Kissing Creek. I'm going to stay for her."

Merrin reached out and grasped his hand, squeezing. "She's a lucky woman."

"We're both lucky," he replied.

Love was one of those fundamentally human things that defied explanation. But there was no getting around it: the time they'd spent together was short but impactful. His life would never be the same again, because she'd lifted the shield covering his eyes. And his heart.

He was a changed man. Ruined and reborn and forever different.

Walking away now—leaving her in Kissing Creek while he chased a lonely, successful life—felt pointless. He'd accused her of not being flexible enough to see how she might be able to have everything she wanted, and yet he was doing *exactly* the same thing.

Ronan looked at his mother. She'd come back after all these years, after all the hurt and bad feelings and mistakes, and it showed him what he now knew…

It was never too late to try again.

. . .

It had been two days since Audrey had visited her mother's grave. Two days during which her life was…not in its usual state. She'd taken time off work. Her focus had been on sorting out her family life, which had involved helping Oliver move in with her aunt so he could live without the critical gaze of their father. The deal was that he would finish out the school year, but college would only happen if *he* wanted it to. As scary as that was for Audrey, she knew her aunt would be a good influence. Oliver needed space and quiet, two things he didn't get much of at home. Perhaps with time to think, the right solution would come.

Georgie had gone to stay with a friend for the week, and only Deanna remained behind, the idea of being away from Audrey for any extended period of time was still upsetting to her. But she'd convinced Deanna to spend one night with Oliver and Harriet, because she didn't want any of them in the house when she confronted her father.

And it had worked—without any guilt for him to hang

over Audrey's head, he'd backed down. Promised that things would change. Could she believe him? Audrey had no idea. But Georgie had less than twelve months before college, and with her grades, there would be plenty of offers. Then Audrey could take Deanna and get a place—something small and cozy. Somewhere with a bedroom that was all her own.

Audrey would *not* be living under her father's thumb anymore. He had to contribute to the family as well. Otherwise he'd have to support himself...and she really hoped he would step up.

She felt good. Well, as good as a woman could with a Ronan-shaped hole in her heart. As wonderful as the image of her own place was, it wasn't the complete fantasy. Ever since she'd done the visualization exercise with him, *that* image had been stuck in her head. Him in her bedroom, with lust in his eyes and love in his smile and butterflies swirling in her stomach. She thought about him every day.

Thought about the truth in his words.

She *could* aim for more. She could dream as big for herself as she did for her siblings. That was why she'd started looking into alternatives to the GED herself. She might not be able to have Ronan—because she would not stunt or slow down his life—but she had to admit that fear *had* been holding her back. Fear had been blocking her from seeing more than one way forward.

But she was doing it now. Getting Oliver out, planning for a place for her and Deanna, starting the search for a way to get her high school diploma. Every bit counted.

It would be slow, but it would be hers. And that's what mattered.

Big Red had mercifully lived to fight another day after the mechanic had towed her in from the cemetery, and Audrey parked the car at the back of Kisspresso Café. Inside, the café was bustling. A line snaked out of the front entrance and onto the street outside.

"What the hell?" Audrey hurried behind the counter and tied her apron at her back. She wasn't due to start for another fifteen minutes, but there was no sense letting the staff drown if she could lend a helping hand. "Did I miss a memo or something?"

"Apparently the college is doing some big event." Audrey's boss, Jamie, poked her head out from the kitchen. "And you know their coffee tastes like dishwater."

"That's putting it mildly," Audrey quipped. "I would have said it tastes like Satan's backwash."

Lana, who was working the espresso machine, snorted. "Satan's backwash. I am totally stealing that."

Audrey got behind the second register and started taking orders to help speed things along. As soon as they'd cleared the line somewhat, she'd help Lana with the coffee orders. Something told her it was going to be a manic day.

"I don't know what I'd do without you," Jamie said as she ducked past, carrying a tray of freshly baked muffins. The chocolate-blackberry scent hit Audrey's nose, and she immediately thought of Ronan and his love of the berry-flavored snacks. "It's going to kill me when you leave one day."

Audrey paused between orders and looked at her boss. "I'm not going anywhere."

"Yes, you are. And as much as it will pain me to do it, I'll show you the door if you don't do it yourself." Jamie laid a hand on Audrey's shoulder before she ducked into the back room.

The comment struck her in the chest, and while Audrey tried to put on a brave face for her customers, inside her stomach was turning and churning. With trepidation, with excitement. With things she hadn't felt in such a long time... not counting her fling with Ronan, of course.

It wasn't a fling, and you know it.

No, it was everything. It was life-changing and world-tilting and soul-soothing. It was the very thing she didn't even know she needed. Ronan had opened her eyes to how she was treating herself, to how she was stunting herself.

You have to stop thinking about him.

Sure, it hurt. But she was stronger than she ever realized was possible. Visiting her mother's grave had shown her that. She was already planning to go again next month. Maybe sooner.

Whatever life threw at Audrey, she could handle it.

But as that confident thought flittered across her mind like a daring butterfly, Audrey looked up to find her next customer approaching the counter. *Ronan.* Seeing him was like a punch to the gut—because he looked beautiful and a little haunted and every bit as perfect as she remembered. His blue eyes were alight, and he wore soft blue jeans and a touchable white T-shirt that gave James Dean a run for his money.

"What can I get you, Professor Walsh?" she asked in her best server voice.

Don't break, don't break, don't break.

"I thought we were past official titles," Ronan said with a slight lift of his lips.

"We were, but…" Oh God. Why did this feel like carving her heart out with a dessert spoon? She would *have* to get used to seeing him. Ronan's contract would keep him around for the rest of the school year, and she needed to check her feelings at the café door. "Sorry. Ronan it is. We've got chocolate-blackberry muffins today. Can I heat one up for you?"

His eyes searched hers. His neat facial hair had a slight reddish tint to it as the sunlight streamed into the café, and for a moment Audrey wanted nothing more than to leap the countertop and tackle him to the ground for a searching kiss.

"Can we...talk?"

"I'm working." She shook her head and glanced along the line of people waiting. "You could have called."

"Would you have answered?"

She looked up at him, heart drumming a thundering beat in her chest. He had hollows under his eyes that matched hers. And a serious pull at his mouth that made her want to reach out and soothe him.

"No," she said honestly.

"I can't go another day without talking this through." He raked a hand through his hair, and the motion was so familiar, it called to Audrey. "God, I...I miss you so much."

Tears pricked the backs of her eyes, but Audrey straightened her spine. She would not cry at work, no matter how much Ronan's words ruined her. Because she missed him, too, with every beat of her heart. With every breath she pulled into her lungs. With every neuron that fired inside her.

"If you're not going to order anything, then I need to serve someone else," she said, determined to keep her cool. But inside she was breaking. How was she going to do this for the rest of the year?

"I'll get a muffin," he said. But when she moved to the pastry counter, he followed her. "Audrey, I messed up. You were right; I should never have gone behind your back."

She reached into the pastry cabinet and wrapped her fingers around the metal tongs that hung there. They trembled in her grip, and the first time she reached for the muffin, she dropped it right back onto the tray.

"You were right," he said. "I should have talked to you first instead of barreling ahead on my own like I always do."

It was validating to hear him acknowledge that, but it didn't change anything. Audrey dropped the muffin into a brown paper bag and began to close the pastry cabinet.

"Anything else I can get you?"

"Another muffin." His voice cut through the aching in her heart, and she looked at him over the counter. There was a determined set to his jaw. "I was expecting you to do all the growing and changing, but I was the one who needed to meet you halfway."

The tears prickled harder now, but she blinked them back, reaching for one of the decadent chocolate-blackberry muffins and dropping it into the bag.

"Every day without you is like being torn apart."

She sucked in a breath, fully aware that their conversation was drawing the eyes of those around them. "Is that everything?" she asked, trying to make her voice as perky as possible despite knowing there was a telltale wobble giving her away.

"Another one." He folded his arms across his chest, and it only served to make him look even more impossibly handsome. Having those biceps on his side was an unfair advantage. "I want another chance, Audrey. I want to show you that...what we have is worth the difficult conversations and the apologies and the stumbling. It's worth everything."

She dropped yet another muffin into the bag, and now it was so full she could barely close the top. "Anything else?"

"Another muffin," he said without missing a beat.

"Are you going to buy every muffin in this café one by one?" she asked, nailing him with a stare.

"If that's what it takes for you to hear me out. Hell, throw in the croissants, too. I'll take all of it." Tension crackled between them as they faced down. Ronan wasn't going to leave this be, and part of that made Audrey's heart swell. Nobody had ever fought for her before. "I'll even take those gross oatmeal things you keep for the llama."

"Fine," she said through gritted teeth. "A hundred and fifty spite cakes coming up."

Oh, if Ronan thought she wasn't going to call his bluff, then he was dead wrong. He wanted to come to her work and force a conversation? Fine. But he was going to pay the sugary price. Audrey grabbed a tray from behind the counter and started piling the muffins and mini croissants and cookies on.

"I'll be back tomorrow, Audrey," he said. "And I'll buy everything in the pastry cabinet then, too. I'll give myself a cavity in every last tooth if that's what it takes."

"Why are you *so* persistent?" she asked, frustration seeping into her voice as she shoved the muffins onto the tray haphazardly.

"Because I love you."

The whole café went so quiet, Audrey could have heard a cookie crumb hit the floor. For a moment, she wondered if she'd actually passed out. Maybe she'd fallen and was currently dying underneath an avalanche of baked goods.

"I'm sorry, what?" She blinked.

"I love you." The vulnerability on his face was the purest and most arresting thing Audrey had ever seen. He looked sincere and hopeful and so freaking sexy that her mind couldn't even compute such a combination of things. "Standing still while you walked away was the most idiotic thing I have ever done in my entire life. So idiotic, in fact, that I feel compelled to take the elbow patches off my blazer."

Despite her shock, she laughed. "Losing your professor badges, huh?"

"Absolutely. Not fighting to keep you in my life is... I don't even know if there is a word that accurately describes how criminal that is."

Audrey looked down at the tray in her hand, scattered with sweet treats. She felt the intensity of all the eyes in the room boring into her, the weight of their expectation and curiosity like rocks on her back.

"You don't want this life, Ronan." She bit down on her

lip. "I appreciate the sentiment, but we've been through this. I'm not going to leave my family. I'm not going to be the woman you're proud to take to faculty events. I'm not—"

"Do *not* tell me that I won't be proud of you." His eyes blazed with passion. "You are the most resilient, hardworking, curious, intelligent woman I have ever met. *They* should be proud to be in your presence."

Her heart fluttered in her chest, hope sparking like the tiniest of little flames, wavering in the air and sputtering to life.

"Every single one of you people in here," he said, turning around and addressing the entire café. "You should all be proud to know this amazing woman."

"Have you lost your mind?" Audrey shoved the tray onto the countertop behind her and marched over to the swinging door that allowed staff to enter and exit the serving area. "You have students in here."

"I don't care." He shook his head. "If anyone at Harrison Beech wants to fire me for finally pulling my head out of my ass, then fine."

She pushed through the swinging door and stood in front of him. Mistake. Because he smelled as good as he looked—like long, hot showers and fresh sheets and earthy, sensual man. She wanted to hang onto her walls, but standing before him was as good as packing them with TNT and detonating the lot.

Her defenses were smoking ruins.

"I love you, Audrey. I never thought I'd say that to someone. I never wanted to say it." He let out a breath. "But you changed that. You changed *me*. I...I want to stay."

"Here?" Audrey blinked. "In Kissing Creek?"

"Yeah, right here."

"No..." They were the words she'd always longed to hear—words that said she was worth waiting for. "But your career. I can't let you do that."

"Too late. I had a meeting with the faculty head today and told him my intentions," Ronan replied. "We're already talking about how to build on the curriculum I've set up for this year. They're excited and...so am I."

"You're staying." It was like someone had sucked the air out of her lungs with a syringe. "But what if I said no?"

"Then I have extra time to work on my influencing skills." A cocky grin morphed his serious expression into something a whole lot more delicious. "I plan on winning you over, Audrey. Every damn day for the rest of my life."

Could this really be happening?

"Tell you what—how about I make this easy," he said. "I'll ask you a question, and if you get it right, then we'll have dinner tonight. How does that sound?"

Audrey pressed her palms to her cheeks. "Are you serious?"

"Always."

"Ask me." Her voice was but a mere whisper. Hope danced inside her like pixies, spinning and twirling and churning all her feelings up into one tornado of emotion.

"How many feet can a llama spit?" His sexy grin brought a sparkle to his eyes, his hands already reaching for hers. "I'll give you a moment to do the calculations."

Audrey laughed, one fat tear finally plopping down onto her cheek. "You're giving me a free pass?"

"I couldn't take a chance, Audrey. Not with something this big. Not with you." He pulled her closer, brushing her long braid over her shoulder and running his thumb along her jaw. "So what's your answer, huh?"

"Fifteen feet," she said, laughing. "And they have really good aim."

Ronan lowered his head to hers, capturing her mouth in a tentative kiss. But there was no need for him to go slow, no need for him to wait and see. Audrey rose up on her toes and wrapped her arms around his neck, arching her body into his.

The entirety of Kisspresso Café erupted in a cheer, and Audrey was pretty sure someone's phone camera flashed. But she didn't care. Couldn't care.

The only thing that mattered was that she was exactly where she was supposed to be—in Ronan's arms. When he pulled back, his eyes were dark and inviting, hinting that dinner might have to wait for other types of reunions.

"Does this mean he's *not* buying all the muffins?" a young girl asked. "Because I really want one."

Audrey laughed and covered her mouth, eyes bright and watery. Ronan grinned and motioned to Lana behind the counter. "Whatever she wants, it's on me. That goes for everyone in here."

"Are you really doing this?" Audrey asked. "Giving up your career for me?"

"My career will be different. But I'm still going to finish this book and see what happens. I'm still passionate about my work, and I'll have to travel from time to time, but if I'm telling you that you can have it all, then it seems mighty hypocritical for me not to do the same." A slow, sensual grin curved his lips. "The thought of having a home base, coming home to you every day, dragging you to bed every night, waking up to you every morning...I can't get it out of my head."

"Me neither," she whispered. "But my family—"

"We'll make it work. Whatever it is, Audrey, we'll make it work. You want to find a house big enough for both of us and Deanna and the twins? Fine. You want me to cook dinner every night? Can do. You want me to worship you every second of every single day? I'll start right now."

His arms tightened around her as he brought his lips down to hers again. Energy crackled around them, and Audrey was sure there were fireworks behind her eyelids as they shuttered closed. Ronan's kiss was soft and deep, and it hinted at more. So much more.

His tongue danced with hers, coaxing her to open to him. To melt into him. To be his, wholly and completely.

"I will do *whatever* it takes," he said, trailing his lips along her neck. "I can't watch you walk away twice."

"You have no idea what you're promising," she said, shaking her head. "Offering to house three teenagers is not for the weak of heart."

"Good thing my heart's a lot stronger than I ever gave it credit for."

"I love you, too." The words burst out of her as she looked up at him, arms around his neck and body lining his. "I'm so glad you walked into the café that first day."

"Are you glad you called me a sex robot?" he teased. "And accused me of being a heartless thief preying on small business owners?"

"Absolutely." Her tone was 100 percent sincere. "I take my job very seriously, Professor Sex Robot."

Who would have known that the future could be so bright and shining and full of good things? She'd cleared the dark shadows from her mind, brushing them away by speaking up for herself and facing her fears. By forging the kind of life she truly deserved.

And right now, with love in her heart and a sexy, perfect man promising to worship her every day, Audrey's future was more exciting than ever.

Epilogue

Wedding rings are placed on the third finger of the left hand because ancient Egyptians believed the vein in that hand ran directly to the heart.

ONE YEAR LATER...

Ronan stood in the kitchen of his and Audrey's new home, a small but cozy townhouse in a newer development at the edge of Kissing Creek. It wasn't quite as convenient as his walk across the leafy Harrison Beech grounds to get to his office, but having a space to call their own made him feel like his life was complete. Besides, Audrey had started her degree at Harrison Beech—part-time—now that she'd gotten her GED. That meant they often drove to the campus together.

Almost all of their belongings were in boxes scrawled with Sharpie and sealed shut with duct tape, but he'd unearthed enough utensils to cook a basic meal for their first night together. For all of them...

Audrey sat on the floor with Deanna, their matching

blond heads bowed as they rifled through boxes marked *kitchen*.

"Found them!" Deanna held up a fork triumphantly. "Now we don't have to eat with our hands."

Audrey shot Ronan a look and closed the flaps on the box. "I would have been perfectly happy to order pizza."

"No way." Ronan shook his head. "This is our home. I'm not ordering takeout for our first meal. It's a special occasion."

Audrey pushed up from the floor and came over to him, the hem of her long skirt swishing around her bare feet. "Best I find the wineglasses, then," she said, planting a kiss on the tip of his nose. "That champagne isn't going to drink itself."

"Can I have some?" Deanna asked, getting to her feet. She'd grown up a lot in this past year, shooting up several inches and developing her confidence. He'd grown to love her like a little sister, given that she shared Audrey's sparkling personality and happy disposition—as happy as a teenager could be, anyway.

"You won't like it," Audrey warned. "It's not sweet."

"But I want to celebrate."

At that moment, there was a knock on the front door, and Deanna ran over to greet their guests. She skidded to a stop on her sock-covered feet and yanked the door open.

"Hey everyone!" Georgie appeared in the doorway, tapping away at her phone as usual. Jane was close behind, along with her boyfriend from college. Oliver brought up the rear.

"I can't believe you wanted me to invite everyone over on our first night when we don't even have things unpacked," Audrey said, grabbing the champagne from the fridge. She wrapped her hand over the cork and gave it a gentle twist, easing it out with a satisfying *pop*. "You're crazy."

"Crazy in love with you," he said, pulling her close for a kiss. "Which means I want your family to feel welcome here."

"Thank you," she whispered. "This house, this... everything—I can't believe it's ours."

"And I can't believe *you're* mine, Audrey." He gave her a little nudge. "Now go and welcome everyone. Dinner will be ready in ten minutes."

Grinning, she dashed off to greet her siblings. Even with them being scattered across the country, they were close. Georgie was off studying at Columbia, Jane was still at Duke, and Oliver had spent six months overseas, doing an exchange-type program with a specialty digital arts school.

They all saw their father periodically, but the relationship was slow to repair. Especially Oliver. Ronan knew that struggle, though he was happy to say that he and his mother were much further along. They spoke every few weeks now, and he visited her and his grandmother once a month. It gave him hope that Audrey and her siblings would get there one day, too.

Deanna came up beside Ronan and snuck a look over her shoulder to see if anyone was watching her. "Everyone's here now."

"Can you get them all to sit down at the table? I'll dish up." He winked at her. "Then it's showtime."

She grinned but quickly smothered the expression. "You've got it?"

Ronan nodded. A small velvet box wasn't the easiest thing to stash in his jeans without it looking totally suspicious. But the apron he'd thrown over his clothes was perfect, with deep, loose pockets perfect for stashing an engagement ring.

He'd taken Deanna to a jewelry shop in Boston a few weekends ago, claiming that they were going to the MIT Museum for a school assignment. In reality, Deanna had helped him pick out the perfect ring, since she knew *way* more about that kind of girlie stuff than he did.

She'd guided him toward an oval-cut citrine, since

yellow was Audrey's favorite color, surrounded by glittering white diamonds. It was almost vintage-looking, a little old-fashioned, which he thought suited her to a tee. She liked old things like dusty bookstores and black-and-white movies.

"Get your butts into those chairs," Deanna demanded, rounding up her siblings.

Audrey had located the wineglasses and the plates, and the table was set in a few minutes. Ronan thought maybe he should have been nervous about proposing, especially with an audience. Having an audience for anything personal was *not* his style.

But this felt right. Audrey's family was the most important thing in her life, and he was fully aware that marrying her meant making her family his own. And instead of informing her father that he intended to ask for her hand in marriage, he'd gone to Deanna to ask for her blessing. Everyone else was in on the plan, except Audrey.

"By the way, you didn't give me a fact this morning," Deanna said with an exaggerated pout as they all took their seats. "But that's okay. I've got one for you."

"Oh yeah?" Audrey asked. "Go on. Dazzle me with your facts."

"Wedding rings are placed on the third finger of the left hand because ancient Egyptians believed the vein in that hand ran directly to the heart," she said with a smug grin, flipping her long blond hair over one shoulder. "Romans even called it the vein of love."

Everyone at the table was silent and looking at Audrey. She cocked her head as if she'd started to suspect something, but before she had time to figure out what was going on, Ronan walked up to her and dropped down on one knee. He fished the box out of his pocket and held it up to her, opening it like he'd seen in the movies. Audrey gasped, and she pressed a hand to her chest, shaking her head.

Don't focus on the shaking head. Just ask the damn question.

"I said I wanted our first night in our new home to be special, and I meant it. This past year has been the first time I've ever felt like I wanted to set down roots and build a life in one place, and that's all because of you."

"Oh my gosh." Audrey looked to her siblings, who were all grinning and giggling. Her hands shook. "I wondered why you were so insistent that we have everyone over on the first night."

"I know what marrying you means. I'm joining your family and mine, and your devotion to your family is one of the things I love most about you. So, of course, I wanted to make sure they gave me their blessings."

"We do!" Deanna said as unofficial spokesperson for the Miller siblings, clapping her hands together.

"Thanks, Dee." Ronan pulled the ring out of the box and reached for Audrey's hand. "Audrey Dorothy Miller, would you do me the honor of sticking with me for the long haul? I want to see every amazing thing you do with your life, and I want to keep loving you until we're old and gray. I want to hear your quirky facts and hunt through bookstores with you; I want to tell everyone who'll listen how we met when you called me a thief and a sex robot."

Audrey laughed, her eyes sparkling. "You're never going to let me live that down, are you?"

"Never." He hovered the ring at the end of her finger, the perfectly cut yellow stone glinting like pure sunshine. Just like the woman he loved. "Will you marry me? It'll make me happier than I ever thought possible."

"For a professor who teaches a class about positivity, that's saying something." She grinned. "Yes, I'll marry you, Ronan. I want to be your wife, and I want to see all the amazing things *you* do with *your* life."

"With our life." He slipped the ring onto her finger and got to his feet so he could drag Audrey into his arms.

He brought his mouth down to hers and kissed her long and deep to a chorus of vomiting noises from her siblings. Laughing, they broke away. Audrey cupped his face, her smile wide and bright and so true he felt her happiness right through to the core of him.

This wasn't a fake holding-it-all-together-smile, because Audrey didn't need those anymore. When she was happy, she smiled, and when she wasn't, she let it all out. She trusted him, and that was the greatest gift of all. And, in turn, he let himself become closer and more in love with her every single day.

"Our life," she echoed. "I like the sound of that."

Acknowledgments

Firstly, I can't write a book all about family without thanking my own family first. To my parents and my little sister, thank you. It's been a rough few years, but no matter what life throws at us we'll tackle it as a team.

To my husband, who is always quick to challenge me whenever I think I can't do something, thank you. Your drive and ambition and relentless pursuit of our dream life is a blessing. I love you more every day.

To Luke and Jill, our family in Canada, thank you. Our nights laughing over boardgames and drinks, our endless catalogue of silly in-jokes and the true friendship we have is something I am incredibly grateful for. And to my Wednesday-night ladies—Shiloh, Myrna, Madura, Tammy, Jeanette, Aliza, and Lou—thank you for being a bright spot in my week.

To Taryn, thank you for everything. For keeping me sane in the ups and downs of this job, for always being there to brainstorm, for being the best cheerleader and sharpest critique partner and most genuine friend a gal could ask for.

To all the amazing people who had a hand in bringing Kissing Lessons to life. Thank you to my agent, Jill Marsal, for all your sage advice. Thank you to Liz Pelletier, Lydia Sharp, and Hannah Lindsey for your keen editorial input. Thank you to the rest of the Entangled Publishing team—Curtis, Riki, Jessica, Bree, Heather, Meredith, and everyone—for all your hard work behind the scenes.

Lastly, thank you to my readers. Your emails, DMs, reviews, and comments make my heart so full. Knowing my stories connect with you is the most rewarding thing in the world. Thank you.

About the Author

Stefanie London is a multi award-winning, *USA Today* bestselling author of contemporary romances and romantic comedies.

Stefanie's books have been called *"genuinely entertaining and memorable"* by Booklist, and **"Elegant, descriptive and delectable"** by RT magazine. Her stories have won multiple industry awards, including the HOLT Medallion and OKRWA National Reader's Choice Award, and she has been nominated for the Romance Writers of America RITA award.

Originally from Australia, Stefanie now lives in Toronto with her very own hero and is currently in the process of doing her best to travel the world. She frequently indulges in her passions for good coffee, lipstick, romance novels, and anything zombie-related.

Discover more Amara titles...

JUST A LITTLE BET
a novel by Tawna Fenske

Smokejumper Tony Warren and his best friend, photographer Kayla Gladney, are both bad at love. They even tried dating each other, but that crashed and burned, too. He's certain he's just a shit boyfriend. But Kayla thinks he's a straight-up commitment-phobe. So they make a bet—hunt down his exes and decide once and for all why he's so unlucky in love. Terrible boyfriend or commitment-phobe. Why does either answer feel like he's still losing?

THE WEDDING DATE DISASTER
a novel by Avery Flynn

I can't believe I'm going home to Nebraska for my sister's wedding. I'm gonna need a wingman and a whole lot of vodka for this level of family interaction. At least my bestie agreed he'd help. But instead, his evil twin strolls out of the airport. If you looked up doesn't-deserve-to-be-that-confident, way-too-hot-for-his-own-good billionaire in the dictionary, you'd find Grady Holt. He's awful. Horrible. The worst—even if his butt does look phenomenal in those jeans...

HOOKED ON YOU
a novel by Cathryn Fox

I'm not in small town Nova Scotia to hook up. I'm here to settle my grandmother's estate and sell the B&B, which I soon discover has been overrun with seasonal fisherman and operated on the honor system. The hard-core fishing folks become an instant family––the one I never had. Then there's the blind pet cow, who has a crush on my hot fisherman, Nate. Okay, technically he's not mine. I have no desire to get reeled in.

THE WEDDING DEAL
a *Heart in the Game* novel by Cindi Madsen

Former quarterback Lance Quaid just inherited the most losing team in the NFL. He's got only a few weeks until draft day to turn things around, and he can't do it alone. Thankfully, his HR manager is more than capable, if only she'd stop looking so sexy while she's yelling at him. When Lance begs her to join him on a trip down the coast for his brother's wedding so they can finalize details—on a strictly business basis—she agrees…after they fill out the necessary forms, of course. Sparks start flying as the team starts coming together, but both of them know anything more than the weekend would be a colossally bad idea—after all, the extra paperwork would be a nightmare.